ALL STRINGS ATTACHED

Joseph Colicchio

ALL STRINGS ATTACHED

Joseph Colicchio

Cedarwood Publishing

ISBN (Print Edition): 978-1-66782-055-2

ISBN (eBook Edition): 978-1-66782-056-9

ACKNOWLEDGEMENTS

Many people have helped me in the long process of this novel's creation. I would like to thank all of them for their time, guidance, and encouragement: Susan Abraham, Jack Colicchio, Roy Colicchio, Don Ginty, Charles Lobue, Artie Martines, Eileen Martines, Mary Jane Nealon, and Laurie Riccadonna.

My double special appreciation and acknowledgement has to go to my wife Pat Vogler. In the years it took me to write this novel, Pat has spent hundreds of hours working with me on it, including having read it cover to cover at least a dozen times. Additionally, she has handled every technological problem which I was incapable of handling on my own which amounts to handling every technological problem. Thanks, Patty, I love you.

WEEK ONE

Monday, July 1, 2008
1.

AT FIRST TOMMY called it a promise. A few days later he called it a plan. His plan became an intention, and, the night before his brother's leaving, when Alex asked if he'd be getting up to see him off, "That's my expectation," Tommy said. By bedtime, expectation was a mere hope, a fading one at that, all but a lie.

Alex grabbed his brother's ankles and tugged. Tommy jerked awake, but after that initial twitch he didn't even turn, just rearranged his bent arms and shifted his head from one side to the other, to face the wall.

"Yo."

"Sorry, not happening. Have a safe trip."

"Take care of mom."

"I will. Call me later."

The horn honked outside 46 Clifton Place, Weehawken, New Jersey, and at 7:15, Alex and his friend Billy were heading west, way west, into and across these United States. Tommy, a week beyond his 17th birthday, rolled onto his back, hands clasped behind his head. He turned again, back onto his belly, and slithered off the bed, spilling onto the floor before pushing himself upright and staggering to the bathroom. An hour later, dismally, he was on a forced march back to the high school, there to set up a summer internship.

Why was Tommy stuck doing this internship thing? Because Collins is an idiot, that's why. And, because of Tommy's own stubborn denial of the possibility that one could actually flunk a course entitled

"Introduction to Life Skills." Tommy's summer internship would suck, but all Life Skills Internships sucked and his actually wasn't as bad as most. In previous years, kids had been stuck working in a converted trailer in a puddled corner of the county, tending to the homeless or crippled or otherwise afflicted; or watching after Special Needs adults who, on day trips, loved nothing more than to run through the aisles of Walmart, to run through the quiet halls of the museum, to run at the red and wait on the green. Things could be worse than spending leisurely days at an old folks' home.

Tommy's assignment was to Bon Secours Continuous Care Facility, a mile north of his home. First, though, he had to get through this interview with Collins, the teacher who'd given him the "D" in Life Skills. Collins called Tommy into his office—a windowless cubicle in the old section of the school—and reached out a hand. Grinning and shaking his head, "Fucking Moore," he said. "Sit down."

Collins was 37, balding, and slightly overweight. He wore a suit to school every day—and on every day but the hottest, wore a multi-colored sweater-vest underneath—but he always looked a mess. "Go through the internship contract, Moore. There are three sections, don't fuck it up, I can't give you credit unless you complete the whole thing in its entirety. So, you know, don't hold me hostage on this all summer. Me and some Chi Phi buddies have a beach house."

"It says there are four sections."

"Oh, sweet Jesus, Moore! Then do all four sections, what's with you? Show some common sense, show some initiative. Look," he tipped back in his chair, holding up his hands, palms to the front, defending against responsibility. "It's on you now. It's your deal. You have an appointment at Geezerville with this woman tomorrow afternoon. They have to agree to take you on. Here's the card. Cathy Degnan, Director of Whole Persons." Collins shook his head, sad what this 21st century was turning us all into. "Director of Whole Persons. What the hell does whole persons mean?" Laughing, "Is there any other kind? Ha-ha."

Moments later, Tommy was outside, on the steps off the side door, envelope under his arm. Sparrows were chirping, the sun was shining off the black metal landing, and next year's freshmen were being marched towards the front doors and Orientation. Some hundred or so miles away his brother was pushing west. Probably Billy was driving and probably Alex had his shades on, feet up on the dash, elbow out the window, America breezing past. New Jersey, Pennsylvania, and then what? Ohio? Whatever state it was, it was flat. Welcome to the Heartland.

Tommy checked central PA's weather: Sunny and 73, temperature would go up another ten degrees by mid-afternoon. Chance of rain: 0%.

2.

ROAD CONSTRUCTION FROM one end of the state to the other.

Ten hours on the road brought them only to Pittsburgh. And worse, when they finally got out of PA, the day's light was fading and they were in the wrong state. West Virginia, not Ohio. They must have gone off course with all the construction, the merges, the lane closures, their own stupidity. Alex didn't care about this, but it sent Billy into a minor panic. Billy had a destination, not Alex. Billy's goal was to get where they were going, and for Billy that was grad school at USC. Alex was in no such hurry. And, well, that should have been a tipoff, even before they'd set out: Billy spoke of driving across America, Alex of driving into it. How could they not have recognized that huge distinction? Foolish.

When Billy checked his cellphone, the GPS kept telling him to turn around. Fuck this! He pulled the Toyota onto the side of the road and consulted an old AAA map. At the next exit, he turned northwest, towards Ohio he presumed.

"Billy no," said Alex, the unfolded map in his lap. "This is cool, we're right. We're where we're supposed to be. This is just a little strip of West Virginia that for some stupid reason comes up north."

Billy wasn't buying it, he shook his head dismissively. Alex was his best friend, but Alex was also a little bit of a space case, a guy who trusted in strangers and acquaintances alike, trusted in a half-torn decade-old paper map, and in every case anticipated his own good fortune. He'd firmly set his sights on this trip but planned nothing about what would happen next. Two hours earlier, Billy had sat with his foot on the brake, fuming about how few miles they'd put behind them and how westerly the sun already was. Alex replied: "Relax, the trip is more about the journey than the destination." That so aggravated Billy. That summed things up.

"I'm telling you—that way was fine. It's on our way. Well, at least it continues west," said Alex.

"Yeah, just leave it to me, okay," said Billy. "We're already *at least* two hours behind schedule."

Schedule?

Well, they'd lost a third hour and Billy couldn't let that be. It was only nine o'clock and they were not going to spend the night in West Virginia, two states behind where he'd planned. Twenty miles of wasted time heading south, back to Wheeling, then sixty-five miles, pedal to the metal on Route 70. There'd be no stopping until they got at least to Zanesville and put a reasonable dent into Ohio.

Tuesday, July 2
3.

TWO MILES SOUTH of the George Washington Bridge, Bon Secours Continuous Care Facility on the Hudson sits just fifty yards from the water's edge, part of a muddy sliver of land that separates the river from the Palisades. All there is between the facility and the drink is River Road and the newly constructed Waterfront Park, a bright and breezy strip of white cement, still-caged young trees, fresh-from-the-wrap benches, and life-capturing steel sculptures—a child heaving a ball, mitt on his left hand, leg in the air; a gent on a bench, legs crossed, reading the day's news; a sailor, in tipped cap and bell bottoms, leaning on the rail, peering towards the Manhattan skyline.

The Bon Secours campus consists of three buildings. At the south end, the domed front building houses the reception area and staff offices, the Grand Hall, the main dining room, and, behind tall accordion doors, the auditorium. Behind that building and connected to it by a broad corridor, the eight-story residential unit is built right against the cliff. The north building, across the parking lot and linked to the two newer buildings by a tunnel, is the Acute Care for the Elderly Center, ACEC (the first such facility in the state), housed in the renovated former Public Service Electric and Gas Building, a brick, factory-like structure constructed in the 1920s.

Bon Secours' doors silently slid open as Tommy approached. In the small entrance lobby, a glamorous 70-something woman sat on a rose-colored satin couch. She was on her cell phone and she was talking about fruit: "No, no, they have to be thrown out. Yes, over-ripe. They have black spots—yes, they're over-ripe, I told you. I can't stand to look at them. They're done, Dorothy. Finito."

Tommy smiled but the woman ignored him. Ignored him stoically—she'd seen this patronizing smile before. He walked past the elevator, opting to climb the twelve carpeted steps to the main hall. Opposite the reception counter, a mounted TV scrolled the day's activities: Mass, 9:00; Trip to Oak Leaf Mall, 10:00; Pilates in the Zen Garden, 11:30; Residents' Council Meeting, 2:30; Prayer Garden of the Blessed Mother, Wine and Cheese Social, 3:00.

A tall, bone-thin woman of mixed race sat behind the counter, her complexion caramel, her features more Asian than African, her shoulders bared and boney. Her hair was pulled back in a knot that doubled the depth of her head. "God be with you," she welcomed. "How may I help you?"

"Yes, thank you. I'm here for Mrs. Degnan."

"Yes you are. And that will be no problem. I'm guessing you're Thomas."

"I am."

She rose and walked towards the back. "Just let me tell Mrs. Degnan you're here." Her tight-fitting, lime green dress, narrow angularity, and oblong head reminded Tommy of a Pez dispenser.

During the school term, during the regular marking period of Intro to Life Skills, Collins had prepared his students for what he'd referred to as "professional level, career opportunity interviews." He warned the class that these would be challenging, no-coddling, real-world interviews. Doubting Collins but certain of his own ignorance, Tommy arrived at Bon Secours with a set of weakly held expectations. He was dressed for the occasion: blue Oxford shirt, blue and gold tie, khakis, brown penny loafers. In the past year he'd finally hit a growth spurt, grown from 5'7" to 5'10" while gaining but ten pounds. His pants were short, his shirt was flopsy, and if God were good, Mom would never again refer to his "baby fat." He'd cologned up and brushed his brown hair off his forehead. He was ready to meet Mrs. Degnan, full set of protocols in place: make eye contact but remember to blink; speak in complete sentences but don't drone on; appear to be intelligent and mature; "and for God 's sake, act like you've got some sense of who you are as a person." It was the last recommendation that baffled him. It was a typical Collins-ism, and therefore taken by Tommy as nonsensical. What the hell's a "sense of who you are as a person"?

"And look, Moore," Collins had warned. "I know you. Please act like you're interested, for Chrissakes, interested in either her or the geezers or yourself or something. I mean, come on, help me out here."

4.

A SMALL PERCENTAGE of the staff and the majority of the bosses at Bon Secours were nuns. The Sisters of Bon Secours, in some intricate and shady relationship with the Newark Archdiocese, basically owned the place. Cathy Degnan is not a nun but nearly had become one.

When Cathy was in sixth grade, in 1979, the Bon Secours order celebrated the centennial of its North American Province with a "Come See About Us" Jubilee. For each of those three autumn days, a caravan of busses filled with plaid-clad girls would make their way to Rose Beach, a tiny seaside town a hundred miles south of Cathy's school, its entire shoreline owned by the order. For knobby-kneed Cathy and her classmates, this would mean two song-filled hours in the bus and then, as the sun sank, two weary return hours home to north Jersey and the Our Lady of Mercy schoolyard.

The Rose Beach Bon Secours nuns who had prepared "Come See About Us" had done a terrific job, their enthusiasm lighting the way to an imagining of the sixth-grade girls' complex inner lives: fits of the tasty excitement of liberation and a relished out-of-the-daily-humdrum day mixed with boredom that ached like a sore tooth, that seesaw of, on the one hand, a day away from school desks and a promising ride to a far-away seaside town—who knew, there might be at least a few boys there and maybe they were less stupid than the boys from around here—and, on the other, the cruel punch-line of being handed over to a colony of nuns, themselves bubbling with effervescent spirituality, their billowing navy blue-and-white swarming like bees. For the nuns, the Jubilee—that word popped from their mouths like happy candy, they couldn't get enough of it—had been the highlight of the year, of the decade, really. These were women, remember, for whom it was second nature to conclude every reference to the future—"Sister James and I will restock the Campbells this weekend," "I'm excited to begin them on prime numbers tomorrow"— with a "God willing." The sisters were giddy with liberation and the incarnation of tangible joy in their lives.

The Centennial Jubilee allowed these Sisters of Bon Secours— virtually pleaded with them—to be un-nun like, to shed their humble, mince-stepping selves and recover (or in most cases, invent) in a not too showy way that long-lost, much maligned, and otherwise sinful and attractive—yes, intentionally attractive—girl inside. The Bon Secours associates—an advisory group composed of lay members and full-fledged nuns—provided them advice: do not comment on the length of our young visitors' skirts; remember, the year is 1978 and the days of arguing over your favorite Beatle are over; and, Sisters, sports talk is fine but please cool it with the pitching windups!

The Retreat House was one block from the Rose Beach board-walk and still had the look of the Victorian hotel it had been until 1957 when the order took ownership. Arriving well before the 10:00 opening prayer, Cathy's OLM contingent was treated to a walk-through of the gloriously clean Retreat House in order to get a sense of the nuns' life-style: a typical Pine Sol-clean Retreat guest room; the basement game room, complete with bowling alleys, ping-pong tables, a gum ball machine, a record player and a dozen albums, from Nat King Cole to Peter, Paul, and Mary to Cat Stevens; the East Wing, West Wing, and Upstairs chapels; the main library; and the window-lined second-floor perimeter hallways with their scrubbed floors and panoramic views. Also preceding the opening prayer—as groups of twenty, thirty, and forty girls bustled and giggled their way down the aisles of the giant multi-purpose room, each one believing itself to be the most awkward, the most watched, and the most and least cool of the two dozen groups present—a slide show was presented outlining the steps of the nun-becoming process from Aspirant to Novitiate to Perpetually Professed, the observing nuns intently scanning to identify the few spontaneously devout prospects.

After the slide show, the girls were brought outside to sun-sparkling ocean air and led onto one of the compound's two softball fields for Opening Prayers: "In the name of the Father, and of the Son, and of the Holy Spirit," invoked Mother Grace—tall, almost giant, somewhere between the ages of fifty and seventy, and subject to quick personality swings, from the heart of sweetness to the dismal scolder of wanton ways and the prophet of eternal hellfire. "Welcome my young ladies. God has blessed us with this beautiful seaside day, has He not? Has He not let us down? Let us praise this day's glory and magnificence."

"Yay, yay, yay!" they cheered.

"Let me begin, my young ladies. Let me begin by telling you a little about my own Bon Secours journey. When I was a girl, even younger than you are now . . .And then when I was fifteen…"

Lunch was served picnic-style—box lunches of sandwiches too long in the heat, bruised apples, and cupcakes with crusted icing— served on ball field #2, the same location that would hold the afternoon's team-building activities: Simon Says, egg toss, keep the giant ball in the air. At 2:50, the designated Group Leader-nuns blew their silver whistles and the girls headed to the boardwalk for Closing Prayers in Saint Anne's Pavilion, a green and white octagonal structure, open on all sides and large enough for its benches to seat all three hundred girls. Moments before closing prayers, an afternoon thunderstorm darkened the seaside with Matterhorns of swiftly building clouds. The storm came and went in moments. As prayers began, hardwood-scented steam lifted from the boardwalk, a golden hue infused the waving beach grass, an ocean breeze blew through the pavilion. It was during this hosanna-rich 30-minute ceremony that twelve-year-old Cathy Degnan was filled with the marvelous certainty that she had been called to the religious life.

5.

AT 9:30 IN the morning without so much as a honk, they'd sped past the exit to the ancient Native-American Serpent Mounds—one of the spots Alex had identified as a borderline must-see site in his days of planning the trip. Instead, their first stop came an hour later in the thick traffic ten miles west of Dayton. The Toyota's windows were rolled down and the sun blinding off the mirror as they sat in the parking lot eating their Whoppers and pocket-pies, sipping their big Cokes through red and white straws. The skies were hazy blue and the temperature a humid eighty degrees and breezy. Billy reluctantly conceded to Alex that they could make one stop that day, but he was adamant that they'd cross the Mississippi by nightfall.

Billy went into the BK to take a piss. Alex pulled out his phone before slipping into the driver's seat. He texted his little brother.

"Big brother here. Just checking in."

"Wassup. About to go in for my interview."

"You're there now?"

"Yeah. I go in whenever the boss-lady is ready for me. Where are you?"

"At a BK in Ohio."

"Okay."

"I'm going to get rid of my phone."

"And why would you do that?"

"I'm gonna run it over."

"But why? Does mom know? You're gonna be completely out of touch."

"To the does mom know question, answer is no, it'd just worry her. To point number two, I can use Billy's phone. Besides, the whole country is wired."

Alex got out of the car.

"You didn't answer the why question?"

"Because you know me."

"What's that mean?" asked Tommy.

"*Thomas. Tom Moore. Ms. Degnan's ready for you.*"

"Oops, I gotta go. Call me from Billy's phone. I'll tell you if I got the job."

"Will do or email me. Now, I have some technology to destroy."

"Whatever."

"Go outside, get some fresh air."

"If I could. Fucking Collins."

Alex knelt on the parking lot asphalt.

"Love you."

"Yeah, you too."

"Bye-bye."

Alex placed his phone under the front wheel and got back in the car.

6.

POWERFULLY AND TRIUMPHANTLY, Mother Grace began: "Yes, yes, these habits are like straightjackets. They are *our* straightjackets, freely chosen and self-imposed. These habits are ours and we are theirs—as it is, as it must be if you are called! Shall we pray . . ."

Next, a pretty college-aged girl, a novitiate six months in the convent, sang the Order's praises, bellowing the word "Jubilee" with all the gusto of a Miss Teen Bon Secours contestant. Three young nuns in white short-sleeved shirts and Blessed Mother-blue jumpers, hair peeking from long-brimmed white caps—extravagantly healthy-looking despite, possibly because of, their beefy paleness—took the stage and strummed guitars, tapped their feet, and exchanged jubilant smiles that pulsed from a mysterious source of joy unknown to the schoolgirls, equal parts creepy and enviable. A young priest with black-haired arms and an athlete's hands raised the host, then raised the chalice. He consecrated both and delivered communion: "Take this and drink of it all of you. Take this cup of my blood, the blood of the new and everlasting covenant."

Their giggles gone, solemnly the girls filed forward.

* * *

As she bounded out of Saint Ann's Pavilion, her twelve-year old spirit singing with the peace and triumph of a life resolved, Cathy Degnan was certain that in the words of Mother Grace herself, she had, that day, been illuminated.

Out of the Pavilion and across the field she skipped. She was the first girl to reach the bus. The door was open and the driver was asleep with an Italian newspaper in his lap. It was a modern bus, one with tinted windows, air-conditioning, narrow aisles, and rows of thickly padded, raised seats. Cathy used the canvas bag the nuns had given her as a pillow and leaned her head against the window. She hugged herself to fight off the chilly stream blowing from the air-conditioning grill and kept her eyes closed as the other girls noisily filed to their seats.

7.

GROWTH SPURT OR no growth spurt, Tommy was still your run-of-the-mill emotionally immature kid. His m.o. was passivity—resolute, stone-cold passivity. He could be pleasant but he certainly wasn't outgoing; he was intelligent enough but not one to strain his brain; he was a follower more than a leader, impressionable more than impressive; he was a good and empathetic kid without being truly generous. He'd give you the shirt off his back, but to get it you'd have to ask, and afterwards you wouldn't be sure if he'd granted the request out of affection or indifference.

In many ways the Cathy Degnan who introduced herself to Tommy that afternoon looked much like the girl who had left Bon Secours thirty years earlier. Her arms were childishly thin and, as she reached out to greet Tommy, the blue-green veins on the back of her hand showed through. At 5'4" she barely topped one hundred pounds. Her summer dress was sky blue and white. On her feet were tan sandals.

Retaining the litheness of youth, speedily she met Tommy in the middle of her office: "Welcome, welcome." Her outstretched arm forced Tommy to hurry in reciprocating. "So what should I call you? Tommy? Thomas?"

By instinct, he'd have replied "whatever," but Collins' voice echoed. He was quick to avoid that error, but not quick enough to fill in the blank with the more adult sounding Tom, a name he couldn't recollect ever being called in his life.

"Come on, Tommy, sit down. Did you have any trouble finding us?"

"No, no. I live right up the hill."

"Oh, sure. Union City, right?"

" Weehawken."

Cathy's office was chilly, spare, and bright—the ceiling white and the walls nearly white, the furniture a mixture of steel and glass and almond-colored wood. On the walls and shelves were religious figurines, all a bit abstract: a white marble cross without a Christ, sterling silver praying hands, the word "Believe" as a shiny brass wall sculpture. The room's one window looked to the southeast, but the ground floor was too low to see over the greenery and across to Manhattan.

"Let me explain my job as Director of Whole Persons. It's a funny title. Basically, you'll be helping me. Believe me, the way this year's been going, I could really use help. Things are improving," she smiled, sighed theatrically. "We'll make your responsibilities such that you can put 'Assistant to the Director' on your resume. Okay, so . . ." She spoke rapidly, rushed even. "Well, first, what is a 'whole person'?"

She told him: "A whole person is a physical, emotional, and spiritual being. My job is to maintain that integrated health. In short, that means keeping people happy and comfortable in the face of all of life's traumas, large and small. That's a noble cause, right?"

"Oh, definitely."

"And how do I attempt to achieve this? By whatever means necessary," she laughed, knowing and guilty. "It's a very fine line, honestly--it's a balance," she said, eyes upwards, as if she were in conversation with a listening self, floating between her squinting eyes and the ceiling. "It's about an equilibrium between truth and efficacy, you know?"

Cathy stared, Tommy stared back. Unblinking and blank, "For sure," he said. She was a little wacky and Tommy was having some trouble following along.

She explained that she attempted to achieve this equilibrium through talk sessions and prayer sessions, through Casino nights and piano matinees. She attended to her people with a nudge down the hall and a hand on the shoulder, with a passing high five, with the flash of her smile, with the mischief in her eye. Sometimes, to cover up the black parts of life, she used white lies, an artful blend of fact and fiction, ministering with a mixture of heartfelt beliefs and manipulation of beliefs where manipulation served the greater good, where manipulation helped her achieve her job in its essence—cleaning up after God, finding happiness and comfort for her people.

"We *are* religious," Cathy insisted in the face of no resistance, turning her eyes to Tommy. "We use all the tools religion gives us. They're very important, in fact they're the best, the purely religious elements are. But we're not doctrinaire. You don't have to be religious yourself, you see, to use religion's tools," she began. "Well, never mind that. Religion is a way, a means. Like I tell people, my job isn't to save eternal souls, it's to save *mortal* souls. You get the difference, right?"

"Yeah."

"Tell me what the difference is."

"You don't want to wait. You want to do some good now. You're not so much about getting to heaven or going to hell. You're about making people happy."

"Exactly, Tommy. Very impressive," she beamed.

He didn't entirely know what it was that he got, but in any case Collins would have been proud.

8.

THE BUS—ALONGSIDE ANOTHER dozen busses—rolled out of the main Rose Beach parking lot and onto sandy Ocean Avenue, all its traffic lights blinking yellow in the off season. By the time the caravan reached Route 1, Cathy had been lulled to sleep by the bus's sway and the whispery chatter of the girls around her. She awoke half an hour later when they pressed to a stop at a Parkway toll booth.

She didn't open her eyes, she didn't need to. The recognition was there already: It was all gone. All gone and now she was worse off than ever. She was chilly but flushed and had to suck hard for air. Her certainty and joy evaporated. Illumination was the stupidest word ever, a nasty joke. Her heart was aching and empty and she couldn't bear to be seen, and when she looked round the bus it was like she could barely attach names to friends. It was a scene out of a twilight dream.

Thirty years later, after Tommy Moore left her office, Cathy recalled that afternoon as she had a thousand times before. That day, as she'd skipped to the bus, she had been too young to tell her true self from her pretend self. Not so any longer. At 42, Cathy knew what she was. She was a pretender. It was all she was and all she would ever be. Pretender was her calling.

9.

AS PART OF the Bon Secours modernization initiative, the Grand Hall was being transformed into a Town Square. Construction was nearly complete, but, still, "Pardon Our Appearance" was the phrase of the day. Around the room's perimeter, the lower fifteen feet of two walls was covered in heavy plastic sheets that protected the sitting area from the dust and fumes of the work going on behind. A third side of the

Hall consisted of a plant-topped half-wall, behind which was the main dining area; and the fourth wall was made of the two floor-to-ceiling accordion doors that opened to the auditorium.

Tommy's interview with Cathy was completed by one o'clock and the walk-through she took him on done forty minutes later. In the Grand Hall he'd await his meeting with the Residents' Council. Cathy had given him a ticket for a free lunch at Here's 2 You, a cafe, newsstand, and gathering place, a casual alternative to the dining room. At 1:45 it was empty except for one worker behind the counter, a pair of old men sitting together arms folded, and a lone woman—clearly not a typist in her younger years—seated at one of the new computers set up along the Palisades-facing windows. Tray in hand, he and his bagel and orange juice found a small round table in the Grand Hall. The Residents' Council Meeting was nearly an hour off.

Centering the Hall was a gas-burning fireplace with an outsized stone chimney that rose through the domed ceiling. The hall's entire floor, except for a perimeter of blue stone, was covered by a patterned golden-brown rug, diverse furnishings scattered across it: floral couches; blood-red leather chairs; high-backed wooden rockers close to the fireplace; and, on the other side of the chimney, nearer to the reception area, three card tables, one covered in a half-completed Peaceable Kingdom puzzle.

After finishing his bagel, Tommy moved to one of the leather chairs, the Bon Secours canvas bag which Cathy had given him—"Have a Bon Secours Day" in fancy script across it—on his lap. A tall woman leaning on a walker passed by him, an unlit cigarette between the wrinkled fingers of her right hand. A man in plaid pants and a pinstriped Yankees baseball jersey sat at a table, doing a crossword. A trio of arriving Hispanic workers, headphones on, hurried towards the kitchen.

The Bon Secours bag was full, loaded with pamphlets, describing both the facility and the Order—mission, ministry, history, programs, progression of care, one pamphlet dedicated specifically to the new Acute Care for the Elderly Center (ACEC). The contents would have been depressing enough on their own. Let's face it, the residents' lives pretty much sucked (and speaking of sucking, their present was Tommy's future, if he should live so long), but what made the stuff more awful was the obvious veneer, the great effort being made to costume this whole aging and dying business in upbeat clothing: photos of braceleted ladies arranging flowers; a coed group power-walking through Waterfront Park; a lady on a treadmill watching Food Network; a toothy grandpa, his balding head freckled with age spots, hugging his thrilled-to-be-there grandchildren. Even the small stuff, the stuff related to things Tommy only understood partially if at all—the hospice, palliative, dementia, degenerative, Advanced Directive stuff—was wrapped in flowery language: "Blessings Hall," "Tranquility Glen," "The Evergreen Neighborhood."

Brutal, just brutal. Brutal to think about. Even more brutal to think about for the first time and simultaneously be surrounded by it.

Four residents—three women and a man—walked past Tommy on their way to the nearest table. Each smiled and offered a "Good afternoon." One woman, perhaps clairvoyant, whispered "Nice young man" to a mirror image of herself, likely a twin. "*Very* nice," the second woman responded.

Yes, what a nice young man, Tommy thought: mentally trash-talking a bunch of elderly folks, very nice young man, indeed. What did he expect the brochures to say: You're old, your life's in the rear-view mirror? Give it up and be miserable? Maybe skip lunch today, instead, lie down till you're dead. He could be such a self-absorbed little asshole:

a moment of recognition, an epiphany Collins would have called it. Yes, that was it: a self-absorbed little asshole he could be.

The twins spoke with Spanish accents and were dressed similarly in open-toed shoes, silky blouses, and long pearls. They wore the same makeup the same way. Their names, Tommy learned, were Ava and Nini. The guy was Sandy, strong, round-shouldered, wearing a plaid shirt, unironed but not particularly wrinkled. He didn't say a word. The fourth was Sara, at 5'3" slightly taller than the twins. She had a dark complexion, high cheekbones and almond-shaped eyes. Her granite-colored hair came down nearly to her shoulders. One of the twins asked a question of Sara, who was apparently a new resident. She paused, wobbled her head. She, too, spoke with an accent, one Tommy couldn't identify. She'd mentioned Oklahoma and Nebraska. Maybe she was Native American.

Tommy went through the pile of brochures for a second time and a third, stacking and unstacking them. He pretended to be reading them while hoping for another text from Alex, eavesdropping on the old folks, and waiting for Cathy to call him to the Residents Council meeting—the sooner it started, the sooner he could leave.

"Nini, we have to go," said Ava. "The Residents' Council."

"Already? What time is it?" asked Nini, leaning back to find the distance at which she could read her watch. The sisters rose quickly. "Sara, you have to talk. You can't try to do it yourself."

"You can't do it yourself," repeated Ava. "Go to CDR and talk about it."

"Go to Cathy's CDR. It's the best thing." Cathy's CDR referred to the semi-weekly sessions of Consolation, Discernment, and Reconciliation that Cathy had months earlier introduced to her "by any means necessary" menu.

Both sisters reached out to touch Sara, anywhere.

"Don't try to do this alone."

The sisters left, Sara and Sandy remained, talking in whispers, Sara speaking into her own folded hands. Sandy also avoided eye contact, nodding with understanding but mostly looking, too, at Sara's folded hands.

Cathy called: "Tommy, the Residents' Council is about ready for you. Come follow me." He nodded before he turned to face Cathy. He remembered to smile, push back his shoulders, and walk at a brisk pace.

10.

THE MEMBERS OF the Residents' Council were already in place when Cathy ushered Tommy in. The library Conference Room's second-floor plate-glass windows offered a straight-on view of midtown Manhattan's skyline, made even more brilliant by the reflection of sunlight off the river.

Cathy announced that she would say the opening prayer, lead the introductions, then be gone.

"In the name of the Father," she began. "'The world will place many tribulations before us. Jesus overcomes the world.' John 16:33. Amen."

"Amen."

The Council, Cathy explained to Tommy, was advisory on all major decisions at the facility and its importance should not be underestimated. It consisted of eight members, but several of them were unavailable for today's interview. She added that the quorum bar had been set necessarily low.

The introductions began.

"We're joined at the hip," said Nini of herself and Ava. They were 83 years old, born in Argentina where they both had been professional women. Neither had any children: they couldn't. God had given them one another. They seemed spry as fifty-year-olds and were planning a trip back to the homeland for late September. Next came Annie, three years younger. She and her Teddy, who had spent nearly half a century as an aeronautics engineer, enjoy walks, uplifting art, and theater of all stripes. Though Teddy spends three mornings a week at dialysis (then three afternoons sleeping off the effects), still they appreciate the beauty of the world, every aspect of it, and practice daily positivity, she bragged. Name a Bon Secours committee and Annie was likely on it. The final member of the Council, seated next to Annie but some distance away, was Carmella, and positivity, daily or otherwise, was clearly not her thing. At 75 years old, she flaunted her youth. She had been married to Ray for 38 years, widowed nine. He was her life. Her 45-year-old daughter, Theresa, and Carmella's two wonderful grand-children now lived half an hour outside Tucson, AZ. There, housing is so much more affordable and the air so much cleaner, "God's air." Everything there is beautiful: the sky, the people, the climate, the view from her daughter's hacienda's front steps, even the little things growing out of the dirt in downtown Oracle. For 32 years, Carmella had worked as a dispatcher at the taxi company Ray owned, a career that now owned her voice—raspy from decades of assuming that the connection was bad.

"Well, now that you've met everyone it's time for me to leave," explained Cathy. With ironic formality, she lifted her slight frame and reached out to shake Tommy's hand. "Good luck, young man. You'll need it with this group," she winked, and with that whisked her way out of the room.

Annie, Council Chair and a woman of erect posture and brilliantly white hair, began: "On behalf of all of us, not just the four of us here, but on behalf of the entire Bon Secours family, I welcome you. Now, I will take the chairperson's prerogative and ask you our first question. So then, please tell us a little bit about yourself and why you believe you'd be a good fit for the Assistant to the Director of Whole Persons position."

Okay, now this was an interview. After making clear that he knew nothing about the qualifications of the other fine candidates (though he was pretty certain that there were no other candidates), Tommy launched into a list of what he had to offer, sandwiching the truth with a pair of lies: he was responsible beyond his years, he worked well with others, he was willing to learn, he was flexible, he had good communications skills. He addressed his "D" in Life Skills on the off-chance that they knew of it: it was completely his fault. He should have given as much attention to it as he did to his academic classes, like AP—"that means Advanced Placement, it's college-level"—AP Psychology (in which he tied for lowest grade in the class with a "C+"), never mentioning his mom's illness as a distraction or excuse.

He'd nailed the questions. Three of the four ladies nodded so enthusiastically he thought they might break into applause. They so obviously wanted to like him. And then, of course, there was Carmella.

The second question came from Ava, or possibly Nini: "Can you tell us something more about yourself, a story or something? Something that we wouldn't know from your application."

"Let's see," said Tommy, suddenly confident. "I live just about a mile from here, up the hill in Weehawken. My mom is a school aide and is also going to school or will be going back to school soon, to Saint Peter's College. She wants to be a kindergarten teacher."

"Education," approved Annie.

"Mm-hmm. I live with her and my brother Alex. He just graduated from Rutgers in biology. Right now he's off on a trip, a road trip."

"And your fatha?" interrupted Carmella. The big woman couldn't get a lot of air in her lungs, so, like an aging boxer who had to conserve his punches, she had to conserve syllables. "If I m'ask."

"He died when I was in first grade."

"Aww."

"S'was he in the ahmy?"

Ava made a tight cross-fingered gesture to Nini that must have signaled something uncomplimentary in the old country. They signaled covertly, or semi-covertly, not so covertly as to keep Tommy from noticing.

"No, he worked in the Post Office, a big warehouse."

"Oh," said Carmella. "Lak'wanna."

"I think so. It was in Hoboken."

"Definitely then," she said with a wave. "It was Lak'wanna."

"Yeah, it was an accident."

"He fell out a window?"

"No, no."

"A forklift accident."

"Yes, actually. A forklift went out of control and pinned him."

Carmella blessed herself.

"My deepest prayers go to you and your fam'ly. I'll make a novena," she said in her husky, gruff voice, confident, it seemed, that her reassurance would all but erase the young man's loss. Tommy didn't know whether or not the finger of the lord had been at work in Carmella's identifying the cause of his dad's death, but yes or no, her out-of-the-blue guess had brought him into her good graces. Now he had all four on his side.

"You were saying—your brother. A road trip?" asked Annie.

"Yeah, Alex. He's traveling across country."

"I hope he's being careful," Ava said in the direction of Nini, or vice versa.

The other nodded. "Youth," she said.

"Well, he's with a friend. He's the adventurer of the family for sure. He's always up to something."

And from there, the questions rolled, the ladies' involvement in Alex's journey immediate and nourishing.

"To be young again," sighed Annie.

"Are they traveling on foot?" asked Carmella.

So there went any sense Tommy had that Carmella's forklift intuition was anything more than a lucky guess, that (a lucky guess) or an item in a long-held file of how men died at Post Office terminals, second only to window fallings. The twins bit their lips to show Tommy they were holding back laughter—they hid things in a very public way, probably had been doing so since kindergarten.

"Answer Carmella's question," Annie urged.

"No, they're traveling by car."

"Whatever y'say," shrugged Carmella as she pushed away from the table. Annie thanked Tommy for his interest in the position. She told him he had an excellent chance of landing the job. She told him he presented himself very well. Pointedly, she thanked him for his patience. She was sure—*if* he was selected—that he would be a boon to the community. Annie and the twins then sang the praises of his soon-to-be boss, Cathy.

"She's an angel, too good to be real."

As they spoke, Tommy thought of Cathy's message to him and her "by whatever means necessary" approach, and their consensus "too good to be real" praise echoed like a suspicion.

"Well," huffed Carmella. "Honestly, as y'know, I had a very different 'sperience with Miss Catherine Degnan." Red faced, she grabbed the edge of the table, pulled herself in, drew herself upright. "She wouldn't help in meh time o' need. I had to go over huh head, to Sister Margaret Mary."

"Oh, goodness. Sister Margaret Mary," scoffed Annie. "Don't make me laugh."

"Yes, Margaret Mary. Missy Degnan's boss. You've heard uh chain uh command?"

"It's a ridiculous thing to . . . hold a grudge about," said the twins in a sentence started by one and completed by both.

"Oh, it is, excuse me. Why's it a ridiculous thing? Because youse say so?"

"Carmella, please," pleaded Annie. "A funeral mass for a dog?"

"Not just a dog," said Carmella leaning forward. "My dog. Before they moved, she was like a little guardian angel to my grandchildren." She spoke aggressively, sure that even with half a lung she could knock the crap out of the other three.

"Of course," said Nini, attentively watched by Ava. "How could we forget, this was Carmella's dog. Your darling Frita!"

"Don't you dare." Carmella pressed a hand to her chest. "Frida was my motha's name."

"Oh, my goodness. I am at the end of my rope," exclaimed Annie, embarrassed by the stupidity of it all. "God bless us."

"Carmella, Miss Degnan would have had a very nice burial for Frita."

"Frida! With a 'd' if you don't mind t'learn English."

"Oh, who cares. And besides, you're the one who insisted on having a funeral mass."

"That's right, that's right, my dear. Do you know The Book, have you ever read The Book? Look it up. Saint Rocco, Patron Saint of Canines. Try to tell *me* about The Book."

"Now I've heard it all," said Annie. "I'm telling you, Cathy would have had a beautiful and appropriate burial service for Frida. Remember the one we had for Casper?"

"Casper, ha, don't make me laugh. This isn't a God damned cat we're talking about. A mass is what I needed and Cathy Degnan would not provide. All this talk about 'consolation'!"

"Cathy couldn't provide. Couldn't, not wouldn't."

"Baloney, Miss Know-It-All. She damn well *wouldn't*. And it is lucky fa me Sist' Marg'ret Mare would. I was getting no consolation, no CDR from your Cathy Degnan, not a drop—'consolation,' fah! so I went ovah her head. Sista authorized the mass, and God bless her for it. It was a small mass. It's not like I expected the archbishop to come. Frida was no saint. I'm under no delusions."

Annie sat up even straighter. "Sister Margaret Mary is not . . . well she is not any source of inspiration. No wonder Cathy is so overwhelmed, she has to do two jobs instead of one. How could she have authorized a mass for a dog and come back and talked to us with a straight face? She would have lost all credibility. It would have been untenable. Oh, bless us. Never mind, Carmela, just never mind."

"Yeah, whatever your blather is about, blah-blah-blah. Sista provided in my hour of need and Catherine Degnan, your Saint Cathy, did not. . . . And Frida, mommy loves you, baby. She is surely looking down and taking names. I have nothing more to say on the matter."

Tommy had a headache but was impressed. Who knew the old crows had so much fight in them?

He caught on to the argument quickly. Annie was right, of course. Sure, Cathy could espouse a "whatever means necessary" philosophy to provide happiness and comfort, she could be flexible with the religious stuff, yes. But there had to be some limit. There are little white lies and then there are blatant absurdities that create holes too great to mend. If you're Cathy you've got to know the difference.

Young as he was, the equation made sense to Tommy, her soon-to-be right-hand man: You can't go around telling residents, on the one hand, that God is solemnly preparing the holy chambers for their own immortal souls and those of their most loved ones, then also tell them that He is at the heavenly gates with a smile on his face and a bag of Liver Snaps for Carmella's Frida in his hands.

It was simple, really. You (God, that is) are either a punch line or you're not.

11.

HEY TOMMY,

Welcome to Hannibal—Hannibal, MO, that is. That's 500+ miles due west of fabulous Zanesville, OH, where we started from this morning. That's still not quite enough to satisfy Billy but truth is he was almost as excited to stop for our mule riding escapade (Yes, mule riding!!!) as I was. I think from his perspective he's thinking, well, at least we're on the left side of the Mississippi even though he's not happy that at this pace CA will take us five days, maybe six. Poor tortured soul!

I have to admit for me the name Hannibal was the draw. Elephants over the Alps added to some vague connection to Mark Twain. Turns out Twain was born here and not only does Hannibal have a Mark Twain Park and a Mark Twain Museum (the white plastic 'stache was way over-priced) but the town has Hannibal Haunted Hayrides and a Double A baseball team, the Hannibal Cavemen. The town also has a three-block long hippie section, our hotel is right on the edge of it, and the Rolling Stones are blasting from an Old West-style bar across the road, singing "And you can send me dead flowers every morning/Send me dead flowers by the mail."

So, you ask me for the highlight of my day. That's an easy one. It was the Mule Riding. All through Indiana and Illinois, we're passing signs for Horseback Riding places. Neither Billy or me has ever been on a horse but Billy's reluctant and I'm indecisive so we keep zipping by them, slowing down too late until we wind up just going, "Aw, damn, aw, damn." But this changes when we get to Carrollton, IL, home of Honeybee Stables. We're on Route 10, a supposed short cut, but actually a creaky 50 mph road. The big sign says, "We have mule rides, too! One mile on the left!" Okay now, mule rides! We have no choice but to stop. Running the place is a woman named Jo, a gorgeous thirty-something (maybe even forty-something) year old, super friendly, long golden hair, sweet smile that just opens up her face, and dressed up like a real cowgirl, muddied cowboy boots, and all (kinda like Mom in her Oakley Moore days).

So, back to the mules. Yours truly gets to ride Cody and Billy gets King James. Here are some notes for you: 1) mules attract flies as big as field mice; 2) the difference between mule shit and horse shit is not worth exploring; 3) if you aren't used to riding a mule, afterwards not only will your butt and legs hurt but so will your balls; 4) either Jo gave us the two laziest mules in the world, or, pure and simple, mules do not like to move, never mind run (or whatever the fuck it is that mules do—gallop, trot, lope, canter?) They'll leisurely amble along, nice and chill, get you relaxed and bam, sudden stop. Hence the sore testes.

It was cool. A great big afternoon of nothing but being and enjoying.

Two hours later, we cross the Mississippi. It is wide, it is muddy, and late this afternoon it was bronze. Thus, on this evening of July 2, 2008, I find myself at Mark Twain Inn. It's just before eight o'clock, shadows are long and across the way, the music is still playing from Friends of *the Dead Saloon. I'm sitting in the motel's check-in office/visitor's center/ breakfast nook/movie-rental center/discount coupon outlet/and internet access depot, but I'm here just until either I get kicked out or Billy is done with his shower. The choice of the evening's entertainment is a no-brainer. Tonight is "Bowl, Bite, and Belch Night" at Hannibal Lanes. I don't know how much bowling or biting or belching you get to do, but however much you get it's all three for $12.95.*

Good luck with your new friends. Hope you can keep up with them. And listen, it'll all be good, don't let the old age home get you down. I'm here and you're there and life is weird, but life is good. Maybe in a couple of years we'll do a trip like this together, me and you, on the road. Hey, it's 2008, and guess what—time passes, yeah, really, it does. Ten years from now it'll be 2018 and maybe our chance will be gone. Let's make a plan, bro, no kidding.

If you need to get hold of me, use Billy's number. Otherwise I'll just keep checking email. I know you'll let me know anything I need to about mom.

Love, Alex.

Wednesday, July 3
12.

THERE WERE BILLBOARDS along the bus routes, stickers on car bumpers, signs on the lawns: Save the Tatas. One-percent of anything you bought anywhere in the world—from Evian to Slimfast to a Five-Hour Energy Drink to the pink case for your iPod—would go to research. Linda resented them. She hated the ads. "Yeah, and save the assholes, too. Remember to wear brown," thought Linda Finklestein Moore, wife of the late Dennis Moore, mother of Alex and Tommy Moore, cancer survivor.

Three years earlier, the doctors had had Linda and her stage 3 colorectal cancer one foot in the grave. First came the chemo and radiation in an effort to shrink the tumor. The treatments had burned her mouth and skin, turned her teeth chalky, left her skinny, white, hairless, and nearly as lifeless as a Macy's mannequin. Linda sympathized with these bald mannequins and their winter hats: she was always cold, too. Occasionally, walking through the store, she'd touch her fingertips to theirs, want to cry. The chemo and radiation were followed by surgery. The surgeon removed two inches of her colon and half her rectum, and for six months she wore an ileostomy bag. There were no internal leaks, there was no infection, there was no sign of cancer, she was in remission.

By the spring of 2008, Linda was still in remission. Just a few months earlier, she had told both boys that after more than three years of bullshit, she was finally letting go of this constant cloud she carried above her and returning to her old self.

But that was several months ago. Not now. On her last visit to Dr. Hammond (whom she'd befriended and taken to calling Gabriella after all these years of nurturing) Linda confessed that she had noticed a change in her bowel movements: they were much more frequent, three or four a day, at least, and they came out like little worms, "No blood at all, no pain at all," Linda was quick to add.

Gabriella shook her head: "Then we may as well order a couple of scans and blood work, okay?"

"Sure," replied Linda, doing half her best to hide her disappointment and anguish.

Dr. Hammond turned to her screen, scrolled: "Next available appointment is for Tuesday, the 9th. And this way you can get it all done in one day."

"Nothing sooner?"

"It seems long but it's less than a week. Honestly, a few days isn't going to make any difference. Could you make it at 1:00?"

And that put a halt to the daily improvement of Linda's spirit. Even if it was nothing, if it turned out fine, at the very least she was back in this purgatory-lite of waiting rooms, needles and tubes of blood, and all the hits of yesteryear playing softly through the intercom while being told to lie still. Back to anxiety, obsession, and a false face towards her kids.

13.

HIRED.

Overnight, the heavy plastic curtains that lined the walls of the Grand Hall had been removed and, voila, the Town Square was born. The entrance and perimeter were festooned in banners and balloons. Down one avenue was Vinny's Italian Ristorante, Frank and Tony's Barbershop and Hair Styling, and Swifty's Dry Cleaners; down another, Eclectica Gifts, Meyer's Confection, and Schmidt's Deli. To all this, throw in the barbershop pole, the striped awnings, the new "sidewalk" tables, and, of course, the colorful window stencils: a mustachioed man in floppy chef's hat twirling a pie, Betty Boop in high-heels and seamed stockings, a strawberry ice-cream cone right on the verge of dripping. Big band versions of songs from antiquity ("Tennessee Waltz," "Too Young," "The Best Is Yet to Come") filled the hall, their titles scrolling across an electronic board.

Same as the brochures, thought Tommy, same load of bull, an anesthetized life, a Disneyworld for the old folks. On the one hand, this new scene was shiny and bright, upbeat in its way, even with the many wheelchairs mixed in with the arm-in-arm women and the solitary slow-strolling men, hands in their pockets, as spry step-counters lapped the slippered, shuffling, and bent; on the other hand, it was kind of creepy, recalling to Tommy the board game he and Alex used to play intended to teach younger kids how to count money.

"Hey," Cathy called from the edge of the Grand Hall-turned-Town Square. They approached each other. "I'm ready if you are." Then she paused and slumped theatrically, waved her arms at all of it. "Isn't it awful? I don't like it. They should have talked to someone from Whole Persons first, that someone being me. These things can have unintended consequences."

"Definitely," said Tommy.

"They're much too obvious, in my opinion. They cross the line and could undercut everything."

14.

SARA BERRY AND Sandy Cassamarrano were the two more silent members of the foursome Tommy had overheard in the Grand Hall the preceding day. Both were scheduled to attend Consolation, Discernment, and Reconciliation for the first time. Cathy knew that first-timers frequently backed out of CDR—in fact, so did a lot of second and third timers. Sandy had been a resident for three years but hadn't previously expressed interest in CDR, and Sara was the new girl on the block. She'd arrived mid-June with her husband Archie. But less than a week after moving in, he had suffered a stroke, a bad one.

Sara didn't hear Tommy when he knocked, she didn't hear him when he rang the bell, and she didn't hear him when he opened the door and softly called her name, "Mrs. Berry?" reading it off a card as though he couldn't remember it independently. This apartment was different from the ones Cathy had walked him through the day before. In the middle of the living room, where the couch would normally have been, a man was lying in a full-sized hospital bed covered to his chest by a baby-blue blanket, his head raised at a slight angle. He was a light-skinned black man, but in patches his coloring was more grey here, more yellow there. His mouth was slightly open in a smile, and in a pretense of wakefulness, his eyebrows were lifted though his lids were shut. Although he seemed to be dreaming, he appeared thoughtful and alert as well, maybe even amused. Must have been having a happy dream.

Sara was in the bedroom, seated in a chair partially turned towards a bright southeast-facing window which, from the fifth floor, offered a long view of the Statue of Liberty and the New York Harbor. Tommy slowly stepped into her peripheral view, or so he thought. Her eyes were closed and remained closed, but there was no droopiness to Sara's face—no indication of a groggy sleep, her alert expression akin to her husband Archie's. Tommy took her to be meditating—meditating or something like meditating. She may even have been quietly humming. On the bureau to Tommy's right were two framed photos, old images of Native American women; the photos, once black and white, were now shades of gray. One picture, cracked and creased, probably the older one, was of a Native American girl, a teenager about Tommy's age. She stood erect in a traditional dress, beads around her neck, moccasins on her feet. The photo next to that was of a mature but still young woman, heavyset, perhaps thirty. She was wearing a prairie dress and her hair was in pigtails. She posed outside a cabin, reeds in her arms, her intelligent eyes impatient with the camera.

When Tommy glanced back at Sara, she was smiling at him.

"You like the pictures? That's my mother and my mother's mother. Those are the two who raised me."

"They're beautiful pictures. I'm sorry I bothered you."

"Oh, you didn't bother me. I was waiting for you. I was told I was going to have an escort. Tommy, right?"

"Yes."

She stretched out a hand for him to help her out of the chair. "Oh, boy, I hope I know what I'm getting into with all this, you know? Off we go to the elevator," she said, giving Tommy an elbow to take hold of. "Off we go to the gabfest."

15.

CATHY DEGNAN GRADUATED from the Academy of the Immaculate Heart of Mary, an all-girls high school in Hoboken just five miles south of Bon Secours, in 1987. She was a bright, pretty, and slightly under-achieving girl—but not so under-achieving that anyone would bother her about it. She had no primary high school activity or clique, only temporary ones which she generally regretted joining soon after she did so: a cross-country runner one year; a member of Miss Elainie, the school's literary magazine the next; a member of the debating team twice, quitting both times. If the teachers at AIHM—still, then, about half of them nuns—had been asked to assess Cathy on just about any scale, she'd have scored no ones and no tens. Even an eight would have been a surprise. Okay, she could be moody, could be too quick with a smart answer—but so could every other AIHM girl. In many ways, she was the 200th girl in a 400-girl school.

One thing about Cathy, though, did make the teachers take note. She was one of the two or three girls per class who professed interest in a religious vocation, in possibly becoming a nun herself. The teachers—nuns and lay teachers alike—argued over Cathy's suitability. These discussions sometimes turned heated, but this may have had more to do with the setting than with Cathy herself, the discussions taking place in the AIHM Teacher's Lounge. That lounge, with its opaque windows, dying plants, hidden ashtrays, and counters dirtied with spilled Cremora, was as dreary and unhappy a confinement as ever there was.

The teachers agreed that Cathy could be contrary. And, yes, they all agreed that in the context of a religious life this might be a problem. But the real debate, the high debate, had to do with the nature of Cathy's contrariness. In describing Cathy's behavior, the phrase of choice was "dialoguing with God." And the central point, argued over with simultaneous petty animosity and erudite parsing, was whether her dialoguing indicated a blessing or a blasphemy.

The first time Cathy ever heard the term she was still in grammar school, shortly after a spiritual despondency settled upon her young soul following the Rose Beach trip. The phrase was uttered by tall, blue-eyed Sister Ellen, Cathy's mentor and champion. As Sister explained it, dialoguing with God was the explanation for the radical swings in her faith. It was a trait God would only place upon the strong, but, Sister Ellen assured her, this hard-earned faith would mature into faith of the richest sort. And that was that, until the phrase was used against Cathy in her sophomore World Religions class. Sister Regina, too, was tall and beautiful but her beauty was stern, not loving and sweet, and she used the phrase as an accusation. With porcelain anger, Sister Regina accused Cathy of supreme and damning arrogance and pride. She reproached the sophomore: "We are here to serve and obey the Lord, not to bicker and barter with Him."

Even Cathy had to acknowledge that the sentence had been well-turned.

As she sped through her high-school years, the words "dialoguing with God" buzzed in Cathy's ears. More and more, though, it was not Sister Ellen's voice but Sister Regina's that rang true, all the more as Cathy was unable to hush herself into silence and humility. Indeed, it was a vice and an especially troubling one when the dialoguing would flare into a shouting match between this seventeen-year-old Karamazov in knee-socks and Great God Almighty. Afterwards, Cathy would feel guilty and forlorn, especially so for winning all the time. She'd have been better off if her heart had followed her mind into atheism, but it couldn't—the presence of the Lord was too intimately ingrained. In the liturgical phrase, His presence dwelt within her, and He would not be evicted.

16.

CONSOLATION, DISCERNMENT, AND Reconciliation meetings were held in the smaller of the two second-floor multi-function rooms. On the blonde wood conference table sat a red pillar candle atop a mat of wicker and green plastic leaves—a year-round Christmas. Also scattered across the tabletop were several books, all with white covers, embossed lettering, and gold or red page-ribbons. Tommy and Sara completed the group at seven. Cathy made quick reference to the two no-shows. One, Josie, had passed on ("She always had a smile for you"). The other missing-in-action, Jessica, had been picked up by her son to attend her granddaughter's AAU Tennis Tournament—she was always at a grandkids' sports event somewhere, and at 77 still sporty herself.

So, it was Tommy and Sara, Cathy and Sandy, Annie from the Residents' Council, and a frail little man who seemed to carry the weight of the world on his curved, bony shoulders, and who, out of kindness, Tommy assumed, wasn't asked to repeat his name though he'd whispered it too softly for anyone to hear. Completing the group was Sister Margaret Mary. Sister was the odd-ball Tommy had expected, just much younger, about 30. She was a tall woman with chipmunkish cheeks, pursed lips, and wire-rimmed glasses set to a head that was too broad on the upper half and too narrow on the lower. Sister Margaret Mary began playing a secret game of quick-glance hide-and-seek as soon as all were seated. When introduced to Tommy, she nodded but abruptly averted her eyes as though they'd revealed too much—though in reality they'd done nothing of the sort, merely made Tommy wonder if he'd missed something that had in fact been disclosed. Except for her scripted opening reading, Sister wouldn't speak for the entire session. She merely smiled and nodded, moved a finger enough to be noticed only to still it as soon as it was; occasionally, she might cast a knowing glance that hinted at an insight which couldn't even be guessed at. Hands folded in his lap, the burdened little man also remained silent and distracted, attentive only to some omnipresent wrong he'd committed who-knew how many decades earlier which floated somewhere, if not everywhere, just above his unhaloed head. He seemed oblivious to his surrounding environment, treating CDR with no more or less regard than he would have an empty room, a marching band, or a ride on an upholstered chair through outer space, his frail frame mere purgatorial baggage lugging around a remorseful but unforgiven soul.

Like the previous day's Residents' Council Meeting, the CDR Meeting had more than a hint of hallelujah about it. The three, Cathy, Annie, and the sad, old gent (upright suddenly, briefly--this opening ritual serving as his starter's whistle) knew how to begin the traditional bible verse quotation prayer. Sister Margaret Mary merely mouthed the words slyly—slyly except for the one moment she giggled and had to cover her mouth. Sara, Sandy, and Tommy followed along: "I am holding you by the right hand—I, the Lord, your God. And I say to you, do not be afraid, for I am here to help you.' Isiah 41:13."

"Sister, have you picked a reading for today?"

"Mm-hmm, I have," smiled Sister. She pulled one of the white books towards her, watching everyone watch her hand. She coughed, wiped something from her eye.

She opened the book and paused. "I say unto you, watch out for people who cause divisions and upset people's faith by speaking contrary to what they have been taught." Her eyes moved person to person. Her voice transformed into a harshly whispered secret: "'Stay away from them. By smooth talk and glowing words they deceive innocent people.' Romans 16, 17-18." Head bowed, she gently rode the book back to the table's center, a Ouija planchette moving on its own. "Stay away from them," she warned. Then "Pop"—her fingers jumped from the book.

For the sake of the newcomers, Cathy repeated the mission of CDR: "Consolation in the face of sorrow. Discernment of God's plan for us. Reconciliation to His divine providence."

To his great relief, Tommy realized that not everyone had to speak at every CDR session. He figured this basically gave him the hour off, and he was sort of right. It would be the two newcomers with the session's lead speaking parts. The ladies agreed to let the gentleman go first, Sara would follow. Tommy relaxed into his chair, ready to sit through whatever grievance, ailment, or nostalgic tale the old man had to tell. In any case, Tommy thought he was ready, but Tommy was wrong.

17.

SANDY BEGAN: "WELL, okay, then. Well then, my whole life, so my whole life, 82 years of it. Eighty plus years of life comes down to one day." Except for a rim of white hair, Sandy was bald. Still, he needed a haircut, strands of white hanging over his collar. He had his from-birth set of tobacco-yellowed teeth that fit comfortably into his mouth. His face and freckled arms were as cleanly scrubbed as every other resident's, but he hadn't shaved in a couple of days and his cheeks were lit with silvery stubble. "July 16, 1977. That's the day. That's the day my son was killed." Sandy's hands, spotted with age but strong, the fingernails ridged and a darker yellow than his teeth, were set flat on the table and he leaned in, hunched towards them, like he was about to do pushups. "My son Joe. That's the day Joe was killed or at least the day we believe he was killed. I was 48, my wife Carol was 45, Joe was 22."

Tommy took a good look at Sandy, attending to the stoic misery in his voice. And just that quickly, Tommy realized he was not ready for this. He doubted he'd ever be. Glancing up, Sandy noticed Tommy's graying pallor and slackening facial muscles and smiled at him reassuringly, almost apologetically, before continuing.

"Joe had just graduated in May with a B.S. in Anthropology. He was talking about writing a book on Native Americans," he said looking towards Sara. His eyes lifted from the table but not quite enough to meet hers. "It was just in the talking stage. He tried to persuade us that this was the reason for his trip, there was something about undeciphered petroglyphs around where some of the Pueblos were, you know, that it was that, and not just the adventure of being 22 and having fast feet. He had gone to UMass and had an outstanding future ahead of himself, and, well, he just needed this exciting experience. And he deserved it. We were all for it. So he was hitchhiking across country, all alone he was doing it. It was somewhat common then. No, of course, I don't mean very common but not so far out of the norm as it would be today. Since those days, our whole society has made a right-ways turn.

"Me and Carol, though, like I said, we were all for it. 'Do your thing, young man. Go for it.' We were anxious for sure but we couldn't control what he did. Hell, we wouldn't have wanted to. It was his time of life." Firmly, Sandy tapped the table with one bent finger. "It was his time. Joe's. With the long hair and the scruffiness and the denim and corduroy everything, he was the epitome of that generation. . . and the kid had such a smile. They're maligned, that generation, but they shouldn't have been then and they shouldn't be now. All his friends were such wonderful kids.

"It was worrisome, too, you know, but Joe was good about it. He called every day or two, and the calls were terrific. He'd just tell us what he was up to and where he was, usually a gas station or something in the middle of nowhere. He got to where he was tired of saying that phrase, the middle of nowhere so we'd ask and he'd say 'Not sure, must be the edge of somewhere.' Sometimes he'd mention a wacko who'd picked him up. That was scary to a mother and father, but mostly these guys were just goofy, at least the way Joe presented them, nothing danger-ous. Of course the phone calls ended with I love yous, usually multi-ples, multiples upon multiples to where him and Carol even got me saying it in multiples. It was like a running joke. We waited every day.

"Hah, phew. Well, the last call we got was on July 10th from a town called Elkhardt which is half in Kansas and half in Oklahoma, which is something we always remembered because Joe literally didn't know what damn state he was in. We were excited though more than anything else, living it with him. So much life.

"Then . . . but then after Elkhardt, the phone calls just stopped." Sandy's palms came up from the table. Pfff-pff—it seemed like the table almost lifted with them, his palm- and fingerprints remaining. "Carol and I waited and waited. Then we prayed and we prayed and we prayed some more. We prayed to God." He lifted his head and this time stared directly at Cathy, challenging her somehow, challenging the C and the D and the R, all of it. The hurt in Sandy's voice was thick. But more than this, Cathy was jolted by his anger, and it all seemed directed at her, God's mouthpiece. "We didn't know what to do," the old plaintiveness in Sandy's voice overwhelming the anger. He'd been taken in again, for that one awful second, taken in with the hope that it could all be undone.

"We didn't have the slightest idea. Whoever imagines being in that situation? We didn't know where Joe was. We had no idea, not within two hundred miles. It wasn't like today with so much technology, everybody carrying cellular phones. He was all alone. He was just that—our son all alone. A kid. We didn't know what to say to the cops, we didn't even know which cops to contact. The state police? The FBI? Who the hell knew?" A few seconds passed as Sandy gathered breath. "When we didn't hear anything from him in a few more days we called the FBI. Now, we were trying to calm ourselves, trying to con ourselves, saying we were just being a pair of nervous nellies. We even kind of made jokes, you know—Joe is out there having the adventure of a lifetime, smoking marihuana, and making love to beautiful girls, and we're worrying to death.

"Anyway, to shorten it, the FBI was very good, they were great. We learned the last time Joe had been seen was in a little dump of a town, Wagon Mound, in New Mexico, in a little cafe/deli sort of place. He was miles from nowhere. It was a meaningless place. The agents described the dirtbag he was with as a little guy with a bandage on his neck, a gauze thing over his throat actually. This scum had picked up Joe hitch-hiking and he's the one wound up killing him. That would have been the 14th, the café thing, July 14th. And then, and then, hmmph . . . anyway, and then they spotted this same car which was a white pickup in the backyard of a shack in Las Vegas, it was a mess of weeds and spare car parts—Las Vegas, New Mexico, not Nevada. He was dead inside there, wrapped up in some sheets on the couch. He had been shot multiple times, all over. Fuc . . . rying out loud. What else? The state and local cops took over. They said he'd been dead at least 24 hours. Well, that detail doesn't matter. What does number of hours matter? What does number of hours mean? Nothing.

"We were out there the next day, and that was, oh, the worst moment of my life. That was my death, too. He was cleaned up. Me and Carol touched him. But he was cleaned up. You know, you know . . . a . . . a corpse. We touched his face and hands, but it wasn't him, wasn't Joe. It was like an awful fake doll." Sandy's eyes reddened. His chest heaved and the big man he had always been became more obvious. "God. Oh, God. We brought him home, buried him in Holy Name which is where Carol is now, too. And that was that. That was that, it was over. Over.

"I still go to the cemetery, I guess now once every couple of months. But I don't stay long, I didn't, not even in the beginning. You know how lost you feel standing there, how useless? What are you gonna do? What? There's nothing to do. I don't pray. Certainly not. And the little stinking bastard? The little scumbag who killed Joe? He just disappeared into the desert, like goddamned tumbleweed. For all I know, he could still be alive today.

"And that's it. And 'it's' what, what is 'it'? It is nothing. Zero, emptiness, nada. That's why I always say to myself what I said just before—it's the only day in my life that really matters. And, you know what's sad—I got a daughter, too, Claire. She was six years younger than Joe, middle of high school. After that, she never had a dad, a real dad, a dad who could love her. I wasn't capable. I didn't have it in me.

She's in California—married to a good man. I have two grandkids, a boy and a girl. I don't even know their ages—the girl Amy is the older--she has to be a teenager by now. But I don't know them, I have no grandkid stories to tell. I'm the kind of grandpa they only hear from around Christmas—I stick two checks in an envelope. It's unfortunate, but it's all my doing . . .

"Well, back to my story. . . Afterwards, every day before Joe died, all those days seemed like a bad trick, a really cruel joke, you know," he looked up and around for the first time, briefly meeting eyes. They should understand, every one of them, damn it. Why tell the story for them to half understand? He turned back to Cathy. "All bullcrap, all deception. And every day since, oh, I don't know, a hollow life, a shell. What have I been doing? Waiting, waiting, waiting. Not life, no. Not living. No."

When Cathy gained the courage to look into Sandy's eyes—to do her job, fulfill her mission—it was too late. Sandy glared past her and into the white wall behind.

"Anything more you want to tell us?" she asked, the quiver in her voice not quite controlled.

Sandy paused, nodded. "So, if I had to describe myself," he said, and wiped the corners of his eyes with his fingertips, checked to see if they were moist. "If I had to describe myself ever since then, I'd say I've been kind of a hard and insensitive person. I don't know. No, no, not that really. No sense being unnecessarily cruel to yourself. Just, I'm missing something. I'm incapable of some things, I have been for a long time. One expression you could use—emotional cripple, emotional cripple. Yes." It was a simple factual statement, not pained, not enraged, a mundane reality. Sandy lifted his gaze from his folded hands to the white ceiling. "I also know this. The way I am, what I just described about myself is not so much because of what happened to Joe, as it is *for* Joe. You don't know what I mean, I bet. It's something of a choice . . . that I am not going to let go. People have told me, friends and priests and whatnot, that I should let go, that I have to, but I tell you right now, that's not going to happen. I'm not going to let go because I do not want to let go and I do not have to let go. Walk away from the gravesite and look forward to the day ahead? Are you kidding me? I refuse! Joe dies and I go on living, enjoying? No. I'm sorry. I'm sorry. No way, not me."

Sandy's throat locked up. There were no more words from him. He heaved and the air blew from him like a rough sob.

Like the simple-minded, more-harm-than-good side-kick she was, Sister Margaret Mary dramatically touched two fingers to each temple and looked to Cathy. "Oh, my. Uh-oh," she seemed to be saying. "What do we do now?" Everyone's attention turned to the group's leader: certainly it was Cathy's job to speak, to guide, to find the correct response to Sandy's confession, to his denial, his refusal. Sandy stared at her directly, his eyes challenging her: "Go ahead, tell me all about Jesus' love. Just tell me all about it." Cathy sat rigid, a frightened look on her face, the look of a kid being bullied into a fight she didn't want. Sister was shaking her head, fingers covering her mouth. Only Sara's face remained soft, both intimate and observant, transfixed and receptive.

"Let us pray a silent prayer," said Cathy. Sandy closed his eyes and shook his head—there hadn't been a prayer in him since 1977. The very notion of praying to God turned his stomach. Cathy noticed this and her guilt by association swelled.

She continued, pulling the white prayer book towards herself and ruffling through its pages though it was obvious that her ruffling was random. "Instead," she said. "Instead of a prayer, let us just think . . . let us just be . . . and contemplate on what Sandy has said, it was so moving. Let's think on what we are here for, ourselves, individually, all of us and each of us—and for . . . consolation, and all. We must trust. We must." She closed her eyes. "We must have faith that God is good."

Sandy's mouth began to move, as though he were chewing his own lips and gums.

"Only Sandy can understand his own feelings," continued Cathy. "How to follow that moving . . . those deeply moving words, I don't know. Would anyone like to address Sandy? No, no? I understand certainly. Well, if not . . . then, well, Sara, we still have time for you. Would you like to share with us?"

"Oh, no," said Sara, reaching out to take Sandy's hand, forcing him to extend it. "I don't think so. I'm a newcomer, but I don't know, I don't think so. What this beautiful man told is so much touching my heart. I don't think so. I don't think I want to talk now. Okay, if I'll talk next time?"

"Of course, yes. Certainly. You're right," stammered Cathy. "Then, let us say our closing prayer for Reconciliation with the Lord."

Sandy pushed back his chair as though he needed a broader view to grasp just what Cathy was suggesting. It was hard to believe that he was going to be asked again to pray. He shook his head. "I don't think so," he whispered. "No, no. I can't do that. I'm sorry." He pushed himself up from his seat and shuffled to the door, waving his hand goodbye, waving everything away, his last glance sweeping across Tommy's face.

"'When you go through deep waters and great troubles, I will be with you. When you go through rivers of difficulty, you will not drown,'" read Cathy. "And this one, this one, too," she added, now looking directly at Tommy. "From Proverbs, remember, remember: 'Do not withhold good from those who deserve it when it is in your power to help them.'" But Tommy was inattentive to her, engrossed in watching Sandy disappear down the corridor. She repeated more forcefully: "'Do not withhold good from those who deserve it when it is within your power to help them.'"

18.

AT 12:30 P.M., four hours and 250 miles after pulling out of Hannibal, at Alex's insistence they pulled into Lawrence, Kansas—nominally for lunch, but while Billy was getting himself a sub, Alex checked into Feyton's Family Motor Inn:

Hey bro, some pretty big news. Well, pretty big for me, anyway. Billy and me are going to split up. There was no fight, God bless us. In fact there was no scene at all. I want to go at a slower pace than Billy. In fact, you could say I have no pace at all, and a few hundred miles a day just doesn't cut it for him. He's excited about getting to USC. He's got profs to meet. He wants to see the campus, set up his apartment, get a part-time job, etc. I understand that and respect it. It's just not where I'm at. I can't say I planned to split up, but I think at some level I anticipated it, knowing my situation, knowing Billy's, and honestly, I don't really mind it. Anyway, the two of us are still planning to meet up in CA, I just don't know when I'm gonna get there.

Well, so much for that. As you can figure the morning took us through MO and into KS. I knew I wanted to split with Billy and Lawrence seemed like the perfect place for me and my wheel-less self to land. A big college town is what I want. It's got cool stuff nearby to explore (nature stuff, cultural stuff, historic stuff). And why is the college part important? Libraries, gyms, bars, cafes, bookstores. Young people to blend in with and not get arrested for vagrancy. Girls. Free or cheap public transportation.

I called mom last night and we had a nice chat, even though I had to make up a story about why I was calling from Billy's phone instead of my own and had to put her off on all of her questions. She's planning out her fall classes and sounded happy and excited for me even after all she's been through.

I'm staying at a motel tonight and it's gonna cost me $33–$33.33 to be exact. A few nights of this is gonna break the bank. So job number one will be to find a place where starting tomorrow I can sleep free or pennies-from-it and hopefully safely. Let the games begin. Starting this afternoon, I'm a lone traveler in Bleeding Kansas.

Love, Alex

19.

DESPITE HER DOUBTS, Cathy had entered the Convent of the Sisters of Bon Secours one month shy of her nineteenth birthday on a Sunday afternoon in August of 1987, after dropping out of Caldwell College in the middle of spring semester. Her parents, silently fearful, dropped her off at noon and, as instructed, were gone by 1:00. She was anxious and questioning and desperate for illumination, but so were all sixteen of the new ones.

Monday and Tuesday didn't go well. This didn't surprise her and certainly she wasn't alone: she could hear crying through the walls. In session, they talked about it those first few mornings. Such melancholy was natural, indeed healthy, a kind of shedding. It would surely be odd if it weren't present.

Wednesday was better. She awoke at peace, if not illuminated. Sadly, though, it was a brief peace that vanished in the bright but airless corridor between the residences and the cafeteria. During that afternoon's respite, she sequestered herself in the dark North Chapel, praying the rosary the entire time. And, reassuringly, this prayerful meditation worked. She was chatty and gay at supper; it seemed like a summer camp and she felt like a leader. But that night, as she washed in only a bra and half-slip, her reflection caught her unannounced and her small frame was overwhelmed with fear. Clicks popped from her throat, her mouth locked open. These clicks came more and more quickly and she couldn't stop them. Pacing did calm her—tiptoed pacing (she must have looked crazy!) in a baby's white socks, so gently not a floorboard sounded. Finally, she could bring herself to sit on the edge of the bed, her heart pounding, hands to her chest. Shortly after two a.m. she fell into a restless sleep, and, when she awoke in the morning, still shaken from her freak-out (a harsh word but so much less so than nervous breakdown) she washed up but kept her eyes closed to avoid the mirror.

Thursday morning's early walk through the woods helped to revive her, to put a lid on the night's horrors. She tried to latch onto some of the other girls' joy, and was uplifted by Wolf Creek's bubbling waters, by the pale sunlight cutting through the trees, by the appreciation of these, God's gifts, and by the salvation she knew was available to all supplicants. She made a commitment to a new outlook, one strong, optimistic, wholly loving, appreciative of every second on this earth, one by which she would convince herself of the shared absolute love between herself and God. Simply, this is who she would be. A nun. This is what she was meant to be and would be. Only be brave, Cathy, you must be brave and open-hearted.

They saw through her, though, the nuns and the other aspirants did. Her effort, her transformation was so obvious. It was a blatant and even unnerving enactment: the chatting and smiling, the sympathizing and over-sympathizing, the consolation she hoisted onto those girls who were still downhearted.

Thursday night Cathy took two precautionary sleeping pills and they knocked her out. She awoke still feeling drugged and had to drag herself to prayers. She struggled all morning, and by noon acknowledged that the most appealing thing in the world would be to simply give up—to call her parents and ask to be taken home. That would be heaven.

After lunch a headache pulsed at the temples and throbbed at the base of her skull. She thought that she might have a fever, she hoped that she did. Mid-afternoon brought her back to the North Chapel, but this time there was no relief. She covered her ears and screamed so loudly the birds on the roof scattered.

Late afternoon, she called her parents to pick her up—she had changed her mind, she told them, childlike, just those five words: "I changed my mind, mom." And they came for her, were there within two hours. She could never love them enough for this. Her only recollection of the ride home was sitting in the back seat, her mother's window cracked an inch, the breeze hissing upon her, every bit of tragic, golden landscape made warm by their love—their love, not God's. Why couldn't He, why didn't He? That would have resolved everything.

At home she showered, then with a towel-covered hand wiped clear circles in the steamed mirror. She saw herself and her heart popped open with love. She was a sweet and human child, pale and frail, but so willing to love, so capable of it. When she walked into the living room, the Mets were warming up for an eight o'clock start and it was familiar and beautiful. She rested her head on her mother's shoulder. Her father sat in his lounger, happiness in his weary eyes—his girl was home again, safe and happy.

It was a room full of love.

God was not there.

He would never be there.

And that would have to do.

That would do fine.

Thursday, July 4
20.

IT WAS THE end of the workday, 4:30 on the Fourth of July. The Town Market's stores had darkened and closed, and just one poor worker remained—a skinny, young Sikh in flopsy linen pants, long and slipping from his waist, his turban off. He was sweeping in front of Swifty's Dry Cleaners. He was all alone tonight—usually there were two. His pace and body language said this sucked.

Cathy planned to be at Bon Secours until midnight. The residents would be watching the fireworks: some would be watching from outside with its perfect Manhattan view across the river; others would watch from the auditorium where they'd wheel in the 64-incher. Cathy was wandering, looking for Henry, Associate Director of Operations, when she spotted Tommy on his way out.

"Hey," she called.

"Hi, Miss Degnan."

"It's Cathy."

"Hi, Cathy."

"Come by later and watch the fireworks with us. Perfect night for it."

"I might, I don't know if I can."

"It should be fun. Not only the fireworks, you know . . ."

"I know, the music."

"Yeah, definitely," she said. "You like folk music, old American-style music?"

"I don't even know," he said, backing his way to the exit.

"See what you can do."

"Yeah, I promised my friends I'd watch with them. But maybe."

Yes, he had told his friends he'd be down at the park. Promise, though—that was definitely the wrong word. Already, he was feeling drawn to Cathy and the band of residents. But no. He was not going to spend 4th of July night at Bon Secours. No thank you.

Cathy's buddy Henry House was seated in a tucked-away corner nook—a pair of blue pastel chairs, a small plexiglass table, a wall-mounted TV: "Have you ever suffered from mesothelioma? If so, call the Mesothelioma Asbestos Law Firm of Hammer and Smythe at 1-800- MESOBUX." After the commercial, a mini-explosion erupted on the screen behind which appeared Wolf Blitzer: "Welcome to the Situation Room. Breaking news just this hour."

Cathy was the one who had talked Henry into applying for the Associate Director position. And, yeah, it would have been better if she had kept to her own business, but it wasn't in him to hold this against her. She wanted to help. She was too eager, though. She didn't know how to pull back; that piece of common sense, common courtesy maybe, was not in her. But if a person is going to have a flaw, well, being a meddling do-gooder was low on the list of possible character defects.

"God will watch over," she'd said, sensing Henry's ambivalence about the job switch, and while Henry was a believer, and accepted that most likely, yes, God would watch over, He'd made no promise about protecting fools from their own folly.

Henry had been employed by Bon Secours since it opened in 1989, first as a Service Worker, then as a Maintenance Worker, then as a Maintenance Shift Manager—which is exactly where he should have remained, no shame in that. It's not like he had been dead-set against the Associate Director position, but Cathy was the one who'd really latched onto the idea. She coaxed and coached and he got the job in late 2006. For the past two years, he'd spent his days and too many nights balancing budgets, mediating between workers and bosses (but not nuns, thank you Jesus: they were off limits), and spending a fortune on books guaranteed to teach you the leadership skills of Jesus Christ, Attila the Hun, Donald Trump, and Oprah's boyfriend.

"What are you so pensive about?" Cathy asked.

"Caught me," Henry responded, chuckling at himself.

He was 52 years old, a black man with a beginning-to-bald head and broad nostrils that flared from a sharp nose. Now, thanks to this job, he wore a shirt and tie to work every day and only recently, at the pleading of his daughter, had he dropped the tie clip. He had a broad chest and shoulders that filled out his shirt so that you could see the impression of his athletic tee beneath. He smiled all the time. Or at least he tried to, hiding any of his own troubles well and from all.

"What's the word?" Cathy asked, taking the second chair.

"No word, nothing really," he said, one finger scratching his balding scalp. "Well, they breaking them up. I figured it. Lauryn going southwest," he said with a swirl of the finger. "Junior going a little more east, a little more north and east." He swiveled his finger towards a different over-yonder. "That's more dangerous out there, near what they call 'the rugged hills of Pakistan.' I hate that damn Pakistan, hate the name, hate the country. Anyway, we just wait and see. We still got a couple days left."

His kids were 24 and 22, Lauryn the older. They'd been babies when Henry started at Bon Secours and had grown up right before Cathy's eyes. Two years earlier they had joined the Marines and were both sent to Afghanistan, where they were in the middle of a nine-month tour.

"Four months left," said Henry. "Not too much." Much of what he said to Cathy was false. No need to cause her any worry. What good would that do? Trying to make the girl feel good was more important than telling her the truth. Losing her parents, losing her ex the way she did—it was clear as day that she'd been staggered by this rough year.

On TV, a military analyst aimed a laser pointer at a map of Afghanistan and Pakistan. Little explosions bloomed red then faded to yellow atop the green and brown topographical map.

The Sikh kid finished his vacuuming and checked his cell phone. He was closer to them now.

"Abil, what are you doing to celebrate the Fourth?" asked Henry.

"My friend is home from the Navy, she's a girl. We're going up near the bridge. But I got to get this done. Lee didn't show up and I got to set up for tonight by myself."

"Yeah, leaving you in a lurch, huh? He on a short rope. I'll help you with the chairs."

The three members of Plain Folk—the evening's performers— appeared at the reception desk, one lugging a covered upright bass, the other two with smaller instrument cases.

"Let me greet them," said Cathy. "I expect you to be singing tonight," she called back to Henry.

"No, I ain't gonna be here."

"Henry..."

"No. I'm gonna miss this year. Gonna skip. I just don't feel like in the mood for socializing. I'll be watching, though, and I'll enjoy it, watching those red-white-and-blue fireworks where they belong, way, way up in the air where they can't hurt nobody."

21.

TOMMY SPENT THE 4th of July evening at the Weehawken Little League Field. The menu was pretzels, Donettes, Powerade, and a tray of brownies Carrie had baked. The game was whiffle ball. The tall banks of lights hadn't been turned on, but the field was bright enough from the rippled reflection of the Manhattan skyline on the river, the red-pink lights of the warehouse terminal just north, and the yellow streetlights atop the hill—bright enough for a twilight game and a return to those days of yore when they were Little Leaguers themselves. Every evening the field was locked up, unless you were in the know. High brush ran along the right field line, even beyond the outfield fence, almost to the river. Concealed by the brush, the two poles where the right field fence and the outfield fence met had been pulled apart, leaving easily enough space to squeeze through.

"Long time," said Jesus.

"Long time, man. Long fucking time."

"Too much, ain't it."

First pitch was at 8:00. There were fifteen kids in all—Tommy's school buddies, several friends' cousins, four girls. They hid the Ballantine Ale under the aluminum bleachers but smoked the pot openly. The first fireworks arched over the river at 9:05 when it was top of the fifth, score tied 8-8. The fireworks made a perfect excuse for that half of the group that wanted to quit the game to do so.

Well, long-haired Jesus wasn't about to leave the game—he was easily the best player with an uncanny knack for hitting with two strikes—and therefore neither did Allie, and when she didn't leave neither did Bruce. When Bruce didn't leave neither did Shale. Spanny would stay put until he hit one over the fence and John and Mickey stayed just to bust his chops. Bobby stayed, too, sort of: he was very high and just standing in the outfield, not really doing anything, not definitively "there." Yoo-Hoo and Charlie left the field because they were into fireworks, truly. Then Carrie left because Charlie had and he was like a brother, nothing more, and Jules followed because she followed Carrie everywhere. When Carrie left, Tommy did, too, not because he had a crush on her but because she had one on him, and he was curious as to what would happen sitting with her by the water. It wasn't just that Tommy had grown in the past year. Recently it had become obvious that there really were bones beneath the flesh of his face and beneath his, gulp, baby fat. He doubted but no longer entirely ruled out the possibility of being attractive to the gentler sex.

The fireworks-watchers left the field and made their way across the rocky patch between left field and the river wall, a collapsing stretch of stone and concrete built the same time as the warehouses, right after WWII. It served as a sort of bench, your feet dangling just above the glimmering black water, though a few in the group sat the opposite way, back to New York and the fireworks, Tommy being one of those. Carrie sat next to him, trying to stretch her toes down to the water and holding onto Tommy's elbow for balance.

Her making-small-talk-to-boys-you-like skills were pretty good, barely, but Tommy wasn't offering much to work with.

"You're working at an old age home? Is it awful?"

"Moderately."

Carrie and Jules shared a laugh over Tommy's predictable one-word response and, when he predictably ignored their laughter, they predictably laughed even harder.

"Well, are the people at least nice?"

"Are they really sad?" asked Jules. "They're really old, right?"

"They're old. Yeah, they're definitely old." The girls stared at him. "Yes. Old. They. Are."

They cracked up. Amused as well, Tommy nudged both girls with his elbows, pretending to be pushing them into the river, evoking the desired screams, clutching, and smacking.

"Come on, tell us!"

The fireworks were banging bigger—smoke and sulfurous stink had reached them. Carrie pulled at Tommy's arm. "I can't even hear you," she complained. "Look at me so I can at least read your lips."

"Some of the people are very nice, really, really sweet. But the place is just bizarre, maybe just to me."

"Well, explain."

"Explain what?"

"Oh, my God," Carrie said to Jules. "The details," turning back to Tommy. "That's why you're so bad with essays."

"I am not so bad with essays," Tommy said as he pulled out and professionally lit a blunt.

"Oh, yes you are," Jules agreed. "Expound."

"Probe, develop, illustrate, Mr. Moore."

Well, so Tommy talked.

He told them about the choking aerosol smell, about the Pez lady, about Carmella's doggy-funeral argument, about the mimicking twins, about the weirdness of Sister Margaret Mary, about the mysteriousness, if not creepiness, of his boss's "by any means necessary" philosophy, about how *long* everything took. It was sort of hilarious. "Some of them the entire day is built around coming down for dinner, some of them waiting for the frigging cleaning lady to come by, some of them with checking the mail which *never* has anything except coupons."

"Stop, you're kidding," Carrie laughed.

"Not. I'm telling you the exact truth."

"I know it's mean but that is so funny."

"Finish the story about Carmella and the dead dog."

Halfway into the story—"And 'This is no damn cat, we're talking about,' the Carmella one says"—the noise grew too great for talking, and "Grand Finale!" announced Carrie. After the three finished the blunt, the sparkling dance on the water was more mesmerizing than the one in the sky and Tommy turned round to view it. Yeah, the girls had really enjoyed his stories, Tommy realized, but his satisfaction quickly shrank before suddenly blooming into something much less flattering. He wasn't much of a story-teller but just now he had used the Bon Secours people about as juicily as anyone could—he'd used all his material except Sandy's story, the one point at which even he stopped short.

The finale concluded to great cheers from both sides of the river. By the time they made it back to the baseball field, Tommy had returned to his usual silent self. Now in fact, he was downright sullen. Angry with and ashamed of himself, nearly to tears, Tommy left early, and Carrie told Jules that she wasn't surprised at all, that some boys just had to play hard to get.

22.

IT WASN'T A club rave, it wasn't a Manhattan disco party, it wasn't a 1950s Hop. But it wasn't bad for the lateness of the evening—nearly 10:00—and the age of the audience. After watching the fireworks from either Waterfront Park, from the auditorium, or from the comfort of their own apartment, fifty or so Bon Secours residents had found their way to the Hootenanny. With Sister Margaret Mary applauding from the wings, Cathy had introduced the performers to the crowd: "Ladies and gentlemen, I give you Plain Folk!" Sister rose to her tiptoes and speed-clapped.

Sandy had had no intention.

He'd sat in his lounger watching the Macy's display, expecting to hit the hay as soon as the show was over. But in the moments that the crowd downstairs was filing into the auditorium and Plain Folk opened their show—"Away from home, away from home/Cold and tired and all alone/Yes I'm five hundred miles away from home"—Sandy found himself restlessly dwelling on the previous afternoon's CDR, mostly bashing himself for his "performance," but occasionally surprised, maybe pleased, maybe proud that he'd opened his mouth and that for once true emotion had been attached to the words that came out. "It was a regular roil of emotions," he whispered, shaking his head, smiling at himself: "anger, surprise, shame, pride, embarrassment. All the biggies."

Though ten o'clock was his usual bedtime, Sandy found himself wide awake, and once those emotions had simmered, he found himself attentive to and curious about the music drifting up from the auditorium. He pushed up from his chair. Brushed his teeth and put on a clean shirt, checked his shorts for wrinkles and stains—wrinkles, really, who cared about those, but stains, they were a different story. He slipped on his sneakers and took the elevator down.

He grew lightheaded when the elevator came to a quick stop. Or, maybe what had made him woozy was the realization that he hadn't told Joe's story to the room or to no one at all, that he had not told it to Cathy and not to Sister, not to God, and no, had not told it to Joe or Carol. Really, he'd told it to the new gal Sara. Funny, that was. Dizzy, a bit, he latched onto the handrail for his first few steps down the hall.

> All along the southbound odyssey the train pulls out
> of Kankakee
>
> And rolls along past houses farms and fields

Passing trains that have no name and freight yards full of
old black men

And the graveyards of rusted automobiles.

Good morning, America. How are you?

Say, don't you know me? I'm your native son

I'm the train they call the City of New Orleans

And I'll be gone five hundred miles when the day is done.

Sandy took a few steps into the half-filled auditorium and stood
behind the last row of chairs, his hands on their backrests to keep his
back from going. A few of the friskier ones in the audience were up
and dancing in the open space to the left and right of the stage. Cathy
was one of them; Sister Margaret Mary was sitting on a radiator biting
her fingernails.

Clapping softly to the rhythm, singing out the choruses as did
most of the audience—red white, and blue confetti in her hair—Sara
was seated half a dozen rows from the stage, one empty chair in from
the aisle, but Sandy stood pat where he was.

But come ye back when summer's in the meadow

Or when the valley's hushed and white with snow

'Tis I'll be here in sunshine or in shadow

O Danny boy, O Danny boy, I love you so

"I love this song," said the man beside Sandy. He was a balding
pony-tailed man in a wheelchair whose navy cardigan carried in it the
memory of ten thousand smokes.

"I do, too. We used to sing it at family parties."

"And I bet you were drunk and sobbing when you did."

"Hah, yes. Yes we were. Both," chuckled Sandy. "Well, anyway, I just wanted to take a gander. I got my gander. Guess I'll be going up now. Have a good evening."

"Stay awhile. Have a seat, make yourself comfortable. Pick out a cute one. Got your eye on any gal in particular?

"Ha, no, I don't think so. You?"

"The one there leaning on her broom, Spanish gal, I think. Probably in her thirties."

"You're a character, buddy."

"Stay down awhile. There's probably just a few minutes to go."

"I appreciate your gesture, but I'm usually asleep by now."

"We're all *usually* asleep by now," said the man, his whiskered face smiling, looking up.

"Thank you for the invitation, but I'm tuckered out. Have a good evening."

"Yes, I will. And you, too, fella."

"Good luck. With everything, you know," said Sandy, tipping his head towards the cleaning woman.

"Oh, I only look. You know that."

Friday, July 5
23.

LAWRENCE NIGHT NUMBER one had been spent at Feyton's Motel; and against Alex's wishes due to the $33.33 price tag, he had spent night number two, the Fourth of July, there as well. Night three would be different.

That morning, Friday morning, at the northwest corner of the KU campus Alex discovered the campus arboretum, separated from the main campus body by two soft hills. If not quite a home base, at least it would be a place to sleep. One curving path wound through the pond-centered Free Nature Zone. There were imported cacti along its south border; orange, lavender, and yellow flowering plants scattered among the ubiquitous ferns. There were shading walnut and sycamore trees, and next to them redwood cedars to which Alex attributed the Zone's rich and soothing smell. Behind some tall grasses and under a pair of walnut trees, Alex dropped down his duffle bag. How well was his secret spot hidden? Well enough that anyone strolling through the arboretum would be none the wiser to his presence, but not well enough that anyone tromping around off path could miss it. What are the chances, thought Alex. It was such a relief to have that bristly strap off his shoulder and that weight off his back. He plopped down and took the odds.

The afternoon was oppressive, and Alex found escape from the heat inside the university's Watson Library—one of campus's smaller libraries dedicated to the biological sciences, a gothic, limestone building more than a hundred years old. It being mid-summer, the library was nearly empty: footsteps echoed in the marble entranceway; the scattered workers, whispering to one another or muttering to themselves, seemed suspicious if not creepy: What *were* they up to in there? Watson's four upstairs study rooms were carpeted, and in each of them was one student—in all cases male, in all cases soundly sleeping, in two cases loudly snoring. Alex entered a snorer-free room. The furniture was walnut and heavy and the chair he chose was difficult to move across the carpeting.

Alex took out his wallet. It was time to assess his finances. Cash: two fifties, a five, and three singles. He had change in his pocket, round it off to $110. And there was his debit card. How much was left on that, he wasn't sure, but it had to be fifty or sixty or seventy. Next time in town he'd get the exact number.

He stared at the Douglas County map on the wall. He'd remain in Lawrence just a few more days, then it would be time to do the hitch-hiking thing. Honestly, it was something he wasn't looking forward to. What was adventure without a little danger, yes? But then again, as he'd secretly suspected, maybe he wasn't quite the free spirit he told himself he was. He walked over to the map. A practice run—tomorrow or Sunday—would put him at ease. He chose a simple route: a quick thirty-mile trip west along Route 24, into an area of upland forests and small and larger streams that eventually found their way into Lake Perry. That should give him enough of a taste. Lake Perry State Park it would be.

SUMMER INTERNSHIP: REPORT ONE

Dear Mr. Collins,

Thank you so much for allowing me to achieve my summer internship position at Bon Secours Continuous Care Facility on the Hudson. I can already feel subtle changes at work deep within myself.

One of the extremely profound changes I have undergone has to do with my understanding of the common expression "the real world." As the result of one short week at Bon Secours, I now affirm that the real world is much more complex than I had previously imagined! In this regard, I would label reality a moving target! I have begun to highly suspect that there are indeed as many real worlds as there are people. In the words of the philosophers, no two people experience the same thing in the same way. You can, of course, take fireworks as one example.

Additionally, I have also learned that the residents of Bon Secours are, despite their age, nothing more nor less than that over-used noun, "people." Yes, a simple and some might say obvious observation but one I have only now come to. The elderly truly are just like everyone else, foibles and all! Remarkably, never before did I stop to think that the elderly were once something other than old. By the other side of the token, I have come to realize that the young will not always be young! (I have to admit that I'm not sure I really, really grasp this at my deepest level. Not that I want to, ha ha!)

My third learning point from this week has been one word— Responsibility! I cannot say this forcefully enough! I am beginning to get a bit of an inkling of what responsibility and community mean. As my boss, Ms. Catherine Degnan has helped me to understand my job is to help out the residents in any way I can and, in her own words, by **whatever means necessary.** *Yes, you can make yourself do or become something even if some of the things that you have to do or become did* *not at an earlier phase of life come natural to you. You can almost make it natural by simply declaring **I should and will** do it. You can get to a point where being a helpful, sharing, and consoling human being is something more than as you might say, a job. It becomes your way. Why not, I ask?*

I might add that openness and communication have also prevailed as I have relayed virtually all of the above to my mother on more than one occasion—the names Sara, Sandy, Cathy Degnan are already familiar to her—which is not my usual wont. I do this, for one, because I truly wish to share with her the profound experience I am having with the elders but also because I know that it makes my mother feel good knowing that I am so committed to this serious work of caring for and maybe even brightening the lives of these individuals, aged though they may be.

With this I will conclude. I will stop by this week to get from you the missing logs that Ms. Degnan has to complete according to the terms of my internship if you could be so kind as to ensure that someone is there with access to them. I look forward to seeing you soon!

Respectfully, Tommy Moore

WEEK TWO

1.

IN A COUNTY that included Jersey City, Kearny, Union City, Bayonne, and Hoboken, it was Linda Finklestein's hometown of Secaucus—associated only with pig farms and slaughterhouses, landfills and Mafia kills—that evoked the heartiest laughs locally and nationwide. It was the least urban of Hudson County's municipalities and in the days of Linda's youth—the early seventies—it was still home to dirt roads, undeveloped tracts of wetlands and wastelands, semi-urbanized hillbillies driving the same trucks the family'd owned since the end of WWII, and all of the county's rural- or road-oriented clubs: The Hudson County 4-H Club (a joke to the rest of the state, as the state club was a joke to the rest of the nation), The Hudson-Essex Motorcycle Club, the Hudson County Chapter of the Lincoln Highway Association, and the West Hudson Horse and Rodeo Association.

It was this last organization and its just-blocks-away presence that created in Linda a love of the Wild West. What could possibly be more magical than stirrups and chaps, an Indian head-dress, a ten-gallon hat, brown-and-tan guitars around a campfire, saying "two bits" when you meant a quarter?

For the first few years of her infatuation, when Linda was just six or seven, it was only her Halloween costumes that went the cowgirl route. But from there it spread, and Linda loved the whole of it. She loved the silver-painted plastic pistols, the holsters and gun belts that looked like leather but behaved more like cardboard, the stiff toy-lariats—throwing one was like throwing a hula hoop. She loved the outfits, especially loved them because they came by UPS and the man rang the bell: the scarves and handkerchiefs and tasseled vests; the hats of brown felt, the carved rhinestone belts, the spurs that jingle-jangle-jingled. Linda would nag and save, save and nag for months to get one of those foot-tall horse and rider models with saddles of real leather and riders so well made they could stand on their own or mount the horse, hands so real they could hold a gun or a rope, a cigar or a prayer book. To get one, she and her mom had to take a bus all the way into Journal Square in Jersey City.

Yet it was a solitary love. Try as she might to get them to, none of Linda's friends ever caught the bug. Beyond playroom make-believe and cowboy-show reruns, there was little outlet for Linda's passion. That's where the Horse and Rodeo Association came in. Though it was grown-man territory, she hung out there for hours after school and half the day on Saturdays, but there were only so many times (like two) that she could convince her friends to go riding, especially when there were no long and lovely trails to conquer. Instead, a rider could choose between the Association's third-of-a-mile track, an unpleasant mixture of mud and dung, and County Road 99 which your horse would have to share with barreling trucks as the old stage-route wound beneath the Turnpike overpass then skirted the bedeviled shore of the Hackensack River before dead-ending at the littered and graffitti'd base of Fraternity Rock. And fashion-wise, there was little support for calico and rhinestones in an age of disco and punk.

Then, in 1982 Dennis Moore moved into town. Lanky and laconic, half a mess but never frazzled, cool in an oblivious sort of way, Dennis was 19 to Linda's 18, somewhere having lost a year of school among his parents' frequent moves. Because he fell in love with this red-headed girl—tall and lanky, too, and with barely a cup size—he claimed to have fallen in love with the cowgirl obsession of hers as well, agreeing that there was no dancing like Western Swing, learning the names of heroes and heroines of the old west (celluloid and real), spending more than one Saturday afternoon on Linda's couch looking through *Western Fashions, Native American Crafts,* or *Old West Design.* They travelled on overnights to beautiful Pilesgrove, New Jersey, for Cowtown Rodeo weekends, and a few years later, Linda and Dennis Moore honeymooned in Albuquerque during U.S. Rodeo Championship Week.

A sweet and unambitious guy, a hippie without the trappings, Dennis was, in Linda's terms—and intended as a compliment—the world's greatest underachiever. After they graduated Secaucus High School, at Linda's urging Dennis went straight to college, Montclair State, just ten miles from home. He graduated with a double major in Business and English, a nice compromise between the practical and the day-dreamy. He wrote a handful of short stories, mostly science-fiction, and even sent a pair out for publication, but with little in the way of genuine passion and even less ambition, once those two were rejected, his literary career ended.

By the mid-eighties, the Secaucus Mail Terminal of the U.S. Postal Service was the county's largest employer. Dennis scored number one out of the hundred individuals who took the Clerk/Carrier test—"See, the world's greatest underachiever"—and began working there eight months after college graduation. Linda, meanwhile, worked as a girl Friday at AJ's Plumbing and Supply, a position she'd held on and off since she was sixteen.

Linda relished Dennis's love and warmth, his good nature, his openness, his presence. She had a sweet, good-looking husband who had a steady job to boot. A year after their marriage, they rented an apartment above a chiropractor's office in the more upscale town of Weehawken. That's when Linda decided to become an enterprise. Enter Oakley Moore, the Riding, Roping, Singing Cowgirl, Available for Parties and Occasions! Well, the riding portion was a bit misleading. For an additional fee, the Horse and Rodeo Association would deliver a riding rink and three ponies that she'd have to promise not to sit on herself—and no fat kids either! The roping was no problem. She brushed up on it and she was fine, but she was even better at the knot tying. None of those, though, compared with the singing. She turned herself into a passable guitar player and grew a repertoire of western songs, all of which worked as sing-alongs. The initial outlay for promotion and all the cowgirl schtick was $2,000. But Linda found the whole thing a blast and Dennis was her biggest fan.

In 1986, Linda became pregnant, and, when she could no longer squeeze into the denim, into the chest went the Riding, Roping, and Singing Cowgirl. Temporarily, she hoped. But no. Thereafter, appearances of Oakley Moore would be rare and free (though Linda's singing of cowboy songs would not be rare), coming out to play on her boys' birthdays and on those long summer days when a backyard rodeo seemed like the only and therefore the best idea.

2.

DENNIS HAD BEEN at the Post Office for six years when he was promoted to a supervisory job, just in time to oversee the phase-out of the old Lackawanna Terminal in Hoboken, a job he was promised would take no more than two years. Thanks to the unions and politicos, however, Lackawanna was destined to die a slow and contentious death. Five years later, in September of 1997, it was on life support with only sixty employees working in the cavernous hulk compared to the thousand who'd been there when Dennis took over. After the four kids who were hired as summer temps were terminated mid-August, a new one, a Black kid named Josh Ulmer, was added as a provisional employee, which meant little more than that he would be kept on if the guys he worked with liked him. Not a problem—Dennis loved the kid. "For whatever reason, he always puts a smile on my face," Dennis would say. "One nutty goofball."

Alex was eleven and Tommy six when Dennis was killed in the forklift accident: it was the first day Josh had been allowed to operate the heavy machinery. By mid-afternoon, simultaneously driving and carrying on a conversation that had begun over lunch, Josh was feeling pretty good about himself—"like an actual man, you might say." At lunch, a guy named Oscar and his friend James had been trash talking hip-hop—a daily nuisance topic—with Josh defending it in his own way: "I just like it. I like R&B, too. I even like The Beatles. I bought a CD just last week. It's personal taste, that's all. I got nothing more to say."

But out in the warehouse an hour later, Oscar was still at it. If he used the expression thug-life once, he used it a dozen times. Josh was maneuvering the lift which was loaded with letter- and small-package-stuffed duffle bags.

"I live by the motto live and let live. Ain't no savage in me, ain't no thug, neither." Turning to Oscar, he showed his own bare arm: "See that? That's black. I'm black, real black. And I'm not like what you're saying. I'm a person who naturally likes people, always have."

More animatedly, Josh continued to gesture and explain when one of the bag straps hooked onto a column of stacked pallets and the lift lurched right. Josh began pulling handles—red knobbed, yellow knobbed, white knobbed. In his panic, he managed to jerk free of the pallets and raise the fork, but he didn't slow the machine, he sped it up. He pinned Dennis Moore to the cement wall where his splintered ribs busted through his chest, blood spurting out. He was a mess, dead before the EMTs arrived.

At their father's wake, the two Moore boys were dressed in churchy suits, seated on either side of their mother. Hunch-shouldered, Tommy, the younger one, played with his Gameboy. When a mournful classmate or family friend approached, he lifted a limp hand to take the one being offered, accepted any kiss that came his way, nodded his head at words addressed to him, then buried his head back in his game. Occasionally, Tommy would stand up, hands on his hips, wobble back and forth like a stiff-backed adult just waking from sleep. It'd seem he was about to take a walk, but he wouldn't. Back down he'd sit and sink into himself.

Alex, the older boy, by nature the more outgoing and buoyant of the brothers, was tall and long-limbed like his mom and dad, the kind of Little Leaguer who could hit a baseball over the fence, over the second fence, out into the street. Unlike Tommy, he moved around the room quickly and nervously—reading memorial bouquets, taking a sip of water, observing mourners in other rooms, expectantly eyeing any sound at the front door. When he would come back to the front row, he'd put his arm over his mom's shoulder and rest his head on her as Tommy looked on, eyes tearing from his mom's and brother's contagious sadness. These were the images of her two boys that most stood out in Linda's wallet of memories.

Since the day Dennis died in '98, she'd raised them alone and faced her own illness with a saving mixture of still fatalism, spitting rage, endless anguish, and, from time to time, the laughter of a drunk watching tragedy unfold at the other end of the bar. Her love for her children flowed from her like radiance from a star, like beauty from a flower. Her boys were fatherless and her job was to protect them from pain and provide them joy. She needed to see them smile and needed to make them smile, but the cancer diagnosis challenged this. The worried love in her eyes, the tilt of her head, the mysterious softness of her touch, the occasional dullness in her expression when her thoughts drifted, these had evolved over time and then receded as her health improved. She feared, with the new news from Dr. Hammond, they would once again rise up and betray her.

Sunday, July 7
3.

SUNDAY MORNING AFTER a rainy Saturday, just three blocks from the entrance to Route 24, Alex's thumb was still fresh when he was picked up by a KU neuroscientist on sabbatical—a bearded, slightly palsied man who drove the entire thirty-mile route to Perry State Park in the right lane (fine with Alex), five miles below the speed limit. The trip was as simple and reassuring as Alex could have hoped for: stick out your hand, smile, get a ride, show off your limited Bachelor's Degree knowledge of brain science, arrive at destination, shake hands and offer well wishes.

At the park's unmanned information center, he grabbed a trail map and chose the uphill route off to his left, the sun at his back. He followed a pointing sign: "Coyote Creek Trail: Playing Fields, Tubing, Swimming—3.1 mile loop, elevation 400 feet." For the first half mile, the path's winding ascent brought him into and out of the shade. Soon, though, the woods cleared, and on a gently sloping field backed by a strip of trees and then bluffs overlooking the creek, a dozen guys and half dozen girls played frisbee, Ultimate. Alex pulled off his already sweaty shirt and sat. He hadn't showered since his last morning at Feyton's. He used that sweaty shirt to mop up the grime and perspiration from his face and neck, arms and chest.

The Flying Zambinis wore red and black, Area Nine the copper and silver of interstellar robots. Some damn good athletes were releasing long parabolic throws and rope-tight line drives that sliced through the players' screeches and shouts.

But there were those bluffs at the far end of the field to watch for.

Two opposing players raced towards the end zone. Initially, the disc sailed to catch up with them, then as it passed the players and the guys had to pirouette, briefly running backwards before completing the spin and bursting into a final charge, it was their turn to chase. But the bluffs! The Area Nine player slowed. The offensive player, though, the Zambini, charged faster and faster, legs barely able to keep up with his momentum. As he passed the tree line and neared the drop to the stream, he spread his arms hawk-like, rolling them left and right, teammates and opponents laughing as they urged him on, "Run, Reno, run! Keep on going. Go, go, go!"

He reappeared, unscathed. Of course he escaped unscathed, didn't you always escape unscathed? It was a fact of life.

The game resumed and a moment later Alex found a frisbee settling just a few yards in front of him. A long-legged, dark-skinned girl in a royal blue head wrap hustled knock-kneed towards him, chasing down the wayward disc.

"Hey," the girl said. She bent and pulled up her socks before grabbing the frisbee. "Do you play?"

"Not much. I'm fine just watching."

"Okay, if you're sure. Have a good one," she said, giving Alex a thumbs-up. "Such an amazing day." She turned and ran towards the game, pumping her arms in the air: "We are the Zambinis!"

"Legs," thought Alex. And "Twenty-two," thought Alex. "Twenty-two years old," he whispered and hopped to his feet. "This," Alex reflected—this right here, these moments. I'll *always* remember them. I'll remember that girl when I'm old and grey—the shape of her legs, the awkward running gait, her invitation to the game. This is what I learned on my summer vacation. "So what's your name," he whispered smilingly, the legs twenty yards gone.

The inner loop trail took Alex further into the uplands. He crossed a rope bridge over a nearly dry brook, then zig-zagged down a rocky path to Coyote Creek, the voices of a playful crowd of bathers coming nearer. The clear pebble-bottomed stream flattened out and bellied into a swimming hole ending at a three-foot waterfall, just enough of a drop to do serious damage to the unwary. Bubbling water, baby rapids, and larger, sharper rocks were at the base of the falls. Another fifteen yards beyond that was a steep descent through which Coyote Creek flowed and then widened before becoming one with Perry Lake.

Alex took a spot on a flat rock in mixed sunlight and shade, his feet dipping in the water and his shirt serving as pillow. Aware of his physical self, filled with his youth and health, he breathed each breath a little deeper. Folks played in the stream and pools: tubers who, like rodeo riders, held on with one hand while gripping their beer cans with the other; water-frolicking teens in bleached blue-jean shorts and sleeveless white T's; pale men and women laid out on blankets, cigarettes in hand; Native American kids and their parents barbecuing a few yards into the woods.

Alex was called from his reverie by a pair of kids messing with his feet. He felt it, identified it, only slowly opened his eyes. Lifting himself, he saw that somehow he had become part of their game, his legs and feet saving their rubber duckies, keeping them from floating over the waterfall and into certain oblivion.

"Thank you, mister."

"Great save," said the other.

"No, problem, boys. Glad to help," he smiled, then leaned back, shut his eyes, and listened—he shut his eyes, loosened up his brain, and listened—savoring the moment.

Monday, July 8
4.

THE TOWN MARKET was bustling and there wasn't a hint of the "unintended consequence" problem Cathy had worried over. Tommy sat outside Meyer's Confection working on a strawberry smoothie as he waited for her to call him in. He had a meeting scheduled with her for 12:00, but now at 12:30 she was still in her office, busy with Sara.

The women had two things to discuss. First, there was the question of where Archie would live: could he remain in Independent Living, could he remain there at least for a short time; how much of a recovery was likely for him; how much care could Sara give; what would she do if he had to be moved to Assisted Living or even the dreaded Nursing Care? And then, number two, there was the still-incomplete Advance Directives for both of them which Sara skillfully and, she thought, subtly had avoided.

Finally, Cathy called Tommy in.

"I wanted to get some feedback from you—I told you I felt like I needed a right-hand man and you'd be it. See, I trust you, you should be proud." Again the wink. Maybe he imagined it. "What did you think of last week's CDR?"

"What do you mean?" he stalled.

She could see it: either he didn't want to answer or had no clue how to.

"What do you mean what do I mean? Did you reflect on it? How did Sandy's story make you feel?"

He shook his head, and his mouth did this thing he feared had come across as a smirk; really, it was just his coming to the decision to speak the truth. "It made me feel . . . .was heartbreaking. It was maybe the saddest story I've ever heard."

"Yeah, I've done a lot of these CDRs, and this was one of the saddest I've ever heard for sure."

"I was counting up the years, from 1977 to today. That's thirty-one years. That's incredible. He's been carrying it all that time. I don't know if CDR is going to be able to change him. Is he ever going to be able to let go of it?"

"He has to," Cathy replied. It was an admonition.

"He has to want to first, doesn't he?" Tommy responded, eyes wide, stating the obvious. "And he doesn't want to. He said as much."

"If he doesn't—if any of us don't 'let go,' if you don't seek reconciliation with God . . . . It's what CDR is all about. Then you waste your life." Midway between agreeing with her empathic and loving observation and coldly staring through her charade, Tommy listened. "Like Sandy put it, you're bitter and you're hurting all the time," Cathy said.

"I know. I get it. I don't know if Sandy is buying it, though."

"*Buying* what?"

"Buying the whole thing. He's rejecting it, rebelling even. He was very angry talking about it, you could see that."

"Yes, he was. What about you, do you buy it? I understand what you mean."

"I don't know."

"It's the best tool I have."

CDR, a tool? Sure, Tommy thought. But just a tool? Is that how she sees it? That CDR doesn't actually draw power from the truth about God and His cradling mercy. It's make-believe, nothing more than a handy tool in a dark universe—one of Cathy's white lies, fake as the

Town Market, fake as the Bon Secours brochures? At his harshest, Tommy saw her as she saw herself, as a pretender. At the same time, he felt something very different, a tenderness. He felt a sympathy that left an ache.

"It was my first time," said Tommy, "and maybe Sandy wasn't the best introduction."

"Uh-huh," Cathy agreed. "Fair. Not the best introduction. But I hope you do come around to my way of seeing it," she said. "Come on, let's get to work. I need to tell you about what's going on with Sara and Archie. It's very complicated. I'm going to put you with her more of the time. I'll give you your schedule later but drop anything for Sara. I mean not that I'm expecting anything in particular. What I mean is for companionship most of all. Or support. We all need support."

5.

SARA BERRY WAS a self-proclaimed "half breed" born in Eastern Nebraska in 1929. Sara's mother and all her mother's ancestors were Pawnee; her father was one-quarter Native American, the rest European, mostly Scottish, he claimed. By the time Sara was born, Native culture had been broken, the people vanquished and bitter. And the Pawnee were worse off than most—some on reservations, but more sprinkled among the small towns of the high plains.

Sara herself was raised in the tiny Native American neighborhood of the otherwise all-white town of Pawnee City in the southeastern corner of Nebraska. The neighborhood, which practically functioned as an in-town reservation, was wholly Indian, but, being so isolated from any larger Indian community, not typically Indian, having developed its own codes and manners, its peculiar blend of assimilation and heritage pride. For the kids of Sara's generation, coming of age through the Depression and WWII, the trauma of the preceding seventy-five years—from Massacre Canyon and the relocation south into Indian Territory to the near annihilation of the tribe in the early twentieth century—seemed remote, the events ancient in the minds of Sara and her friends, and the full impact of those times on their own existence lived but unaccounted for.

Even then—just as she did now as an old woman—Sara viewed her heritage with a mixture of love, compassion, and occasional heartbreak mixed with the dose of skepticism all children reserve for anything taught them by their elders. Often she would engage in imaginative leaps to the mythic tepee'd villages her mother, her aunt and uncles, her grandma had known. Only recently did she realize how much Indian she'd actually absorbed. Her childhood friends and her family and she were Indian in the way that in conversation their hands danced to accommodate their words— "You kidding me?" and "Hell with you!" were as much signed as spoken. And they were Indian in the way they laughed and in why they laughed—Laurel and Hardy were the kings of comedy; momma's tickle gesture would send the kids running for cover; a spilled bottle of beer could keep the house in hysterics for hours. They were Indian in the way they felt the earth under their feet, Indian in the way they sat spread-legged, palms on the knee, on the porch, singing in low voice and staring far, far away.

Mary Whitehorse, Sara's mother, was a servant to Pawnee City's mayor, and her father, Pete Endicott, was the mayor's chauffeur, when he needed one, occasionally his gofer, but most often plain out of work, during which time the thin, unshaven man would look towards the hills and grumble, smoke, weep, and read the poetry of Henry Longfellow. It was the family's connection to the mayor, though, that allowed Sara to attend Southeast Nebraska Technical College where she earned a two-year degree in Secretarial Studies. There she met and married Ernie Berry.

In '53, two years after they graduated, she and Ernie, along with their baby daughter Ella, moved east when Ernie was offered a union job at General Motors' New Jersey plant. It wasn't long after they moved that Sara, too, was offered a GM job in the Personnel Department's secretarial pool, and they lived comfortably in Robbinsville Township, just one town over from Trenton where Ella would attend Trenton State College. Later, when Ella was off and married and they were retired, or at least semi-retired, she and Ernie spent much of their time traveling, seeing the country from their light blue station wagon, collecting colorful state stickers, often meeting up with friends, most frequently with Archie Grandling, the man to whom Sara was now married.

Ernie had been the picture of health until the day in 1996 that a heart attack took him, leaving Sara with a mortgage-free home, a love of travel, and no one to share either with.

6.

CATHY WAS MORE disappointed in Sandy's absence from that afternoon's CDR than she was in Sara's, though it was Sara who was scheduled to have the day's speaking role. After the morning's discussion, which had been filled with morbidity—a discussion about advanced directives and long-term care—Cathy had hardly expected Sara to join the group. Sandy was different, though. He could change the character of the sessions. She especially wanted him on her side.

Instead, Sandy sat in his apartment at his cafe-sized kitchen table with Wake Parish, a resident who'd occasionally stop by for a coffee and maybe a snack, to read Sandy's USA Today or *National Geographic*. To be one guy with another. The kitchen, a half-room right off the entrance, was a good place to chat and relax with Wake. After all, he wasn't the kind of guy you'd want to get in the habit of inviting any deeper into your apartment.

The other residents shunned Wake as much as he shunned them. True, some of the residents may have agreed with Sandy that the white-sneaker, golf shirt and khakis conformity of "the joint" could be stifling, but they were unanimous in their belief that Wake took his distaste too far, that he was "anti-everything." They were right. Wake was that, Sandy agreed. But honestly, as negative as he was, Wake was harmless, a softie, and an often appealing change of pace, the black sheep of the place. No harm, no foul, as far as Sandy was concerned. Of the various nicknames the ladies had created for him, The Black Shadow was the one that had stuck, though sometimes with a quick shake of the head and a nod in his direction, a whispered "weirdo" would do. You couldn't argue this. No defending Wake against that minor charge, either.

At 68, Neil "Wake" Parish was one of the youngest residents of Bon Secours. Indeed, he was younger than some of the residents' children. He was tall, 6'2", and weighed 245 pounds. He was not muscled and was not fat, his pounds were spread everywhere—neck and shoulders, ankles and thighs, fingers and toes. Wake wore all black except for his habit of alternating his socks between black and white. Fact: he'd been known to walk around in his black shoes and no socks at all. He'd been dying his brown hair ink black for as long as he could remember, a fact unchanged by the accelerating infusion of grey.

Wake's dad had been a mid-level St. Clare's Hospital Human Resources administrator, his mom an accounts supervisor, also at Saint Clare's, the hospital that had been affiliated with Bon Secours since its inception. After Wake's dad died (when Wake was 56) and his mother's health began to falter, Wake and his mom Birdie moved into a

Bon Secours apartment not very much different from the Guttenberg apartment they'd been living in for half a century. Five years later, Birdie Parish died.

As far as lives of nearly seventy years go, Wake's had been fairly privileged. No tragedies had befallen him and he'd had no cruel burdens to bear, none beyond those which a birth certificate contracts you to. But Wake was not okay with this. Face it. The terms of existence sucked. From a young age he had divorced himself from that nasty little thing called life—he'd have none of it! He lived bitterly, he lived solitary. Now, as always, he was in a strange position relative to his own existence—disdainful of it, absent from it but stuck with it, an under-nourished soul forced to lug around that big body day after day after glorious fucking day.

"Now what are you so angry about?" his mom would inquire.

"Angry? Me? Oh, no, Ma, not me. There's nothing to be angry about, not a single thing."

Or, "You never smile, Neil. Where does all the bitterness come from?"

"Oh, nowhere, absolutely nowhere . . . Mom. Look around, please, just look around. My God, your name is 'Birdie' and you're asking me what I'm bitter about. What's wrong with *you*?"

There was little that could be done for him, with him, or to him. By the time he was in his mid-teens, Birdie and Big Neil decided to simply let him be. Let him and his headphones sit in the living room's recliner and blast his music. If he closed his eyes and contorted his face, so be it—different strokes for different folks. If he passed out and snored, even better, just move to the kitchen. In truth rock'n roll was his only interest, the darker side of it, late sixties, early seventies mostly.

Without other interests, without real friends, without joy or work or responsibility, with a contempt for the terms of existence (about which he'd been given absolutely zero choice), and a blended pity and disdain for anyone who failed to see things the way that he did—which pretty much included the entirety of *genus hominem*— Wake Parish maintained the arms-folded perspective of a hermit overseer, owner of a worldview stubborn and pure as a saint's. To hell with it. To hell with all of it, thank you.

He took his Nescafé black, three sugars. Stirred with the tiny spoon Sandy had left in the saucer.

"Why'd you go to that CDR the other day?" Wake asked, his Jim Morrison T-shirt tight around both waist and chest. He leaned down to the table and blew a breeze onto his coffee.

"Oh, I felt like something different. It was boredom mostly."

"What did you think?"

"I guess, well, it was well-intentioned."

"But childish, for children, though. Am I right?"

Sandy poured his own coffee, grabbed a box of Lorna Doones from the cabinet.

"I don't really want to talk about it. Let's say it was fine."

"Got ya." Nodding as though he understood the true message behind Sandy's noncommittal words, Wake ran both hands through his shiny hair. "Yeah, yup. We both know nothing comes of those things. Nothing comes of them."

"I don't know if I think that. I don't know whether it does or not. Like I said, it's well meaning. It may help some people."

"But I notice you're not going back today." Wake stretched his legs across the floor, crossed his big boots at the ankle.

"That's right." Sandy checked the time, lit green on his microwave. "It started already. No, I'm not running down there but I did consider it."

"But in the end you didn't go."

"Obviously."

"So why didn't you go then?"

"Oh, I don't know why I didn't go, Wake, for crying out loud. Embarrassment and fear maybe."

"C'mon," laughed Wake. "I know you're kidding. You know as well as I do nothing comes of those things."

"Wake, how many times can I say it: I don't know that. You may know that but I don't know that. I told you why I didn't go. That's the truth. So let's just drop it, just drop it, my friend."

"Hey, absolutely, Sand. Absolutely. Your call, buddy."

"Here, have a cookie. Do me a favor, have a cookie."

"Now you're talking," he chuckled. "I love Lorna Doones. Okay if I snag two?"

7.

IN SARA'S ABSENCE, Cathy turned to Tommy.

"Tommy. You're a member of the group. In a sense at least you're one of us, just a younger version." Tommy's blank face went blanker. He didn't want to make too obvious his desire to avoid participation, but he wanted to make sure, too, that there was no way he might leave room for his reaction to be misunderstood as willful engagement. He wanted to help, felt that Cathy needed him, but, no, "by whatever means necessary" did not apply to him, not yet.

"Come on, Tommy. Tell us something—open up to everyone about something new and wonderful," she joked. He was pretty sure she joked.

Quicker on his feet than he'd anticipated seconds earlier, Tommy jumped back to the topic that had bailed him out once already: "The only thing I can tell you more about is my brother's cross-country trip. He's in Kansas right now."

"Yes, please go on," said Annie. "Of course we'd love to hear. He's with his friend?"

"Billy? Not anymore, not really. They split up and so he's on his own now."

"Oh, well. I'm sure he'll be fine," said Nini.

"Of course," asserted Annie.

With enlivened eyes and grandparental curiosity and concern, they soaked in Tommy's tales of his brother's adventures. Their faces revealed an involvement in Alex's distant world that amazed Tommy. A few sentences and they were transported; he wondered if this might not be a consolation gift to the aged—a greater capacity for immersion in imagined worlds, a talent for living inside a dream as compensation for their limited physical world and their personal memory being chipped away by time. Special ability or not, though, they were fully dwelling in this mythological tale of youth and exploration and, for now at least, enjoying the hell out of it.

The attendees were Cathy, Tommy, Annie, Nini (Ava was "coming down with something") and the soft-spoken, put-upon little man, Sal—Tommy had caught his name this time. And there was one newcomer in the group, Jessica, the woman who'd been at her granddaughter's tennis tournament the previous session. An obvious exercise freak, she smelled of Ben Gay and wore grey capri yoga pants and a sleeveless pink exercise top. It was Jessica who proposed that they become pen pals with Alex. Everyone was gung-ho for the idea, Tommy, too. He offered to email Alex their questions and bring the responses back to them.

Annie followed up: "I propose that we not burden either of these young men and that we limit ourselves to one question apiece, and no multiple-parters."

Cathy looked on, pleased and smiling.

"I agree with Annie," said Jessica as she unwrapped grape Gatorade gum. "We mustn't interfere in the brothers' lives, after all they're the young ones not us. I move that we establish the definition of a single question. After all," she said, "what we may initially call a single question runs the risk of growing a lot of branches. That would be unfair, as I say they're young, living their lives, they're the ones out in the world." She pressed her palms together in an isometric exercise.

"Right," replied Annie. "We mustn't abuse the privilege."

"No problem," said Tommy. "He won't mind."

"Jessica and I will confab a definition of a single question for Wednesday's meeting," said Annie.

"That's perfect," added Cathy. "Well done, and what a breath of fresh air it will be!"

8.

TWO OF SANDY'S molars were missing—one on each side, at least he was pretty sure it was just one on each side. The bottom fronts were crooked and worn, and the two top fronts weren't tight in the gums: he now sliced his apples, stripped corn from the cob with a steak knife, and used scissors to cut what he used to rip with his teeth. He'd been laying his tongue in the same cavity for two decades. He'd smoked for fifty years, drank for just as long, and worked his whole life around tools and dirt and soot. If he ever again had the good fortune of kissing a woman, she'd know his whole life.

And he understood Wake, borderline sympathized with him. While Sandy's rebelliousness didn't approach Wake's it was real nonetheless. He shaved only most days and refused to make a fetish out of scrubbed ankles and museum-quality fingernails. His iron hadn't worked for a year. If he was going outside and the forecast called for some low-percentage chance of rain, he'd leave his umbrella in the stand, just to bug them.

Unrelenting, "Cathy's okay, but she pushes the CDR too much," said Wake. "She pushes *everything* too much."

"She is what she is, Wake."

Wake sat with his back to the wall, legs stretched out towards the refrigerator. He lifted his right boot, placed the heel on his left-boot toe. "She knows it's all bull. She's play acting, my friend." He took out a Pall Mall and put it between his lips without lighting it.

"Let her be, Wake."

"I'm just making a point," he said waving his right hand, the one holding the unlit cigarette.

"I get your point. It's not like I don't see what you're driving at."

"About the CDR, I heard the new woman went, too. The Indian gal. Indigenous they call them nowadays."

"Yes, I like her. I imagine she's there now."

"You know her story, don't you?"

"Just that her husband has health problems."

"That's putting it mild. The man had a stroke two days after they got here, a bad one I hear."

"Damn it. Now I feel bad for not going."

"Don't matter that you won't be there. There'll be enough crows there, they can fill you in."

"It's not just a matter of getting information, Wake. I would like to be there, maybe offer support."

"How?"

"I don't know, for goodness sake."

"Eh, I guess there's just something I'm missing."

"No argument from me on that, my friend. Lorna Doone?"

9.

SINCE THE EARLY seventies, Archie Grandling, who also worked for GM, had been best friend to both Ernie and Sara. Archie was a gentleman, so much so that he made Sara feel that he was the only gentleman she had ever met. At 5'8", 145 pounds, Archie was a smaller man than Ernie. He was African-American with a tight, rust-colored Afro and a gold ring on his left hand. He dressed well and smartly, doffed his cap (whether he was wearing one or not—and if he was wearing one it was most likely a maroon and beige checkerboard beret), kept himself a trim package, shaved twice a day, and wore cologne you couldn't find in the local drug store. He loved alligator belts and suede shoes, and he was a gourmand when very few in his circle knew what the word meant. He loved having friends over, and he especially loved watching them take their first sip, their first bite. When he had Ernie and Sara to visit, he'd spend the entire day shopping—utterly enjoying his hours at the outdoor market down in Princeton—and would turn the evening into an ensemble that coordinated not only the appetizer, the main course, the wine, and the blend of tea, but the lighting, the music, his own appearance, as well, indeed his very person: conversationalist, chef, butler, confidant, host.

He had never been married and as far as Sara knew never had a special lady friend. He, too, loved to travel and had accompanied the Berrys on trips to Bar Harbor and Palm Springs, the Great Smokies and Santa Fe. After Ernie's death, Sara sometimes felt that Archie was her only friend. When he proposed in '98, Sara joyfully accepted.

Before their marriage, Archie had been friends with Sara for thirty years and, of course, never said "I love you." Given the circumstances of their marriage, Sara being the one coming off the trauma of losing what Archie knew to be the love of her life, she should have said it first. She knew it as soon as they stepped off the altar. Hours passed. Then days, months, and years, and it only got harder. She should have said it because it was true. Sara loved Archie. It didn't have to be the same love she felt for Ernie. That's what confused her at first. But she loved Archie, there was no other word for it. She loved him and for sure she should have told him. Then he would have known. If she had said it, then he could have said it and they could have said it to one another, over and over, day after day. Even now, with Archie lying in bed and nearing the end of life, she could only muster the courage to say the words when he was asleep, and even then she couldn't simply speak the words but had to mask the phrase inside a lullaby's melody.

10.

ARCHIE HAD HIS stroke two days after he and Sara moved into Bon Secours, and while it was unexpected, it certainly hadn't been sudden. Months of sporadic headaches and eye trouble had preceded it, those symptoms the result of an undetected aneurysm: one of the arteries of his brain had developed a bulge, like the rubber of a stretched and weakened inner tube. He and Sara visited the doctor during their preparations to move into Bon Secours. The doctor referred Archie to a specialist for further testing, and those tests were scheduled. Just not quite in time.

On their second night in Bon Secours—as they talked enthusiastically about decorating the new place—the stroke hit. Archie's head had been throbbing so they decided to eat supper in the apartment. The ache went through his jaw and into his shoulder. He had trouble sitting upright so Sara led him to the bedroom where he lay down, eyes closed. He drifted in and out of sleep while watching a baseball game, Sara near him on a bedside chair. Anytime she asked how he was doing, "Pretty good" or "A little better," he'd respond. He got out of bed at nine o'clock but things worsened with his first step towards the bathroom. By that time the aneurysm had ruptured and blood was leaking into his brain. He struggled to form words in order to call Sara's attention. When he tried to turn towards her, he felt a crinkling like tiny beads at the base of his skull. He wanted some orange juice, and Sara helped him into the like-new kitchen. But at the refrigerator he peed himself, not knowing it until he felt the warmth against his leg. Sara held the juice container in one hand, Archie's arm in the other. He nudged her towards the bathroom and spoke the words "wash" and "awful."

He sat on a stool in the shower, shivering as the warm water ran over his legs and Sara cleaned him up. Afraid to cause trouble, to call attention to his situation, afraid of what might happen to him if he did, Archie convinced Sara to put off calling for the medical staff. So she dressed him in his pajamas and the couple lay back on the bed. Archie closed his eyes, comforted as Sara held his hand and took a spot next to him.

"I'm going to rest my eyes," Archie whispered. Sara put on her glasses and read a home-decorating magazine. This was after all their new apartment, and they would need new things.

An hour later, Archie again tried to make it to the bathroom, and this time the stroke hit him full. He jerked into a stiff, upright posture before vomiting and collapsing onto the carpet in a prolonged contortion. Sara called to the front desk and within minutes he was rushed to Acute Care's Emergency Room, the med-techs running the wheeled stretcher through the tunnel that connected the two Bon Secours buildings.

Tuesday, July 9
11.

BY TUESDAY MORNING Alex was getting antsy. The time was coming soon, maybe as soon as the next day, to continue on his journey. He had his duffle bag on his back and was heading down 11th Avenue towards the laundromat. The showers had ended hours earlier and now the grey clouds were blowing off to the east, replaced by refreshing blue. In the distance the high school marching band was practicing, and the sun shone through the walnut and chestnut trees of the block, but the leaves and squiggly things that had fallen from them were mushy underfoot.

Passing what he took to be just another house filled with students and recent grads—a yellow cottage, its porch peeling paint and its face saddened by the rain—he heard music: "There's a darkness upon me that's flooded in light." It was the Avett Brothers, oh he knew them well, had seen them half a dozen times, even dragged Tommy along and turned him into a fan. The song was "Head Full of Doubt": "In the fine print they tell me what's wrong and what's right/And I'm frightened by those who don't see it." Alex took a step inside the rusted gate. Turned out the music wasn't coming from someone's home. Inside the house was a copy shop, a throwback to the old century.

Climbing the rain-softened wooden steps to the porch, Alex could see that there were three boxy white computers in the window. Alex dropped his dufflebag onto the porch and entered. The Avett

Brothers, a chance to write mom an email, and a pretty girl seated on the countertop—yeah, this suited Alex just fine.

12.

CATS WHO COPY was on 11th Avenue between Illinois and Indiana Streets, midway between the KU campus and Massachusetts Street, Lawrence's main drag. The owners, Dave and Seth, claimed the title of "The Ben and Jerry of Eastern Kansas's Copy Industry." Grandiose and absurd, the claim was the perfect gimmick for a college town. Dave and Seth, who did resemble feral versions of Ben and Jerry, had started their business at about the same time as the more famous ice-cream boys and carried themselves with much of the same hippie, stumble-upon ethos, only more so, defining success as simply being able to pay the bills, keep the business open, and dress as raggedy as you wanted to.

While still in their early twenties, they opened their first store in 1977, managing to scrape together the $3,000 start-up. Those years— the late seventies through the early nineties—were the golden age of copy centers. Their employees grew from one to twenty—mostly part timers—their stores from one to three, and their annual profits from $2,000 to $200,000. Business was booming.

Nineteen ninety-two was Cats' high-water mark. Then the copy shop industry began to change and Dave and Seth were unwilling to change with it. They resented the expectation that now they'd become not only the go-to place to have copies made, but a stand-in post office, as well: "Yeah, I'm sorry. I do have a stamp in my wallet but I don't think it'll stick. The nearest post office is on 12th and Mass. Street." And a communication hub: "Sure. We have a Yellow Pages in the back. I can copy the whole thing for you if you like. A nickel a page." And stationery store: "Boxes? We don't sell those, but you'll probably find some behind the liquor store." Once before and once just after the turn of the century, the boys hired a Digital Technology Coordinator. All they could do themselves with one of the new computerized copiers if it was misbehaving was discard it, donate it, spit on it (Dave), kick it (Seth), curse, pray, or voodoo it. But those tech coordinators were given tiny budgets—really no budgets at all, just begging privileges—and treated poorly, like party crashers, and none lasted more than a few months.

By 2008, there'd been an influx of competition: there were two Staples within five miles of Cats, there was a Federal Express/Kinko hybrid, and there were handful of smaller shops—everywhere from strip malls to hospital lobbies to gas stations—dotting the Lawrence area, half of them not even using the word "copies" in their advertisements. Monetarily, things had gone seriously downhill, back to the '77 level, which honestly is where it belonged.

When Alex arrived in Lawrence, Seth and Dave were back to owning a single messy shop—a mess of empty boxes, a mess of electrical cords covered over in duct tape, three months' worth of recycling. By 2008, grey and divorced (both of them) and living together in a pretty posh cabin in the rolling hills northwest of Lawrence, Seth and Dave had no patience for anyone's bullshit, customers' or employees'.

That's where Jackie Boone fit in. She got the job because she reminded Seth of an old girlfriend—"In your dreams," laughed Dave—and kept the job by never pestering them. She did her job just the way they liked it, competently and pleasantly enough, without any undue enthusiasm or curiosity and with no inclination to embarrass them by going above and beyond.

13.

THE LIST OF difficulties caused by the stroke was long: Archie would always have trouble processing visual information. His ability to speak would be diminished, precisely how much they couldn't say. Motor coordination would be tough and frustrating but there was reason to expect that eventually he would, for example, be able to dress himself. Even under the best of circumstances, though, he would need someone present to monitor his trips to the toilet and he would always need help bathing.

After the stroke, Archie spent two nights in ACEC before being returned to his apartment. But that's where things got dicey. Right now he and Sara were in independent living, but post-stroke Archie required a level of monitoring and care, including nursing assistants and physical therapists, not considered appropriate for the independent setting. The options were baffling and bad: move him to nursing care there at Bon Secours for rehabilitation and hope his stay would be short; shuffle him back to ACEC, but that was an inappropriate use, too—ACEC was intended for only a few days at a time; move the couple to assisted living, intending it to be a permanent stay, but that seemed terribly cruel, to be moved out so soon after moving in. Or, leave Sara and Archie in the apartment, hope that he showed improvement, continue to provide Sara plenty of support, and pray for the best. This is what Cathy wanted, it was what Sara wanted, she was sure it is what Archie wanted. The question was whether or not Cathy had the clout to pull this off.

This choice of forestalling a permanent decision had gone on for the better part of a month, until what was Tuesday of Tommy's second week, when in the darkness of early morning, Archie suffered a secondary stroke. Then there was decisiveness. The morning nurse had just begun her commute to Bon Secours so it was Sara, alone, who pulled the alarm and held Archie in her arms. Within minutes, ACEC's emergency medics were again in the apartment, and ten minutes after that Archie had been stabilized. The nurse, who arrived just at that point ,assured Sara that there was no imminent threat to his life, but Archie had to again be taken to ACEC, right away.

Cathy got the call about Archie as she walked from the parking lot to the building. After she checked in on Sara and Archie, just as he was about to be whisked from their apartment to ACEC, the first person she called was Tommy—who'd been busy stuffing envelopes for a Bon Secours fundraiser. Stick with Sara, she told him, as much as you can, don't worry about anything else. What exactly was expected of him, he didn't know; but a week into the internship, he understood that simple nearness could be a benefit unto itself.

After three hours at her barely conscious husband's bedside, Sara returned to her apartment to change out of her pajamas. Tommy awaited her at the door and when Sara reached out to him he hugged her stiffly. Sara thanked Tommy, understanding that such a touching, physical gesture was not part of his nature. Then, as the three-member housekeeping crew exited, Tommy and Sara entered.

It's not that Tommy was shocked by Archie's removal; even without this second stroke he had expected it sooner or later. More than the suddenness of the move, it was its swift completion that rattled him. He'd imagined that the transformation would be a major undertaking. But now in the living room, it was like Archie had never been. The bed was gone, housekeepers had cleaned, rearranged, and deodorized in a floral scent. The apartment was sweet, innocent, and fragrant. Just another day. They'd even left piano music playing on one of those all-music cable channels.

When Sara stepped out of the bedroom, back into the living room, she had Archie's Advance Directive in her hand. She took a few deep breaths, nodded. "Ready," she said. Tommy took her by the arm, and they left the apartment.

Wobbly at first but more steady after a few steps, with Tommy's help Sara made it to the elevator where she rested her head against his arm. The doors opened, they stepped in. Tommy pressed LL. They exited underground and together walked the tunnel to ACEC.

14.

CATHY FOUND HENRY in his usual corner nook. "May I?" she asked.

"Sure, but don't start with me. We're not going to revisit that topic of yours," warned Henry.

"The awnings, the balloons, etc?"

"Yes."

"You know that I'm right."

"No such thing. The people have spoken and they love it. Hey, something bothering you?"

"The new couple. Sara and Archie."

"Yes?"

"Archie had another stroke. He's in ACEC."

"And you're worried about that, in a place like this?"

"I'm just distracted."

"Why you letting this one get the better of you? Just be good to yourself. A little love and kindness never hurt."

The TV was on, Wolf Blitzer again.

"I don't think he ever sleeps," said Henry, nodding at the screen.

"He's a vampire. Look at the color of his lips."

Wolf turned sideways to the camera, holding rolled-up papers in one hand. An interactive topographical map of Afghanistan popped up behind him. Next to Wolf stood CNN's military expert, a former four-star general wielding a laser pointer. He pointed it at the map, and up came red-lit spots here and there. In a booming voice, he explained the unfolding events.

"Ah, they'll be okay," said Henry, vocalizing the conversation he'd been having in his head. He turned to Cathy: "Lauryn and Junior'll be okay. Okay as you can be in hundred-and-ten-degree temperature. I hear from one or the other of them almost every day. Today's technology makes it possible—it's crazy. They separated them yesterday. Let me figure the time over there. Yeah, well, however many times I figure it that's how many times I forget, but they must be sleeping now. That's what I always figure. If I'm awake they're likely asleep."

"Where are they splitting them up to?"

"Junior's going to Lagham Province. That's all he could say, all he was allowed to say. You heard of Lagham Province?"

"I think so."

"Lagham Province, Lagham Province. It's part of the news's background noise, over and over, Lagham Province. Lagham Province is the rugged hills they always talking about, the 'eastern rugged hills,' right near that damn Pakistan. Lauryn, she headed a little bit west in the direction of Kabul, got to keep that other bullshitter Karzai safe."

"I'll tell Father before mass. We'll pray for them."

"Oh, that's wonderful," he said and patted the back of Cathy's hand. "You go ahead and pray for them."

"Come on, Henry."

Henry sighed. "I don't think He's listening, Cathy. I'm not one of your old ladies. Big man ain't listening. You're listening to me alright, but Him, He ain't listening to me—not that I've noticed."

"You know better."

"No, not really. I don't know better, honey."

He made a motion like he was about to stand, but only pushed himself so far as to get into a more erect position, his hands rubbing his thighs. "Lauryn, I got a feeling knock wood she gonna be fine. The females I don't think see the direct combat action like the men. I don't know for sure. Where Junior's going though is a very tough area, very tough. And that's the way it is. Lots of operations in that region, and you know the way it happens out there. They just wait for ten American boys to die and then they say, oh, no—we didn't need that little bit 'o dirt. Why don't we just pull out for now? You know what Blitzer calls Lagham Province?"

"No, I don't."

"The Devil's Arcade. Is that one hell of a name, when people got their children going there fighting? It must boost ratings, boys dying, boys in danger. And don't you tell me what I know you want to tell me. I told you He ain't listening. I've seen no evidence of that."

"Henry, pray."

"'Henry, pray.' Yeah, sure 'Henry, pray.' Unfortunately, truth is truth, honey." He paused, lifted his eyebrows. "And you know something else? I believe you and me are on the same page."

15.

"HI," SAID ALEX.

The girl seated atop the counter turned to him, big muffin in her hand. "Hi," she responded with a smile but without the least hint of "can I help you."

"Are these computers available for customers? Okay if I use one?"

"Sure," she said, wiping muffin crumbs from her lips. "You log in and then you pay by time. It's all taped on the computer. There's always something wrong with them, though, and I don't know how to fix them. You sure you want to use one? There are *real* computers downtown." She lowered the music.

"These are fine," said Alex, stumbling over the wires taped across the wood-plank floor. "I'm just doing email."

Alex pressed the power button and after a long delay and a nervous buzzing the monitor lit.

He sat at the computer but wisely didn't sign in, realizing that his mind was more on the girl than on writing an email to Mom—and he was, after all, paying by the clock. He spun round on the stool.

"Hey, sorry to bother you, but where'd you get the muffin?"

"Here, you can finish this. I cut it in half. I've been eating it forever. Mae's makes them so big. It's basically a bran muffin with other good stuff like carrots, raisins, nuts."

"Sure, thanks."

"Take. It's a little gooey." She handed him a crumpled napkin.

Back at Computer #A, Tommy signed in and logged into his email account. "Dear Mom," he typed, but right away, realized his mistake. He began talking to himself: "Alex, you're all talk and no action. This is it, this is what you wanted. If you can't loosen up now, well, come on, if you can't now, when can you? What happened to adventure?"

So he spun around again, got off the stool, and did this awkward little shuffle in the middle of the floor.

"By, the way, my name is Alex."

"Pleased to meet you," she said, reaching out a hand. "I'm Jackie. You a student?"

"No, done with school. I'm traveling." Nice ring to it. And assuming it was she who'd put on the Avett Brothers, he still had that whole conversation in his pocket. "What's the 'Odd Job, $75' sign about, above the computer? Is that something here?"

"Yeah," said Jackie Boone. "See those overflowing boxes?" There were three of them. "I was doing a job yesterday that got jammed, then I started again from the wrong spot, then it jammed again, and I started again from the wrong spot. Honestly I don't know if I started from the wrong spot, I just assumed it since it was so haphazard. It just went on and on. You looking for work? Dave, one of the owners, said I could just hire somebody to do it, off the books."

"I might be. So it's just sorting through all the pages and straightening it out. Seventy-five dollars sounds pretty good."

"Oh, it'll take longer than you think, a day or two. It's in a foreign language so you can't read what you're doing."

"I'll do it. You're doing the hiring?"

"Basically. Like I said, Dave told me to just find somebody. I told him because it was the machine's fault I wasn't going to do it myself. Basically, I can hire you—but as long as it gets done by Friday," she said with a droopy pointer finger somehow humorous.

"I'll do it," Alex repeated. "When do I start?"

16.

WHEN SARA AND Tommy reached the second floor of ACEC's Gladiola Wing, Archie's nurse, a tiny African woman, was busy connecting all that needed connecting and muttering a mixture of prayers and curses. She raised the bed rails, snuggly tucked the sheets, and set the bed to what she thought would be a comfortable position for Archie. She clicked the TV to minimal volume—the Catholic prayer channel—blessed herself, dimmed the lights. She blessed herself again and half genuflected, continuing to mutter as she left the room, avoiding eye contact.

Archie opened his eyes to find Sara and Tommy at his bedside. Though he didn't know Tommy, he asked no questions. The words that did come from him were soft and slurred, and they came out just a few at a time. "In a hospital" sounded more like "n'ospit?"

"No, no," said Sara. "Remember, we just moved. This is Bon Secours, our home."

He shook his head, ". . . 'member." He lifted his eyes, and when they met Sara's, he seemed to awaken. "Thank . . . It's you. . . . 'appened?"

"This is your therapy. You don't remember? You had a stroke," she said to him, a touch of teasing sternness in her voice, just as if she were speaking to him when he was well. "You don't remember you had a stroke?"

He nodded, okay. He tried to move his hand but couldn't free his arm from the tight sheet. From his semi-paralyzed position, he tried to take in his surroundings. "I'm not home."

"I told you. This is your therapy room, where you get treatment. Rest. It's okay, I promise." She turned. "Tommy, you come back in a little bit, okay?"

"Sure. I'll go down the hall."

"Rest, Archie," she said and petted the side of his face. "You sweet man, I love you."

"Love, too."

"Oh, my sweet perfect man."

17.

DEAR MOMMER—

All is well here in the breadbasket of the nation!

I'm in Lawrence, Kansas, and have decided to let Billy go ahead to California while I take some time to chill out here. What a great college town! Things are going really well and I expect to remain here for two or three more days and that's the main reason I'm writing, other than I miss you, of course.

So, here's my report from the Midwest. I've been camping for the past few nights in a beautiful nature area right on the Kansas University campus. There aren't very many students around, so there's not only the beauty of where I've been staying, there's also a lot of peace under the stars. Also, I just got a job. I'll be working at a copy shop a block from downtown. It's just a temporary thing but it'll help in replenishing the wallet. I've also met a girl, so even though Billy is gone I have plenty of companionship. Her name is Jackie and she is very responsible as she has a managerial position at the company I'll be working for, and she knows her way around Lawrence.

I'm having a great adventure and I hope that you're happy for me (without being worried!). As for my usual philosophizing, of course I'm doing that. And yes, for sure, I've had my moments: thinking how fleeting everything is in this world and how permanent every experience is inside me. Being twenty-two is cool, I feel like this is my time.

BTW, there is something wrong with my cell phone—it won't take a charge and that's why I'm not calling. I'm going to bring mine in to the Verizon store but just don't worry if I don't call you or answer if you do. I'll call after I get it fixed but failing that I'll be sure to check in via email every day if possible.

Anyway, I hope everything is great for you and I'm glad you're feeling good. I just wanted to check in and update you. Off I go now, gotta get to the laundromat before it closes.

Love, your oldest boy, Alex

18.

AS TOMMY HEADED for the lounge at the other end of the floor, there was no avoiding the smells—of rubbing alcohol and creams, of disinfectants and bleach-soaked mops, of dirtied linens and gowns. In every room the TV was on, tuned either to ESPN or the Catholic Channel.

Tommy hesitated at the lounge entrance as soon as he realized he wouldn't be alone there, but then moved forward, unsure whether it was embarrassment or a sense of responsibility that pushed him on.

"Good afternoon, everyone. Hi," he said, surprising himself. There were five people in the room, none answered back, two smiled. Tommy sat in a corner chair and picked up a year-old *People* magazine.

A stylishly dressed woman, her red hair sprayed stiff and her make-up well applied, as though prepared for lunch at a fine restaurant (or, Tommy imagined, prepared for a return to the other building and a grand entrance at which, her banishment ended, she would be welcomed back to the land of the living) was playing patty-cake with a little girl he took to be a granddaughter or great granddaughter. Also at the table, looking on, was a much younger woman, likely the little girl's mom, keeping a watchful eye on the two, nodding, encouraging the girl to be a more enthusiastic player.

An elderly man, thin but sturdy-seeming in leather slippers and plaid pajamas (his own pajamas, not ACEC issued) sat at a table against a bright window, playing solitaire, oblivious to his surroundings. "There's a ball game at four," he said to no one, no one in particular or no one at all. He shuffled the deck and dealt out another hand. "If the game's close, I may not even go down for dinner, just eat in my room. I have a choice on that matter, you know." He stared at the card layout and shook his head, tapped two fingers on the table. "A 46 and 37 record, no that's not bad at all, just a game and a half back."

Whether it was two minutes or five minutes or ten that he'd been in the lounge, Tommy had had enough. He popped up and walked to the window two down from the old man. The locked window faced southeast, towards New York Harbor and the just-begun Freedom Tower. It was all blinding, a silver monochrome that stung his eyes.

"Black seven on red eight," said the man just as Tommy passed. "Red six on black seven. There you go. Now you're talking."

* * *

Back down the hall, Tommy sat outside Archie's room, waiting for Sara. She was singing to Archie. The words, Pawnee likely, came to him in muffled tones, sounding like "No-la-kee, no-la-kee. Ina-mana, no-la-kee," a death chant or lullaby, one or the other, he thought. He closed his eyes and rested his head against the wall, and soon Sara was singing to him, too.

Half asleep, Tommy startled when the door opened. Sara seemed out of it, mesmerized and weary. "You take me back to my room for now, okay?"

"What was that you were singing? It was pretty."

"Oh, my grandma taught me. She said it was the song the mommas would sing to themselves when their boys were off on their own, doing their initiation rites."

They were silent in the elevator, and they were silent as they walked through the corridor, left foot, right foot, Sara bumping against Tommy's hip. Walking the blue carpeted hall to her apartment, "Suppose I see you tomorrow, after I see Archie?" asked Sara. "For a break. I was thinking about the old days and I have some stuff I want to show you. In the café downstairs, maybe around three?"

"Definitely," Tommy answered without hesitation.

When they reached the apartment, Sara pulled Tommy towards her for a kiss. "You don't forget me, friend." She stroked his hair. He put his arms around her and squeezed tight, his nose pressed to the top of her head, his heart beating against her body, soft, warm, trembling, and old as the hills.

19.

THERE WAS BAD news from Afghanistan: "In a story CNN continues to lead on, in an operation intended to highlight the fighting capacity of the Afghan military, three hundred Afghan regulars attacked the village of Bad Pakh, Lagham Province, fifty miles from the Pakistan border. First reports from the BBC indicate that the operation has gone disastrously wrong."

Wolf promised that there was plenty more breaking news and that CNN would have all of it "back here at the Situation Room immediately after this short commercial break."

The Taliban had been tipped off about the attack and had split then routed the Afghani unit, nearly half its fighters either fleeing or defecting to the Taliban side. The remaining Afghanis were not so much a fighting force as a survival one. Their deadline to surrender and secure safe passage having passed, the fighters were being slaughtered, their white flags shredded and bloodied.

"In the carnage thus far, *at least* fifty Afghani fighters have been killed, approximately that same number of innocent civilians, and reportedly scores, perhaps hundreds, of Taliban rebels. These are preliminary numbers. Stay tuned for our ongoing coverage."

At the request of Afghani military leaders, a Company of U.S. Marines, two hundred fighters from the 2nd Battalion, had been sent in to extricate the surviving Afghani regulars and liberate Bad Pakh, a flat, dusty town of 1,000 situated two miles from the purple foothills of the Nuristan Mountains. But the arrival of the Marines was no more of a surprise than the Afghani fighters had been. The Taliban allowed the Marines to roll into town.

Along Bad Pakh's Main Street, in front of homes and market stalls and Old West-style plank sidewalks, several hundred locals— young kids and nervous mothers, white-bearded elderly men, the occasional teen in NBA gear—gawked, spoke in hand-covered whispers and giggles as the American troops entered. Three miles away, U.S. jets strafed the hills. By sunset, rebels had begun to come out of their hiding places inside the town, and a fevered hatred for the Americans—blamed for the deaths of husbands and mothers and sons—grew more overt and aggressive, and with it came sniper fire and small-explosive dust plumes.

By the time Cathy was ready to leave work, Henry had gone into hiding. There was no sign of him, no response to any message. As she stood and reached into her bag to check for her keys, Wolf called for her to stop: "More breaking news: The fate of two hundred Marines trapped in the blood-soaked town of Bad Pakh, Afghanistan. Details to follow."

20.

CATHY LIVED ON the fourteenth floor of One Hudson Plaza in Edgewater, an eighteen-story glass and pinkish-stone hexagonal tower two miles north of Bon Secours, two miles south of the George Washington Bridge. For most of the twentieth century, time had forgotten Edgewater. It was part of the same narrow slip between the Hudson River and the Palisades on which Bon Secours was built, the town having been kept alive only by the freight line that passed through it and the small businesses and warehouses that served the trains. Edgewater had been a working-class town cut off from the world, generally dilapidated and often muddy, its Main Street, River Road, a pot-holed and little-known alternate route between the GW Bridge and the Lincoln Tunnel.

In the mid-eighties, though, investors creeping north from Hoboken and Weehawken discovered Edgewater, and when it became the northern tip of New Jersey's Gold Coast, things changed rapidly. Except for the two hundred yards passing through downtown, the road was smoothed and widened, the speed limit raised from 25 to 40. But downtown's modernization took on a back-to-the-future theme, from antique street signs and wooden shingles swinging above the shops, to brick sidewalks, crackled-glass streetlights, and even a stretch of cobble-stoned sidewalks. The old warehouses were either torn down or gutted and turned into condos or corporate parks. The docks were rebuilt, and the yachts were moored. The bodegas became specialty shops, the luncheonettes bistros. Ralph's Tavern, Mosquito Park, and Railroad Beach disappeared. St. Moritz on the Hudson, Skyline Promenade, and One Hudson Plaza rose up from the mud and rubble.

The glass doors of One Hudson Plaza's lobby were Easy Touch—poke one with a finger and it breezed open. A uniformed doorman and fresh flowers, snowballs—blue and white in vases, pink and white in vases, lovely—greeted you when you entered. "Hey, Mario," Cathy tapped her nails on the concierge's granite-topped desk. Typically it wasn't until she reached the brassy bank of elevators—a chamber of distortion mirrors—that her anxiety swelled. So, rather than use her pointer finger to press, she'd use her thumb. There was less trembling in that digit. It had been like this since her husband's death. She'd worry that her hand would tremble and then, of course, it would.

It didn't matter which elevator she took, they all clunked unnervingly when they passed the sixth and twelfth floors, as though it were there that separate building blocks met. Recently, she had developed the habit of knocking on her apartment door before entering, always pushing the door shut behind her rather than letting its slow hydraulics do the job. She'd step inside then wait a beat, two beats.

She was too upset by the news of the entrapped Marines to eat dinner, knowing that Marine 2nd Battalion was Henry Junior's. From the kitchen, she brought a bottle of red wine and turned on the TV. The news was startling: the Marines had engaged in numerous skirmishes with the Taliban fighters. One hundred and sixty of the two hundred Marines were safe, back at the base that had been set up at the edge of town. Ten Marines were dead and thirty were unaccounted for.

Wednesday, July 10
21.

IT HAD BEEN a long, laborious, hysterical, headache-producing day of work at Cats Who Copy.

The problem began with a rabbi walking into a copy shop. He taught at a school of Talmudic studies, and he needed one-hundred copies of a thick document written in Hebrew. The rabbi wanted the book from which the text was being copied to be splayed—two pages of the book onto one legal-sized copy sheet—and he wanted double-sided copies. Jackie had made the first copy, directly from the book, no problem. When she dropped that original copy into the delivery feed, pressed collate, pressed double sided, pressed legal-sized paper, pressed a hundred copies, then pressed start, the machine almost immediately jammed. Jackie cleared the jam and for a while things seemed fine, with little damage done. But, especially on a creaky old machine, it takes quite a long time to complete such a job. Even with the utmost attentiveness, the job would have been a tricky one. Alas, Jackie did not provide utmost attentiveness—instead she was drafting and emailing an excuse note, a blatant lie, to her Biology professor—and the catastrophic mess that was the copied manuscript just compounded itself. Looked at by the uneducated eye, there was no telling front from back, top from bottom, left from right, and Jackie was sure she had screwed things up royally.

It was Alex's job to sort out the mess, and he was still not finished after one long day. That was surely frustrating, but the workday had given Alex time to get acquainted with Jackie, and that had landed him a place to sleep other than the increasingly damp Free Nature Zone—had landed him the storage room in the back of Cats, which, while not offering a shower, did provide a bathroom and a deep slop sink for washing up—and it had earned him a dinner date.

Brown haired, hazel eyed, long limbed, and athletically built, Jackie was born to wear sandals and jeans. She grew up the only child in a family that bounced from place to place, and she learned to read people quickly and well. At twenty-three years old, Jackie carried herself with an inherent skepticism and listened to small talk—especially guys'—with a cocked head, a knowing smile, and eyes a touch squinted, as though disingenuousness and irony were givens.

They walked towards Wholly Roman Pizza, a popular college spot on 16th and New Hampshire, nearer to the highways that circled Lawrence than it was to downtown. Their shadows stretched long and mesmerized Alex.

They ordered individual pies and headed for Wholly Roman's back deck where there were six wooden picnic tables, each with its own yellow and white Corona umbrella, each umbrella tipped towards the sun, setting above the mostly barren, purple hills.

Either the rules concerning the serving of beer were very peculiar in Kansas or the operation Wholly Roman had set up was boldly illegal. They didn't serve beer from inside the restaurant, but they did from a cooler on the deck. A blonde, mop-haired kid, an adolescent Tom Petty, sat atop a red cooler (Coronas $4.00), his cell phone in one hand, a wad of bills in the other, one of those annoying pouty-mouthed sixteen-year olds who you'd just bet has already had more sex than you'll have in your lifetime.

Alex had learned this much: the best way to a woman's heart was to show interest in everything she said. Ask questions, but then remember your job's not yet done; remain interested and try, try, try to remember her responses. What he found out was that Jackie had bounced around so much because her father was what she called a migrant academic, an instructor of physics, specifically quantum physics, some extremely bizarre stuff. She'd been born in Austin and there had been a lot of stops before her dad landed a lectureship at KU. Finally, he stayed put long enough to qualify for tenure, but that was not to be. He'd retired in his tenure year, at 62, so that, as his resignation letter explained, "I can dedicate the remainder of my life on earth to the exploration of Space, Time, and Space-Time, my true calling."

In short, Jackie's life had been three parts university park, one part trailer park, always transient. In May she had graduated, finally . . . Well, had graduated except for the matter of one science course she was supposed to be taking over the summer. She was registered but wasn't really going to class or doing the work. Still, you never know—maybe the guy would pass her anyway.

After her first bite of pie, without any trace of it being an admission, Jackie mentioned her boyfriend.

"Oh, really." Ugh. "What's he like, and where is he?"

The guy's name was Corey. He was a 27-year-old Ph.D. student spending the month with his parents in Ottawa. He was wonderful, she said sort of reluctantly, as if an admission, but he was over-sensitive and cared too much what other people thought. He never learned to say no and flaunted that trait, mistakenly as far as she was concerned.

"So Canada."

"Yup. And I do miss him though I hate to admit it. I'm operating under the assumption that what I'm feeling is likely some form of love, but . . ." she said with a shrug.

When it was Alex's turn to speak, he fell back on Rule 2: Don't try to be charming or cute, assume you're interesting. He talked about this trip: about his decision to ditch his phone (she scoffed at that), about the mule ride (she was mildly amused that he found this so amusing), about his decision to split up with Billy and get to California on his own (about this, she was very supportive).

Alex was a cute guy, his eyes innocent and searching, but confident, willing to go eyeball to eyeball, softly and openly. He was younger than her—one year—and he had a totally undeserved sense of his own worldliness, believing himself to be an hour older than the moment wisdom was bestowed.

Just as the string of colorful overhead bulbs lit, "Get a beer?" she asked. "I can pay for the pizza, you want to grab the beers? It's okay, I am the one with the *permanent* job, after all."

"Fair," he said.

He took two steps towards Tom Petty Junior then spun around: "Hey was that you playing the Avetts yesterday?"

"Yeah, of course. You're a fan?"

"Yeah, big time. From before, from the beginning, you know."

"Okay, hurry up back. I got something to tell you about."

Alex hustled over to the beer-boy but the kid was too experienced with sunset Romeos to let himself be rushed. Little prick, thought Alex, he was on his phone, grinning, making time no doubt with some equally jaded, cool adolescent girl on the other end. Come on, how long does it take to grab two beer bottles from a cooler of ice?

"About the Avett Brothers," Jackie said. "They're playing up near Lincoln this Monday, and I would love to go. It's called the Prairielands Music Festival and it's not that far. But I'm chicken to go by myself."

"Wow, wow. But that's like five days from now."

"And, so? What were you just telling me about frustration with Billy being in such a hurry? It's a chance to see the Avetts at an outdoor festival, and there's no reason for you to leave such a great town so soon. As it is, you're working tomorrow, then it's the weekend."

"Game, set, match. We'll do it."

Friday, July 12
22.

DYSPHASIA IS THE general term for eating difficulties that result from a disruption of the swallowing process. Neurological dysphasia is typical in stroke victims and dysphasia complications are among the leading causes of death for that population. Swallowing is a complex process. Of its three phases—the oral, the pharyngeal, and the esophageal—it was the middle one that was most dangerous to Archie. During this phase, aspiration can occur after the food and drink have left the mouth. At the entrance to the throat, a little flap called the epiglottis is supposed to fold back, making sure the food enters the esophagus and not the windpipe. If this complex neurological process doesn't occur in sequence, food gets where it's not supposed to be, in the windpipe. From there, it may make its way to the lungs where infection will almost certainly occur, or it can jam right in the passage causing suffocation. Suddenly, swallowing had become a very complicated task for Archie, and it would be up to Sara and the nursing staff to retrain him.

Sara was with Archie by seven a.m., leaving his side only to use the bathroom or get some water, padding about in hard-soled felt slippers. Each time she'd leave, Archie would ask as best he could, or his eyes would do the asking, "How long will you be?"

He seemed less depressed than he had on his first day in ACEC. Perhaps it was Sara's reassurance. Perhaps it was that he was fatigued, emotionally spent. Could have been the medication and resulting alleviation of pain. Still, Sara could see the great damage the second stroke had done. He looked like a dying man—grey, bruised, catheterized, multiple IVs in his arms. Sara fed him thickened fluids and mushy meals. "Awful," he'd whisper. "Phooey." Occasionally, he'd hold onto her hand as she lifted the food to his mouth, and Sara would instruct him in the art of chewing and swallowing.

After lunch, after a pair of brief ACEC visits from Tommy—who'd spent the morning tossing a beach ball with a crew of seated residents and the early afternoon calling Bingo numbers—Sara sat in a window-facing chair reading *Harry Potter*, book one, and anticipating her planned afternoon meeting with Tommy at the cafe.

When Archie roused, they watched a DVD, "An Affair to Remember," starring Cary Grant and Deborah Kerr. For an hour, they slept through the movie, her hand atop his on the arm of her chair pulled close to the bed. Together they snored until the nurse brought Archie his afternoon snack, chocolate mousse—ugly chocolate mousse: it looked like the hair you'd place atop Mr. Potato Head.

Sara lifted a spoon of it to Archie's mouth. She placed just enough of the spoon into his mouth for him to get a taste of pudding. They did this for several spoonsful, Sara watching the mechanics of his mouth and throat with each one.

"Slow, slow. Swallow."

"Awf'l."

"Come on."

He shook his head: it really was quite awful.

"Oh, okay, wait. I'll be right back. You wait and see."

The tall metal meal cart was half in/half out of the room three doors from Archie's. While the food service person's back was turned, Sara lifted the lid from one of the trays. Grabbed a brownie. Chuckling and with a giddyap in her step, she hustled back to Archie's room. "I have a surprise for you," she smiled mischievously, and Archie widened his eyes.

23.

IN THE PAST year, Cathy had lost both parents and her ex-husband. Her mom and dad had been sweet, generous people whose love for their daughter was pure and unremitting. It was both the fact that they died and how they died that was so awful—her dad going suddenly just as he was bringing solace to her mother through her own ALS deterioration. It seemed such an intentionally cruel act, but that behavior on God's part was par for the course, Cathy thought. It was her husband's death that shook her more profoundly. This death did not fit in with her worldview. In this death, it was she who'd been complicit.

She met Jim at Fordham. He was a student in a Continuing Ed course she'd been hired to teach. Jim Walsh was the most Irish-looking guy in the world, a round-faced, curly-haired athlete, thirty-two when she met him and already well on his way to being bald. The relationship moved from the classroom to dinner dates to the bedroom. They were married in 2000, divorced in '06.

When they met, both, it could be said, were on the rebound—Jim from a woman who after a three-year live-in relationship told him she was tired of him. And Cathy, too, rebounding—this period really just an extension of the long rebound from her broken love affair with God, a tough act for Jim to follow. She sought something to fulfill her, something with a name solid enough to define her, a name as emotionally concrete as "Calling."

"Married" worked. Maybe "mother" someday.

She knew that throughout the courtship she hid parts of herself from Jim, presenting herself as energetic and charming, as enthusiastic, as someone who would lift him.

Then they married and "lift him" she did not. Month by month, Cathy's resentment of him built. No matter how harshly she admonished herself, the needless resentment grew. By the end of the third year, she was considering divorce. They'd visit her parents and she'd dispute his every comment. Out dining, indecisively, he'd order wine and she'd look away. He'd shower and she'd be disgusted by the wet floor, the wet towel, the slimy soap. In their love making, either she would give herself away to Jim or she would not, and she hated both.

Jim tried. He absolved, adjusted, acquiesced. Then he apologized and accommodated. Eventually Cathy had to recognize the truth: It was not that she couldn't live with Jim. It was that, with Jim there, she couldn't live with herself. She was judgmental and unforgiving. At every opportunity, she would make it clear that, just as his ex-girlfriend had, she too was tiring of him.

For the failure of their marriage, and, much worse, for Jim's death, there was no one to blame but herself.

Early on a Saturday morning in February, just a few months after the divorce, Jim drove onto the western spur of the Turnpike. The spur curved as it rose eighty feet into the air, a roller-coaster of a road. He steered the car towards the East Newark ramp and at eighty miles per hour drove head-on into a concrete divider. Cathy found out the next day when she received a Sunday morning visit from the State Police Investigation Bureau She was listed "Wifey" in his cell phone. She was tearful and trembling and the cops apologized: if it hadn't been for the speed, they would simply have written it up as an accident.

24.

SARA LIFTED THE broken brownie to Archie's mouth. When he opened up, she held it so he could take a nibble. "Chew, chew. In the back, with your molars. Careful, this got crumbs. Feel it in your mouth."

With each bite, Sara stroked Archie's throat gently, massaging it, encouraging the muscles to work. "No, you're not doing it right, Archie. Chew more and go slow."

He lifted his hand and held her wrist as she moved the next bite towards him. His last-second tug was just strong enough to turn the nibble into a full bite. But the full bite was too large, especially laughing as he was. The laughter quickly gave way to a huffing curse as he spit up the wet cake all over himself and all over Sara's arm, and he kept right on coughing, trying to clear his windpipe of the crumbs that remained.

Sara cleaned him up. "You think you're funny and see what happened?" She scolded as she reset the pillows beneath his head. "I be right back," she said, exiting the room for a fresh washcloth and towel from the linen closet down the hall.

When Archie regained his normal breathing, he eyed the brownie and smiled his newly lopsided smile. Slowly he raised his right hand towards a chunk of brownie and lifted it, his hand more like a claw than a hand. The brownie slipped from his fingers and fell onto his chest, and there he couldn't adequately lift his head to see it. He felt along with his fingers until he got hold of the chunk, carrying it with all five fingers. It came into view then disappeared just before his opened mouth. It was a perfect drop, too perfect, like a boulder falling into a well, and it lodged deep in his throat. Archie panicked, he reached for the alarm buzzer but couldn't find it. He struggled to spit up the fat chunk of cake but his gasping was greater than his coughing, and the brownie was sucked deeper into his esophagus. He jerked forward then back, and began to cry as he felt his efforts growing weaker.

25.

TOMMY ARRIVED AT Here's 2 You Cafe, a few yards down from the Town Market, expecting to meet Sara there. A recent addition to Bon Secours amenities, Here's 2 You had a wide-open, come-and-go-as-you-please front—no doors, no glass, no wall. With big-leafed artificial plants, long windows, breezy cool ventilation, a coffee and pastry counter, and four brand new black-bodied PC's--thin, shiny, and sleek--Here's 2 You had the feel of an airport lounge, and this seemed to uplift the chatty residents who frequented it. Sandy was busily working at one of those fancy new computers.

"Have you seen Sara?"

"No, isn't she with Archie? Did she say she was coming down?"

"Yeah," said Tommy. "She said she had pictures or something she wanted me to see."

"I'm typing something for her now. It'll be a little gift. After I heard about her husband, I felt bad." Tommy didn't ask if what Sandy had heard was about Archie's first stroke or about the preceding day's.

"I googled and found something online. It's something from Native American culture. I'm not sure if it's a poem or a prayer, but it's lovely. I'm trying to make it look nice. I hope it's not too generic."

"That's so nice of you, Sandy," Tommy said, nodding and staying put, forcing Sandy to meet his eyes. They exchanged nods and smiles. Tommy felt that he was getting the hang of this and actually finding some reward in the process.

26.

IT WAS EIGHT o'clock when, wine glass in hand, Klonopin-twins downed, Cathy stepped onto her balcony. The setting sun turned the Manhattan skyline a brilliant bronze. A cruise ship backed away from its pier and, turning down-river, began to glimmer as well. Just north, heavier purplish clouds darkened the sky above the George Washington Bridge and its strand of blue lights.

"Hi, Phil," she said, spotting the name on her buzzing phone.

"Yeah, Phil Chezz from Acute Care."

"What's up, Phil?"

"Ah, well there's been a death. Archie Grandling. I know you've become friendly with his wife."

"Oh, God."

"Dr. Perez declared him a couple of hours ago. It was a heart attack—that and he was aspirating some food. I wouldn't have called you except for the wife. She asked for a service Sunday."

"How is she?"

"Yeah, I'm really not sure. She seemed okay, who knows. Like I said, she's hoping for a service this weekend and she wants him cremated."

"So do you want me to call Stabile's?"

"Yeah, I'm thinking maybe they'll do it for you. Maybe the son Eric, and if you can reach him tonight maybe they can get somebody here tonight or first thing in the morning. I didn't want to call you at home so late but . . ."

"Not a problem. I'll call Eric. I think he'll do it for me."

"We'll need the ashes back early Sunday."

"Right."

It was a rare job, Cathy's. It was a rare job where having a body-burner with a soft spot for you paid tangible dividends.

27.

ALREADY WHEN TOMMY arrived at the Little League field that Friday night, Bruce and Hector were there with the bats and balls. Surprisingly, Jesus was a no-show, and so far Carrie and Jules were, too. Five more kids showed up twenty minutes after Tommy, kids in cars, kids with beer. Just like always, they hid the case under the aluminum bleachers along the third-base side. Two of the light towers were out, which was convenient since they only had enough players for four on a side and now the fielding solution was simple. Hitting anything to right field was an out.

The playing was intermittent, and the only real excitement was in making a diving catch in the outfield, beer can in right hand, going after the ball with the left, or watching a well-stroked whiffle ball sail over a baseball-distance fence. But even those minor thrills were spent by nine o'clock. The group made its way from the bleachers to the waterfront and there skipped rocks across the dancing black Hudson. They sat on one of the old piers, this collection of sixteen- and seventeen-year-old boys, they drank and smoked, and as the night wore on things became more and more ridiculous. Everything did, their pasts—their failures with sports, girls, school, fighting—and their futures— mocking each other's likelihood of ever having a successful life . . . Shit, of ever being functional: *You* married? *You* raising a kid? *You* in the Air Force? *You* being a fucking psychologist? *You* not being an alcoholic?

"Bleak, man. Look at us. It's looking bleak," and that was hilarious. "The world is doomed!"

Tommy drank his share of beer but stayed away from the pot, worried that it might lead him to the same type of guilt-provoking Bon Secours-talk that had done him in 4th of July night. By nine-thirty, just after three of the guys had walked off—to where no one knew—Jules and Carrie arrived on bikes. Quickly they took charge with a brilliant plan, a plan outlined in the Mystic Age magazine Jules carried. They told the five boys to lay on their backs on the pitcher's mound, evenly spaced, like spokes of a wheel. Then they walked around the boys, holding a super-serious conversation about the colors of the boys' sneakers and the reflection of light off their glasses. They were trying to properly arrange the message, or so they claimed—who knew if those two were serious or goofing, well, I guess they kind of knew—trying to properly arrange the message that they'd be sending to the really, really smart aliens a million miles away.

"Don't, Tommy," warned Carrie. "Don't raise that arm. One more time and I swear we'll all be eradicated. Kaput, mo-fo!"

"What are you talking about?"

"Let me lay next to you, I'll show you. You're so in need."

"Just so you know, I'm gonna take a nap."

"I don't care. It doesn't matter." She knelt beside him. "Just give me your hand, I'll move you as appropriate. We hardly saw you at all this week."

"Early to bed, early to rise. I've got work."

"God, you're impossible. Well, I miss you."

Saturday, July 13
28.

AT DAWN, THINKING about whether or not to call Tommy, thinking about the earliest she could call, Cathy hustled out of One Hudson Park. The sky was pink and blue now, but it had rained overnight and River Road was still splashy as she crossed to the Starbucks situated on the ground floor of St. Moritz on the Hudson.

When Tommy had arrived home, five hours earlier—"sheets to the wind" he and his friends liked to call it, and having been kissed once, kissed twice, kissed thrice—he took a piss that had him standing so long the arm which was holding him up went numb. Stumbling out of the bathroom and tasting a mix of kisses and beer, he forgot to bring his phone with him. When it rang at seven a.m., Linda tried to but couldn't ignore it, not a call this early, not with Alex on the other side of the continent.

That previous night just before 9:00, as Tommy and his friends were laughing their asses off over what failures their futures were sure to be, Linda had received a call from Gabriella. It would have been late for a doctor to call but not so for a friend. She, Dr. Hammond, had been at home going through email messages when she came across the results of Linda's MRI. "Hi, Linda, is it too late?" she asked by way of introduction. Of course it wasn't too late. Gabriella had promised Linda she would call as soon as she heard anything, and so . . . .. Yes, the MRI had shown a small mass, well, a small to medium mass, three inches higher in the colon than the original tumor had been. There was no way of telling whether or not it was cancerous. "Oh, I want to cry," said Linda. But, Dr. Hammond insisted, you can't take too much meaning out of this one thing. Linda covered her eyes with her hand and asked about the blood work. Not ready yet. It takes a while. Probably this weekend. It will be in the system by Monday morning. Dr. Hammond suggested that Linda come in early Monday before her first scheduled patient. Together they'd review both the scan and the labs and decide about a biopsy. Okay, said Linda.

It was starting up again. Damn, the whole miserable experience was starting up again.

After a night of troubled sleep, early Saturday morning Linda answered Tommy's ringing phone. "Hello." She carried the phone with her and sat on the edge of her bed.

Cathy was still in Starbucks, finishing her second coffee. Her eyes were shut, her back to a brick wall. For nearly an hour she'd been debating "if" (one moment) and "when" (the next) she should call him. She knew how upset she was; she knew her judgment was screwy. She knew both coffees should have been decafs, not just the second. Was calling weird, or was it sensitive and reasonable? The debate—actually more a guessing game than a debate—wore on until an impulse, "Where's my phone," made the choice. Of course Tommy would want to know. He cared for Sara and would want to help. Of course. Of course he'd want to know. Maybe he'd even want to come in on Sunday to be with her for the service.

"Hi, I'm trying to reach Tommy. This is Cathy Degnan, his supervisor from Bon Secours."

"Okay. And? This is his mom."

"I'm sorry for calling so early. He's not awake yet by any chance?"

"No, by no chance. It's seven o'clock. Is there something the matter?"

"Well, yes and no," said Cathy. She stared out Starbucks' front window and doorway; executives in flip-flops and plaid shorts were coming in on this Saturday morning. "Not a problem with Tommy. Not at all. Tommy's been awesome."

"Yeah, and . . . so why are you calling? He's off today, right?" Jesus Christ. Linda's foot wagged, goddamned stress. Bon Secours, Cathy Degnan, Sandy, and Sara. It was all Tommy talked about.

If she'd been worried about Alex and his adventure, Linda had been worried about Tommy as well. He was not the most upbeat or carefree of kids, he was a wayward sort. She feared that he was a kid too easily blown by the wind rather than one who set his own course, and she feared that in looking and hoping for a clearer sense of himself, Cathy Degnan's invitation—her invitation to a calling—would be too easy, too soon, and would curtail all the wonderful trials and opportunities, the clarifications and confusions just coming into his young life.

Linda shook her head and stared at the phone as she talked into it, aggravated. It was moments like this that made her miss smoking, it was moments like this that would make anyone's hair fall out. "If it's really urgent I can wake him," Linda said.

"No, I wouldn't say it's urgent."

Okay, then--so what was it? Seven in the morning, for chrissakes.

"Um, okay, look. What is it? You do remember what time it is, right? Is it *so* important?"

Cathy felt herself flush, she massaged her forehead. "I'm sorry, Mrs. Moore, I should have waited. I've been up so long . . .."

"It's okay. Don't worry. But is there a good explanation?"

"I've been up so long."

"Relax. Tell me, what happened?"

"Okay, the short of it. Well, tell Tommy that Archie died. He's a resident and Tommy and his wife have grown close. I couldn't decide if Tommy would want to be there with her . . ."

Oh, my.

Did this lady want him to come in on the weekend? No. Forget it. He'd been spending enough time at Bon Secours, enough time with people five times his age. Enough time with Cathy Degnan.

"It's his day off," said Linda. She rose from the bed and stared at Tommy's closed door. "There's only so much of this stuff a seventeen-year-old should have to be around."

"Yeah, yeah. For sure." Suddenly, Starbucks was full, extra-crowded with strollers and walkers, with families stopping in before heading to the shore, to the lake, to the mountains. Cathy grew claustrophobic, clammy, more sad for than angry with herself. "You be the one to decide. You're his mother, after all."

"Correct. I'll decide what to tell him when he wakes up," she said.

"Oh, and just one more thing. If Tommy is interested, there'll be a little memorial service for Archie tomorrow afternoon, one o'clock. It's entirely up to you and Tommy. It's not up to me."

"Right, that is correct."

Sunday, July 14
29.

THE CENTERPIECE OF the Prayer Garden of the Blessed Mother—a patch of grass and white concrete between the residential building and the abrupt rise of the Palisades—was a larger-than-life statue of the Virgin Mary set on a pedestal of cement pavers. The Blessed Mother's slightly tipped head and welcoming hands encouraged visitation and benignly oversaw the curved rows of white benches facing her.

Technically, Sara was on her own. Bon Secours couldn't sanction individual memorial ceremonies, only the group service held monthly for all recently deceased residents. Cathy, of course, helped in any way she could—getting a security guard to bring out a folding table and cover it in a white tablecloth, herself carrying out the heavy bible from the chapel, making sure that, as Sara requested, the continuous loop of low-volume hymns honoring the Blessed Mother was turned off, not merely down. "And, oh, Cathy, you carry Archie, please," Sara requested, referring to the urn and remains. "It's too heavy."

To begin the service, Sara approached the table from the residence's side door. Cathy placed the urn on the table, alongside one of Archie's suitcases, open and tilted, propped up on the over-sized bible so the congregation could see inside. At one o'clock on the button, Tommy entered the prayer garden from the back, through a white-painted arbor covered in pink flowering vines, his need to be there winning out over his mom's admonitions.

The gathering was small—Cathy and Sandy and Sister Margaret Mary, Annie and her Bill, Nini but not Ava, Phil Chezz, and the neighbors immediately to the left and right of Sara and Archie's apartment. Entering the garden just a moment after Tommy, also through the same arbor, were a resident couple he hadn't seen before—a long, angular man in a Panama hat and a seersucker blazer, and a woman in a Southern belle's dress and a pink hairband that held back her grey-blonde hair. Like a wedding couple, they elegantly glided past Tommy arm-in-arm and slipped into the second row.

Sara waited behind the table, over her shoulder the towering Blessed Mother. She glanced back and leaned forward then away, feigning surprise at the looming Mary.

"Good afternoon and thank you to all of you for coming to this." She held her notes in both hands but only occasionally looked at them. "I went to grammar school in Nebraska, long time ago. I had the same teacher fourth, fifth, and sixth grade. Mrs. Black was her name. She loved Ralph Waldo Emerson and she taught him in every year and even in every subject. So we, all us kids learned three things in grammar school—to add, to subtract, and to quote Mr. Emerson. If I couldn't find a quote from him to apply to Archie, my goodness, how ashamed I'd be! But don't worry. I picked just one even though I could find you a dozen. The one I picked I remembered anyway, it's the shortest one, one sentence, like this: 'Every natural fact is some expression of a spiritual fact.' To me, Mr. Emerson, you're talking about Archie Grandling. Let me tell you why and give you a little lesson. Everything Archie ever did, *everything*, every step, every word, every look and whisper—like when he look at you this way or look at you like this—everything was an expression of the Archie inside, too. And when I talk about the Archie inside, I am talking about a spiritual fact," she said unequivocally. "Every material thing, every mannerism, every everything . . . every habit, every good thing about him expressed his spirit. Now for specific examples, I mean his precision, his discipline, his quietness, his wanting to please his friends—he liked everybody, everybody—his sneaky little sense of humor. Yes," she said, nodding at the audience. "Archie was Archie through and through. You didn't get a chance to know him, I know, and that is too bad. He was a walking and talking physical spirit. But I think we all are, too, maybe. I don't know. You know what I mean by a physical spirit then. Yes? Nod your head.

"Look at Archie walk across the room. You see how his posture is very straight?" Comically, she straightened up when she caught herself slumping. "That straight. His posture is funny to me, you see, because that straight posture is Archie. He's straight and proper, see, like erect, but you see his feet too, so quiet, barely touching the carpet. He notices you so he turns his head and with his eyes and a nod he says, 'Hello, sir. Hello, young lady,' and they say 'Yes, and a good day to you, also.' Maybe you notice his mouth and lips, too, kind of thin and kind of long, and right away you think this is a man who likes to smile. 'Yes, I would be glad to talk if you like to, happily, but I wouldn't want to impose.' If you look at Archie with a smart eye you can see everything, all of him. Archie was himself, whole and lovely. You just need the smart eyes. It's just how good *you* see."

Sara asked the audience to come up and look at the old valise, brown leather with brass corners and an inside lined in pink satin. The unknown, gentrified couple were the first to rise, doing so with such smiles they seemed to think they were the guests of honor. Only Tommy inched further towards the back as the others moved forward.

"This picture, this is Archie with his mother and father when he was eight years old. See how stylish he doffs that newsboy cap? And this, this is his high school diploma, he was very proud of that. This, here's Archie with Yogi Berra, the great baseball player. They were born the same day way back in 1925. Look how healthy they look."

Tommy backed out of the garden and onto River Road. He turned south along the uphill- then downhill-winding road. By the time he crossed back into Weehawken, he found himself running home, blinking his eyes, tearing to wash the sting from them.

SUMMER INTERNSHIP REPORT: WEEK TWO

Mr. Collins—

I know that unfortunately you will be receiving this epistolary report on Monday, not our agreed upon Saturday deadline, but I hope it finds you in good spirits and that you will excuse my tardiness because when I woke up Saturday morning my mother delivered me very sad and unexpected news. This news was the death of one of the Bon Secours residents by the name of Archie Grandling, and I would like to dedicate the opening portion of this report to Mr. Grandling.

Archie Grandling was the husband of a woman named Sara who in my short few days at Bon Secours I have come to consider a friend despite our differences in age. Spending a lot of time with Sara (who goes by the last name of Berry) is one of my primary responsibilities. Of all the unexpected things, Mrs. Berry is a Native American. Who would think to find one in Edgewater, New Jersey? She is a wonderful woman who regardless of the adversity she has been facing is always looking out for me as much as I am looking out for her. I think she can see that this is all new to me and tries to ease my way. I feel that I have learned from her, and I already am feeling old beyond my years.

Thanks to my two weeks at Bon Secours and especially the events of the weekend, I have constructed what I call my All-Strings-Attached Theory. You can see this theory in action in the Archie Grandling case. It goes like this if you will bear with me, sir. Archie's illness makes Sara upset. Seeing her upset upsets me. She sees me upset and she tries not to be so upset and in order to relax me. This puts a smile on my glum face. I then take this better demeanor and go about my business being nicer to the other residents, trying to make them smile because now after what she did I feel the fool not trying to make them feel better. If there are all these strings attached to one death in this little outpost known as Bon Secours Continuous Care Facility, well, you can imagine the big picture, or as a wise man once said, "Do unto others."

Now, in the second half of this very lengthy weekly report, I would like to transition to my work-related narrative, specifically a tale of my second installment of Consolation, Discernment, and Reconciliation. Last week, I told you about the long-ago tragic death of one of the residents' sons at a young age. Well, at this week's CDR, by luck and misfortune, it was my turn to speak myself. This was unexpected, but as you always tell us in Life Skills, expect the unexpected. Miss Degnan turned to me for rescue when two of the participants didn't show up. Thinking on my feet (something else you hammered into us in LS) I launched into the story of my brother Alex's cross-country trip. I was a little confident because the previous week when I mentioned it the elderly seemed interested. I am pleased to say they were very into it. To wit, as of a few days ago Alex split up with his traveling companion and this added what you might call a little undercurrent of deja vu to the tale given what Mr. Cassamarrano—the gentleman whose son died—had talked about the week before. I think they picked up on this suspense right away but were still so excited for Alex taking a very strong live-it-while- you-can stance that I thought was remarkable for their age. Before I left work on Friday, they gave me the set of questions for Alex that I promised to get to him and will email today.

This is all-strings-attached on a much larger scale. We can see how the connections extend, from the Bon Secours residents here in New Jersey, through me, to a young man by the name of Alex Moore who they've never met and is now on his own in Kansas (of all places) almost 2,000 miles away.

I will sign off now except to let you know that I have called the high school twice because I still don't have the work logs I need to complete as part of the internship contract. But to no avail. I get no answer or am told to call back later. If you could please contact your administrative aide about this and I will stop by once again today after work to pick it up. I thank you.

Respectfully, Tommy Moore.

WEEK THREE

Monday, July 15
1.

TOTING ALUMINUM-FRAME BACKPACKS—BOTH were Jackie's, her old one having replaced Alex's duffle bag which remained at Cats Who Copy—they walked a half mile down Illinois Avenue to the Xtra Gas Station and Economy Stop, two low cinder-block buildings (gas pumps here, diesel pumps over there), set on an asphalt patch before the yellow-brown prairie past the edge of town, just a few hundred yards from the Route 70 ramp. They hadn't even made it to the highway when they were offered their first ride.

A 5,000-gallon tanker-truck, new and sparkling, its cylindrical, silver trailer sporting a sky-blue and black raptor logo, left the gas station moments after Alex and Jackie had. It rolled towards them, crunching stone and kicking up dust.

"Good morning, young lady and young gentleman. I'm going north." He was a middle-aged guy, probably early fifties. His un-truck-driver-like shiny clean shave, boutique cologne, and fancy watch, his dress belt, pressed slacks, and tucked shirt surprised them.

"So are we," said Jackie. "Heading up towards Lincoln."

"I can help you out, but I'm not going that far." His chocolate-col-ored-hair was gelled and parted into a wave; it was recently clipped but buzzed a bit too high around the ears. "I go north to Auburn—that's about halfway—then west to Beatrice. That's where I dump."

"Ultimately we want to get to Fremont."

"Well, you should be good with me. Let me take you to Beatrice—then you jump on 77 for fifty miles right into Fremont. There'll be lots of trucks heading through there on up to Lincoln and Omaha."

They knew the route the driver referred to. It was part of a cross-plains route they had considered. It wasn't exactly the original plan, but then, they had already gone through three original plans.

"Sounds good," they agreed. "Thanks."

"Fan-tastic. Let me give you a hand up. My name's Layne."

"Alex."

"Jackie."

"And a more attractive young couple, I've never met. Climb in . . . Up . . . Up. Take a look at your accommodations. Ain't that sheer luxury? Known throughout the upper Midwest as Layne's Lair, heh-heh. Sleeper cabin's all yours."

It was five feet deep, all mattress except for a carpeted well up front into which they shoved their packs. The walls and ceilings were made of textured plastic, the sort Alex had seen along the way in Feyton's Motel's pre-fab shower—stain-proof, easy to wash, cream colored. There were two pillows in striped burgundy and white cases and a rose-colored lightweight blanket atop the fitted sheet of the mattress, a three-inch thick slab of plastic-covered foam. At the head and foot of the bed there were small windows, round-cornered rectangles in the sidewalls. The air-conditioning kept the little love nest humming and cool, even chilly.

"Hey," called Jackie, leaning forward towards the driver. "This is pretty good."

"'Pretty good.' I see you're into understatement. You kids make yourselves comfortable," Layne grinned. Winking, he closed the plastic accordion-door to give them added privacy. "Relax and enjoy yourselves."

Jackie took off her brown boots, rolled her socks down to her ankles, unstuck them from the balls of her feet. She settled into a curled position against the window, knees up. She plugged the earphones into her iPhone. She pushed the buds into her ears and dreamily observed the countryside: "Made up my mind to make a new start/ Going to California with an aching in my heart." Alex relaxed, eyes closed (except for occasional peeks in Jackie's direction), feet to the floor, hands folded behind his neck. It was so awkwardly inviting there, even the air-conditioning encouraging them to share their warmth.

Nine-thirty, ten o'clock, the miles rolled under them. The truck bumped and glided, rolled and swayed with the slightest bend in the road, the sun occasionally slipping through Jackie's side window, turning the beige interior to yellow. Eventually, Alex the Bold defeated Alex the Meek. Simply, he had to put a stop to this. It was more weird not to kiss her than it was to do so. Alex slid towards Jackie and tapped her on the shoulder. She turned with a smile and expectant eyes. Alex leaned in, one hand pressed against the window, one hand on Jackie's calf. He unplugged her from the device and kissed her gently on the lips. She kissed back in just the same fashion—softly puckered, gentle and brief, tender and promising. Shifting again, Alex withdrew and finally took his shoes off. He rested his body against Jackie's legs and ribs and side. She traced her fingers along his arm.

Their eyes were closed when the truck slowed at an intersection—a rare STOP sign in the middle of nowhere—and Layne pumped the breaks as, even more rare, a station wagon approached the intersection from the east as he approached from the south. Alex reseated himself, and while doing so he noticed a small surveillance-type camera mounted in the corner of the Lair, its tiny red-light blinking. Alex again unplugged Jackie and pointed at the camera. "Huh? What the fuck?"

It hadn't been on moments earlier. It hadn't been on, had it? This was not normal. Since when did trucks have interior surveillance cameras?

There was silence from Layne up front—no music, no humming, no crackling radio talk show.

"You okay back there?" bellowed Layne.

"Yeah. We're cool," replied Jackie.

"What kind of music you kids like? I tend to soft rock but I got a whole juke box up here. Really, any sort of music. You'll be surprised."

"No, nothing, thanks," replied Alex.

"Nothing! Nothing? Really? Well, all right, whatever you say. I'm just the chauffeur."

Jackie pulled Alex close and whispered: "Relax kids, enjoy yourselves.' Fuck that."

Through another fifteen minutes of silence, Alex and Jackie sat as still and observant as birds on a wire. Then a pfft came from beneath them and the cab seemed to sag. The truck slowed onto a crushed-stone shoulder. Layne drew back the divider separating him from his passengers.

"Okay, birds. This is where you get out."

"We're in Beatrice already?" asked Alex.

"No, we're not in Beatrice. We are in Table Rock, makes Beatrice look like midtown Manhattan. You're about halfway to Beatrice."

"What happened to Beatrice?"

"Oh, nothing—three churches, two go-go bars, a gas station, a funeral parlor, all still there. I just a minute ago got my orders changed. Nothing personal." As he leaned to open the passenger-side door, Alex and Jackie could smell the Noxzema smeared under his shirt collar, and the skin beneath, they could see, was red in blotches. "Now they're telling me to dump a thousand gallons in Seneca. That's in the wrong direction for you guys. Ah, well, you win some, you lose some."

"We're in the middle of nowhere," said Jackie, shimmying towards the door.

"Well, yeah, just about. That's Table Rock, right there."

Population 342 ("and counting" some wise-ass had scribbled). Incorporated 1856. Theatrically, one hand above his eyebrows, Layne scanned the area like an Indian scout. "Heep big heep of nothing. They got a cafe on that first block if you want to get something to eat. Not much shade, though, and it is awful hot. You win some, you lose some. Oh, well, at least it's dry heat," he laughed. "You'll get a quick ride. You're good looking kids and there are plenty of us on these roads. By and large, we're harmless. Enjoy Table Rock, may be a once in a lifetime chance," he chuckled.

They tossed their packs to the ground and jumped down.

"Hey, yo," called Layne. "Shut the door, the a.c., the a.c.! Last thing I want to do is start sweating like a pig. Good luck, birds, and may the Lord bless you every minute of the day."

On the short walk into town along a road caked with dried mud, "You think he was a pervert?" Jackie asked.

"Well, either a pervert or, if not, my money's on he's an alien researching earthling behavior."

2.

FOR A SMALL town, Table Rock had a huge town center—deserted but huge, way too huge. Someone some decades earlier had christened the nearly rectangular expanse of grass, stone, and weed The Table Rock Village Green, but little remained of those grand revivalist dreams, nothing but a cement oval surrounding a clanging flag pole. Around the Green, Table Rock's downtown consisted of overgrown vacant lots (verging on junkyards) and a few hundred-year-old buildings. Included among these was the town's own Historical Society and Museum and a boarded-up hotel: a fading sign announcing that Jesse James and William Howard Taft had slept there. Shorter blocks and smaller buildings ran perpendicular to the perimeter. Into waste high grass and rubble, these streets faded rather than ended.

Layne had dropped them off where Route 4 branched off from 65, presumably on his way to Seneca. On the walk into Table Rock, they passed small homes (abandoned or inhabited, it was hard to tell); one-time farms where a few animals wandered, making a reverse journey from domesticated to wild; Horace's Old Junk where the 20th century rusted; flashes of birds racing from hiding spot to feeding spot and back.

As they paused to locate the diner Layne had claimed to exist, his big truck came barreling back towards them, roaring down Pawnee Street. But it wasn't towards Seneca that he turned. It was back onto Route 4, right back in the direction they had come from. Seneca was a lie.

"Fuck him—weirdo. We're much better off."

Having gotten that first ride so quickly, they had no doubt they'd still make the concert in plenty of time to see the Avetts. It wasn't even noon and with a little luck, they figured, two more rides would get them to the festival—Table Rock to Beatrice, Beatrice to Fremont. Monday night was closing night, and the Avett Brothers were closing night's closing act, scheduled to come on at nine, but for sure it would be later than that.

Backpacks heavy on their shoulders, Jackie and Alex pushed open the curtained glass door of the Table Rock Café— three tables covered in blue and white plastic, and a sparsely stocked grocery section with nearly empty shelves of dry goods, all the expiration dates blacked out, paper Chinese Lanterns and yellow Fly Trap Sticky Tapes hanging from the ceiling. Music, loud and tinny, provided by WQEV, Eastern Nebraska's Home for Classic Rock.

Along one café wall stood an old Frigidaire with a rust pock-marked handle and a "No Lettice Today" sign taped to its door. A beefy, fortyish woman—a local Marilyn Monroe who'd let herself go—in a halter top, too-tight cutoff jeans, pink underpants peeking from the waist, and Roman gladiator-type sandals placed down her book, *A Christian Woman's Guide to Breast Feeding*, then took their orders.

"Would you like that to stay or to go?" she asked sweetly, happy to have customers.

"To stay."

"In here, or there's a table out back, under a tree. It might be cooler but whatever your preferences. I'm just mentioning it. I'll put it on a tray either way."

They looked at one another: "Out back."

The woman nodded, "Surely." Then she turned away from them and laid the wax paper on the prep counter. She sang, too.

> But I still haven't found
>
> What I'm looking for
>
> I still haven't found
>
> What I'm looking for

She was nodding and singing. She turned, catching Alex and Jackie's eye. The woman shook her head, scrunched her shoulders, and smiled, timidly coy: "That could be story of my life,"

The woman made their lettuce-free sandwiches on round rolls, put them on paper plates, added limp pickles, and put the plates on a tray. "There's salt and pepper on the counter alongside the napkins and cutlery and there's everything else—we got mustard, mayo, ketchup, our own blend in the fridge." They added a Sunny D 20-ouncer (one free with every two sandwiches). She rang them up but not having the right change in the register had to dig into her handbag. "When you're done just put the garbage in the barrel. You'll see it right outside."

"Thanks."

"Bye-now! Have a blessed," she said, waving to them from the side door, like she was seeing them off on a wagon train along the Oregon Trail. "Enjoy while you can."

3.

THE LAST THING Henry wanted to do was unload his problems on Cathy. He knew that she was frail, still reeling from the deaths of her parents and the apparent suicide of her husband, and what with Archie's death and providing support to Sara she'd had no rest over the weekend. Nonetheless, he knocked on her door. Her weekend couldn't have been worse than his. Cathy was a friend, maybe his best friend outside of family. Who else could he talk to? He would keep his emotions under control. It wouldn't be so much that he was unloading on her as simply informing her. He'd keep to the facts. After the conversations they'd been having, to tell her made sense. Not only would she listen and understand, and thereby help Henry, but she'd known Henry Jr. since he was a toddler and she would want to know. She would be upset if he *didn't* tell her. It's called friendship.

"Hey, can I come in? There's news about Junior," he said, swiping his forearm across his forehead, mopping up the sweat.

"Yeah, yes. Of course!"

She saw right through him. This wasn't the Henry of just a few days ago, regardless of how worried he'd been then. A person can't control the whites of their eyes and when Henry was this upset his reddened badly, always had. It had taken only that long—a few steps, a single utterance—and he'd done what he'd told himself he wouldn't.

"He's one of the ones they don't know where he is. He's MIA. I got the call early yesterday. They were very nice, respectful, of course, very military, but all they could tell me was 'he's not accounted for.' So we're left in limbo. For all they told me, he might as well be in Timbuktu. He could be fine, on the one hand . . . . Could be anything. Fourteen dead now, as of this morning. Two more of the wounded passed today. Two less lives. Stupid and useless suffering all around. Who can explain it?"

As Henry tried to tie off the hurting part of himself, his face twisted with a pain strong enough to reshape bone. Cathy moved around the desk, pulled a second chair close and sat next to Henry, her hand on his forearm.

"Cathy, the other day. I shouldn't have said that," said Henry, his eyes blinking.

"What did you say?" she asked.

"About God not listening. What if I was wrong and I've angered Him? He knows how to punish. We must pray. Cathy, pray with me."

"Yes, Henry. Love God, trust him, and he will help you. Faith is a gift, Henry. It's a gift we give to ourselves."

"Let's pray," said Henry, his agnosticism abandoned.

"God is great, Henry. God is all good."

"Let's pray. Let us just pray,"

"And bow our heads," said Cathy. "Father in heaven, hear our pleas and in your wisdom and mercy grant us . . . ."

4.

IN THE LANDSCAPE surrounding the Table Rock Cafe, there was little that wasn't a shade of brown—the only noticeable exception being a grey stone outcropping which glistened with traces of orange-ish iron ore. Hot as it had been an hour earlier, it was even heavier and steamier now. But the cafe woman was true to her word and they were in the shade, beneath a lone maple tree, just up the rise from a brook that separated them from the rocks. There they sat—sandwiches, blue-trimmed napkins, Sunny D, shade and a breeze. Awesome. Beautiful.

Alex decided to check messages and emails. He borrowed Jackie's phone. "Here," she said, "If you can get a signal."

"Jackie, look at this. My brother Tommy. I told you where he was working?"

"Right. The old age home."

"Check it out. I got an email from him," he said, shaking his head, scratching his unshaven cheek. "He's got people there who are asking me questions about the trip. They want to interview me for some inexplicable reason. It's like a whole list. It's in an email."

"Let me see."

"*Hello, my name is Annie Costain and I'm president of the Residents Council of Bon Secours on the Hudson where your wonderful younger brother is working.*"

There were five questions in all.

What made you embark on this adventure?

Have you made any new friends?

What has surprised you most about the trip?

How are you getting around without a car?

Where are you now?

Alex's thumbs tapped out responses to their questions, "Damn, I could write a book."

It was only with the final question that he struggled. Alex knew exactly where he was while also having no idea:

"Table Rock, Nebraska. That's north of Mexico and south of Canada, East of the Pacific and west of the Mississippi, AKA, it's the middle of nowhere." He chuckled at his response. "But that's fine with me," he concluded.

Jackie stood and circled around Alex. She pulled on his shoulders, tipping his head back, and leaned down for a kiss.

5.

THEY CAUGHT THEIR second ride nearly as quickly as they caught the first. The driver was a Mexican kid, probably younger than they were, driving a white Cadillac, grooving to Elton John's greatest hits: "Daniel is traveling tonight on a plane, I can see the red tail-lights heading for Spain, Oh and I can see Daniel waving goodbye." The kid welcomed Alex and Jackie. He told them that his name was Jose but that they should call him Mex. He had short black hair and a white scar along his right cheekbone. He wore black dress pants and a white dress shirt, top buttons undone, his athletic tee shirt visible beneath, sleeves rolled up over hairless reddish-brown arms. He sang along with Elton: "'Lord it looks like Daniel, Must be the clou-ouds in my eye.' Beautiful, so beautiful, and beauty has power, man. So, tell me, where we going?" he asked. "We all going west, I suppose." But before they could answer, "Ah, fuck," muttered Mex. "Again? Really man, again? Like come on, for real?" He spun one of the knobs on the dash, bumped his palm against it, two, three, four times. "Fucking air conditioner," he said, turning to glance at them. "Useless piece of shit. So sorry, my friends."

They settled in, Alex riding shotgun, Jackie in the back. The car smelled of funeral bouquets, perfume, Pledge.

As it turned out, Mex was being paid to drop off the long caddy at Beatrice Limousine Service. The job was earning him sixty dollars but truth be told it wasn't for the money he was doing this. "The really reason I took the job," he explained. "The real reason is to see my baby cousin. She's one year old, Josina. Problem is, you know, I got to get back to my hometown, Clarinda, in Iowa, on my own dollar. For real." Taking the bus home would have cost him nearly as much as he earned for driving the limousine, and that was not happening. Nope, on the return trip east he'd be traveling by thumb, the same way Alex and Jackie were traveling now.

"Oh, and on top of that—not enough, right?—the limo boss, dude named Butch, him and his friends sitting around there at the shop, they even make me promise not to get the car dirty, just to be insulting—even scribbled a quote 'contract,'" Mex said lifting his hands from the wheel. "They think they the Pony Express. Jerkoffs, you know. Fucking with me because I'm Mexican. I told my uncles the way he treats me and they tell me all I got to do is say they word and they'll take care of Butch and whoever else. But I'm not like that, I'm peaceful. We do it your way, Butch the Bitch. For now, you know, you know what I'm saying? For now, bro. Where you heading?"

"We're going north to Fremont," said Jackie. "There's a music festival up there."

"Very cool," he said approvingly. "You and your lady. Man, you know, us Mexicans love hippies."

"We're not hippies," said Jackie.

"Mexicans and hippies are like love brothers. You can trust me, I'll get you to Beatrice no problem. From there it's a straight shot to Fremont."

Halfway there, mid-afternoon, Jackie fell asleep across the long seat. She lay on her back, knees bent, boots off.

"To be honest with you," Mex confided to Alex. "The really reason I'm going to Beatrice? Well, that you might say would be to see my aunt more than it is to see her baby, little Josina. In honesty," he said chuckling, "I don't care too much about Josina. I mean she's cool but what does a baby know? But it's her ma, though. Let me show you." Mex took a thin wallet out of his shirt pocket, took a picture out of the wallet. "Good looking or not good looking? She got the long black hair, the big lips, just an amazing woman. And plus she got a sense of her own style, you know—the look, the moves. She knows what catches a young man's eye. You believe this woman in this here bathing suit has three kids? You can't believe it, right? She's only like maybe 32 and you can see for yourself, she is one beautiful woman."

Jackie opened one eye, rolled onto her side, her back to the conversation.

"I'm telling you, they don't make them like that anymore, not these days. I guess I need not say any more about why I'm in a hurry to get to Beatrice. . . .. Fucking A, man! For real? For real? This air-conditioner is such a fucking prick. The thing busts my chops, it really does. Million-dollar car, right, and the air conditioner is out of function. There is no excuse for that. People don't pay this kind of money to be hot and sweaty, fucking Butch. I tell you one more thing, though—Mex is in no hurry to get back to Clarinda. No bullshit. I'm in a hurry to get laid, and that's about it. But I tell you, once I get my ass in that bedroom I ain't coming out, ha-ha. I be in there all day, sorry Josina. No lie. That's one thing about me. I only speak the truth. My uncles taught me: a lie curses the lips it passes through. I'm telling you man, ha-ha," said Mex, growing drunk on his own legend. "This is a real-life reality TV show you walked into, Alex, man."

The air conditioner came on and Mex stopped poking at it, instead poking at his phone which was playing the music through the car's stereo. "You know what, to the Mexicans, well the Iowa Mexicans, or okay, the Clarinda Mexicans, ha-ha, Elton John is like king. My uncle's uncles, they all love Conway Twitty, but now the torch has been passed. Who it'll be next, no one knows," he said, shaking his head, amazed a little at the way the world worked. "Nobody knows. But us, if it ain't Mexican music it's Elton. Just listen—'He was born a pauper to a pawn on a Christmas Day, When the *New York Times* said God is dead.' The fucking *New York Times*. I mean God is dead, as reported by the *New York Times*, that is heavy shit."

6.

"THE PHANTOM" IS another name the ladies of Bon Secours sometimes applied to Wake Parish. Quickly, out of the blue he could appear—unexpected, unannounced, uninvited—then at the first turn of your head be gone. "Wake sightings" they called them: sighted in a distant chair, facing, but only half-facing, a picture window; sighted eavesdropping on a soft-spoken conversation from behind the latest issue of *Art Forum*; sighted peeking, nonchalantly, from behind the fireplace, not responding to your "hello" if noticed; sighted statue-still but observing you in plain sight, as though his stillness rendered him invisible, a phantom.

Typically, Cathy's ubiquity—her voice calling, her laugh resonating, her quick steps encountering someone somewhere—was much the opposite. She was intentionally present, engaged, and visible. But this day, Monday, July 15, she was absent and Wake had noticed, and this activated his inner sleuth: late morning, not seeing her come and go, Wake sat on one of the couches right up front, across from the reception desk. Later, alongside the wheelchairs and walkers, he watched ESPN in the common room. Back and forth, back and forth, he strolled past Cathy's office— where was she? He passed through Physical Rehab, waved hi into the Rec Room. He was in and out of Here's 2 You, which is where he spotted Sandy. Sandy had seen her in the morning, but no, not since then. "Thanks for the update, brother," nodded Wake.

Throughout the day Wake had been seen just about everywhere, but no one noticed him at three o'clock outside the chapel door. It was there, though, that finally Wake found Cathy. She wasn't alone. She and Henry were kneeling together in the first pew. Cathy pushed back from the kneeler and sat praying with her hands in her lap. Henry continued to kneel. Wake could see only the back of Henry's head, but he caught enough of Cathy's profile that he could tell her lips were continuously moving, moving quickly but parting little, each word a bead of the rosary.

7.

IN THE THICK asphalt heat of the recently repaved Beatrice Limousine Company parking lot, Mex untucked his shirt before explaining: "That over there, that's Ella Street. Turn right there. Wait," he said, spinning to orientate himself. "Yeah. From there you got, let me see, two and a half blocks—and then there's really nothing, anyway. Well, there's no more of town. That last block is Ravine Drive and at Ravine you go left from where you gonna be and that'll bring you right to 77 North, and that, that'll be the road to Fremont. You got all of that?"

"Yeah, got it all. Thanks."

"God bless you and keep you tight, right in the pocket. Enjoy your time, my friends, because nobody, not nobody knows what tomorrow holds."

"That's true, very true, and wise," said Jackie. "Thanks etcetera. Give our love to little Josina."

"Oh, yes, that's my girl. You can see it, right? The love I have for her. Peace and love my friends."

"Mm-hmm," smiled Jackie.

And so it was. Mex walked through the Limousine Company's steel back door. Alex and Jackie took slugs from their water bottles, splashed one another, helped one another with their backpacks, headed for Ella Street and 77 North.

"I thought there was supposed to be no humidity in the southwest," complained Alex, squinting into the sky, holding out his palms as though he expected rain to be falling on them. "Dry heat--what the hell?"

"I don't know," said Jackie. "Maybe it's cause we're in Nebraska, approximately six hundred miles from the southwest."

"Well, it's brutal." As they started their trek up 77, a line of darker blue-grey clouds crept over the western horizon. "I wouldn't have the heart to be like Mex."

"Little Josina is his daughter, you know."

"Yeah, I was thinking that. It's sick, only visiting your daughter as an excuse to get laid by your aunt. I started out liking Mex," Alex admitted.

"Please don't call him Mex. He's not your friend."

8.

MORE THAN EVER, since he'd spoken up at CDR Sandy had been thinking about his son Joe, and about how the years had accumulated, about how large the ocean had grown between that day and this. For the first decade or so after losing his son, Sandy had been hoping, searching for the one insight that would explain it all. Or, better than an insight to *explain* would have been an insight or a drug or an awakening to just make it all right—no explanation needed. Make it go away. But for twenty years now—oh, at least twenty years—he hadn't searched for any such awakening. He had settled stone-like into this sad excuse for a life.

For all these years, all these decades, he hadn't allowed himself to be happy, never even tried.

No, that wasn't true. Not exactly. Not entirely true. More of his old self-pitying bullshit. It's not as though he hadn't chuckled over a beer in thirty years, not as though watching Mariano Rivera pitch didn't give him a thrill, at least now and then, not as though there wasn't that string of days down at Point Pleasant Beach with his daughter and toddler grandchild some years ago when the world seemed right and his soul opened up to clean salt air and the ocean's fragrance. "I always loved the shore," he whispered, "ever since I was a kid." Try as he might, though, he could never recapture those simple days, that one moment in time, down the shore. Those few days, when things were different, they had just sort of happened to him. He had never gone seeking them, never tried to make happiness happen. He was a tourist among those moments.

Joy. True, penetrating joy, had eluded him, eluded him by far. Even laughter? He couldn't remember the last time he'd had a good laugh. To laugh hearty would have been wrong. It would have been wrong and terribly frightening. He tempered his laughter, wound it down quickly.

Years upon years. All these years, he had been talking to Joe, or trying to talk at least, and sometimes, usually with the help of bourbon, able to convince himself someone was listening, able to swim in this sweet dream of contact and communication. He would tell Joe how awful it was, how God-awful unfair it was: "You, dead? My boy gone? You dead at twenty-two years. You dead and ninety-year-olds out there playing golf, alive," he said, his hands jerking into the air. "Even me. Alive. Bullshit, bullshit. Fucking bullshit." Other times, he'd talk without the anger. Maybe telling Joe simple stories, sometimes about his own past, though the only days Sandy allowed himself to talk about were those when he himself was under twenty-two. "Have I told you I was a lifeguard for two summers? I must have been sixteen and seventeen. I have such strong memories of it, hard to believe. Remember, I grew up just half a mile from the ocean." If he talked about the present, it was about mundane things: "I think I'll cook my own breakfast this morning. Coffee, juice, an egg on toast." Or, "I met a young fellow at the Target. Really nice young man. Reminded me of someone . . . Uh-huh, yup. I know, I know."

On such a beautiful summer late afternoon as this, an hour before his early supper call, Sandy strolled the River Walk as he frequently did. The sky was clear and a deeper blue than it had been earlier in the day; only a few large, dispersed clouds floated overhead. The sun was sinking but not yet hidden behind the Palisades, its light a glowing margin brightening the ridge, the cliffs dark, hulking, overlording. As Sandy turned from the water to face the tall cliffs, he felt a coolness across his face. "Joe," he said nonchalantly, as loud as you would to a friend across the walk. "You talk, Joe. Instead of me talking to you like always, let me listen. Go ahead, I'll listen. You tell me something."

There was no message from the grave.

But as Sandy drew in a deep breath, he leaned forward and his neck relaxed. His head lolled up and down, looking at the grass, looking at the hill, he rolled it left and right as though swaying to a lullaby. A truth whispered in his own voice came to Sandy. It was so obvious what Joe wanted from him, and it wasn't this. It wasn't such debilitating, gutting sadness. That is not what Joe would have wanted. Think. He loved his father, he loved Sandy, he loved *me*. Think. Use your head, Sandy. Joe would want his father to be free, to be happy, to live *his* life. He wouldn't have wanted his father to waste all those years. He wouldn't want him to waste its remainder. He should allow himself things, life's good things. This beautiful afternoon, the river on one side, the cliffs on the other, the blue sky, enjoy it—why turn it always into a somber occasion? Sandy collapsed onto one knee and began to cry. Now on two knees, Sandy's crying stopped, transformed into dry convulsing. He held his hands to his heart, slowed his breathing, drew in breaths cool and deeper than he had in many years.

Finally, he heard yesterday's voice, Joe's voice: "Dad, let happiness in, please let it in. Stop hurting yourself. Be good to yourself. Laugh, dad." Sandy's wet eyes twinkled as he lifted his head and searched for the sun.

9.

IT HAD BEEN months since Tommy had found himself in the terror zone—the name he gave to the relentless anxiety he felt through the worst of his mom's illness. He suspected that she had been in to see Hammond earlier in the week. He'd seen a prescription slip on the kitchen countertop but couldn't make heads or tails of the code scribbled on it. He knew when his mom's scheduled maintenance checkups were and the time wasn't now. Plus, there were evenings all of a sudden that she was in the bathroom four or five times, a recurrent theme from her earlier colon cancer. And that morning before his work she was preparing to leave the house early, at the same time Tommy was. He asked a simple question: Where are you going? The more her response to the light questioning switched back and forth between arch nonchalance and high-pitched defensiveness the more likely she was hiding something, and switch between nonchalance and defensiveness she did. This worried son's game of connect-the-dots sent him rushing home from work.

River Road turned right and began its uphill ascent at the green and gold "Leaving Edgewater" sign. Moms with strollers came down the hill towards him, hip hop boomed from a double-parked convertible, kids played soccer in North Hudson Park, their screams and laughter echoing. Tommy walked faster, up the hill, but, as he broke into a trot, he stubbed his toe where the sidewalk was split and nearly tumbled, half fell over, scraped his palms on the ground to keep from scraping his face. He picked himself up.

He needed to be home.

10.

SEVENTY-SEVEN NORTH IS a shoulderless, one-lane road in each direction. After half an hour's walking, Beatrice seemed barely more than a stone's throw behind them. At least no one had tried to run them down, though one boy did shoot his water pistol at them. (It was especially good parenting, Jackie noted, that the mom had slowed down to give him a better shot.) Unfortunately, those like-spirited, festival-bound cars with room for two hadn't materialized. By the time a white convertible flew past, Alex and Jackie managed to get their fists half lifted but their thumbs never made it upright. Alex halted and pulled off his backpack, throwing it onto the roadside. Jackie did the same and joined him lying in the three-inch grass, stiff as straw.

"Josina's story reminded me of my own a little bit," said Jackie. "In that I didn't know my biological dad, either."

"So the space-time dad is actually your step-dad?"

"Yeah, technically, but in all other ways he's 'dad.' Supposedly the other guy's name is Paul," she continued. "But I don't trust my mom on anything that has to do with him. I mean, how bad is she willing to make herself sound? She says he's Italian and I believe that. It makes sense. How else to explain the fact that I tan so beautifully, as you can see. My mom gets red as a beet."

Alex plucked a blade of grass, began chewing on it.

"So what we know is your dad is an Italian guy named Paul."

"I don't even know that for sure. To me it's all just like a legend. Anyway, the legend I've been told is that they met in Austin at a UT lecture—probably it was a bar in reality. The Austin part is probably true, since I was born there."

"That would be 1980-what?"

"They met in '84, I was born in '85. The so-called 'Paul' taught at a community college in New Jersey and he was in Austin for a conference. He taught Sociology."

"You could find him if you wanted, if he's still alive." Alex turned onto his side, facing Jackie, his back to the sun. "You could do a search. Paul, NJ community college, Sociology prof. It's possible he's still teaching. If he was thirty then, he'd only be in his fifties now."

"I think I'm better off just with my fantasy or imagination or whatever. If I ever found him I think it would freak me out, he's just been an imaginary figure for so long. I don't know, to actually meet him . . . ?"

A Mountain Dew delivery truck blew past and from her cross-legged, seated position Jackie raised her thumb, only to be greeted with a smile, a nod, and a middle finger.

"You're assuming that him and your mom was something like a meaningless Radisson Hotel one-night fling," Alex said. "Maybe him and her really had a loving relationship. Do you know that they didn't?"

"Could be...no, I don't know they didn't. I don't know anything, not even if he knows that I exist. Come on, let's get up. It's honestly possible he doesn't know that I even exist."

"And possible that he does."

"Yeah, of course. That's implied."

"It's possible that she was writing him and sending him pictures of you all these years."

"Yes, but stop. You're freaking me out." Jackie stood and reached down to give Alex a hand up. "I can't explain how weird it makes me feel to think that he actually existed, that he was a physical presence, never mind that he might still be rambling somewhere out in the swamps of Jersey."

Like a cowboy carrying a saddle, Alex slung his backpack over a shoulder. "Shall we?" invited Jackie, resuming her thumb-out position on the shoulder of 77.

Four cars in a column approached and Alex and Jackie wagged their thumbs with renewed enthusiasm—"We're good kids, we won't hurt you, we can be entertainment, look how nice we smile!"—but the lead driver was only doing forty in a fifty-five zone and the other three cars zoomed around him so swiftly and angrily they didn't even notice the young road-warriors seven-hours deep into their adventure.

"Fuck," said Alex. "It is so hot."

"I knew nothing at all about my father until I was about fifteen," Jackie continued. "Then my mom used him as a cautionary tale."

"How so?"

"She was afraid I was having sex, so the message was, 'If you don't want something like *you* to happen to you, you better stop screwing around.'"

"Hmph. Great for your self-esteem."

"Look," said Jackie, pointing straight ahead. The clouds there were white and grey, blue and a much darker blue, stacked atop one another. Not right where Alex and Jackie were, but not far ahead, the dust was swirling, little tornados of brown scampering across the road. "Feel how it just got breezy and cooler? There's meaning in that."

"Yeah, and what might that meaning be?"

"Means we're gonna have a big fucking storm—wind, rain, hail, prairie shit flying around. . .."

"The end of the world," Alex joked.

"I don't think so."

11.

WORN OUT, TOMMY stopped jogging when he made the turn at the top of the hill. Two blocks later, as the nearly flat roadway curved again, on the porch he saw his mother down on all fours, scraping off paint to beat the band.

"Mom, mom! *What* are you doing?"

Five years earlier, their home's chiropractor/landlord had moved out, and with him went all regular maintenance and run-of-the-mill repairs. When the wooden porch began to splinter and its steps to split, the landlord replaced them with a concrete stoop, plain and cheap as could be. "Poverty Park" Linda called it. By the following summer, Linda had a plan and she and the landlord worked out a deal—if he bought the supplies, she and her boys would do the work. Two days of scraping, sanding, and painting; there was nothing to it. The stoop looked great—sky blue steps and porch, midnight blue railings. Well, it looked great for four days. And then, wouldn't you know it, the rain came. Who'd have thought you actually had to listen to what the Home Depot-guy said about prepping, first this and after this, that? He'd talk your ear off. The paint immediately started to blister, and now sitting on the porch was like sitting on potato chips.

Linda rotated her torso and limbs, moving from all-fours to a sprawl that had her long legs out straight, her left hip and left elbow on the deck, that hand holding up her head, and her right hand working a narrow paint brush back and forth. She was outfitted in the rattiest clothes she owned—paint-splattered tennis sneakers, an old pair of Alex's or Tommy's basketball shorts, a flannel shirt with the sleeves cut off. A mustard yellow bandanna was tied around her neck—an old cowgirl kerchief from her Oakley Moore days—nicely fashioned-up by the specks of dried blue paint already highlighting her red hair. Knowing what she must have looked like to him, Linda, after acknowledging Tommy, quickly resumed her scraping with exaggerated vigor, comedian that she was.

"I couldn't take the porch anymore. It's disgusting."

On the porch beside her was a broader brush, a scraper, a dustpan, old newspapers, a bowl filled with colored water, and the trashcan from the kitchen.

"Well, take a break. You're sweating, your face is all red."

She did as ordered and rolled onto her back, breathing heavily.

"Fan me," she said, handing Tommy a section of newspaper.

He fanned her and then, with the muscled part of his palm, brushed the sweated hair from her forehead, glancing away quickly when their eyes met. "I don't know what possesses you sometimes," he said as he folded the paper further and fanned again.

"Half an hour work and I'm wiped out. Don't get old."

"You've been seeing Dr. Hammond."

After Tommy helped lift her to sitting, Linda allowed her body to fall against her son's.

"Yes, I have, super-sleuth."

"Why the visit, or is it visits?"

"Guess. Tests, tests, and more tests."

""So why now?"

"Because she's extremely conservative. You've met her."

Tommy pushed her shoulder off his. "I'm hot," he explained. He shook his head, hesitated, taking a second to choose his words. "Yeah, I'm sure you're right," he lied. "She is being super conservative. That's not a bad thing, right, mom?"

"Nope, not at all."

"I'm going up. Gonna put on the air conditioner and try to catch a nap. Love you."

12.

THEY COULD HAVE been killed. Fuck yes, they could. They could be dead. Damn, turns out indeed it could have been the end of the world.

Though their hearts hadn't yet fully settled, Jackie and Alex approached Fremont Airfield no worse for the storm they'd just passed through. The hail had put a crack in one of the van's back windows and temporarily turned the front windshield into a silvery cascade of ice-marbles and water, no more transparent than wax paper. Alex had never been through anything like this, a wicked onslaught from a ripped-open sky, an attack of ice pounding then scattering onto the roadside, a storm that had lasted long enough to carry daytime into evening.

Just moments after the wind had arrived, just seconds before the rain did, a pine-green van pulled up and its back doors slid open. The driver, a L'il Abner sort of hippie, welcomed them: "God is good, my friends."

"Oh, shit," thought both Jackie and Alex. "But then again . . .."

They climbed in, dragging their packs and squeezing into the back bench seat.

"We come to rescue you from the coming storm!"

Welcoming them aboard, "A hard rain's gonna fall," sang one of the two women and the two young girls in the van as though they'd been singing it (predicting it, beckoning it) for the past hour, the past day, for all their lives. The side door slammed shut and within moments, hail clattered all around them.

The driver's name was Mark, and he refused to pull over during the storm—he barely slowed down. In fact, they never dipped below fifty. It was a kind of rebellious game to the group, a joy-fest, an "ecstasy," Mark's sidekick Toby explained to one of the little girls. Of the two women, one was fully invested in the ecstasy—"I'm floating out of my body, I'm outside the car, I'm one with the hail," she muttered; the other woman seemed less invested in courting death. She turned, eyes wide and terrified, and reached back to take Jackie's hand—offering and asking for comfort. "It'll be okay," she whispered for her own benefit and Jackie's.

Sometimes the van was and sometimes it wasn't in lane, and whether it was or wasn't mostly a matter of guesswork except for those times that the right wheels drifted off the road and the thumpety-thump of the sloping prairie elicited a communal yelp of the sort you might hear at the End-of-the-Times Amusement Park. Yes, this was freedom. This was an ecstasy.

Making things worse, at least from Alex and Jackie's perspective, they'd only recognize the occasional on-coming car or truck when its dim glow then suddenly brash lights burst through the swirling grey torrent, closing from twenty yards away, rattling the van. Or, worse still, if the road curved or if the hail came especially hard, they'd not spot the lights at all, unaware of the danger until an eighteen-wheeler barreled past, a righteous spirit swooshing by with a blast of the horn, threatening to blow them off their Old-Testament mystery tour.

"Well, gosh, wasn't that something," whispered Jackie dully once the storm had passed and the low sun turned the horizon pink.

Toby, gaunt and bearded and wearing a dirtied, misshapen cowboy hat, shared the front seat with Mark. The two women, just behind, Becca and Judith, wore peasant blouses and calf-length skirts. Each had a chain and crucifix tattooed around her neck and onto her chest. Both were dirty blonde and meaty. Bible-thumping, hippy farm girls, they could have been twins, except for the fact that Becca seemed as crazy as Toby and Mark, while Judith, with her alternately disbelieving and pleading eyes, did not. Also along for the trip were Eden and Lilith, both six years old and wearing homemade denim skirts and suspenders along with mismatched socks. After the excitement of the storm, the little girls fell asleep, knees bent, sole-to-sole across the van's middle bench which they shared with the two women. All four adults seemed in their late twenties or thirties, only Toby's ponytail salted with grey.

They called themselves The Mission and proved to be talkative, funny, and generous companions. Surprisingly, Mark slowed down the van considerably in the afterglow of the breathtaking storm. "We came straight north through Law'nce," he said. "Too bad we didn't know you were looking for a ride. We're part of a free-range community, one of only six left in the contiguous forty-eight." They were driving to the Prairielands Festival to see The OOHB, The Original Outlaw Hippie

Band, a rocking bunch of drum-pounding, fiddling fools. The OOHB thumped the Bible, too, just as the Mission did, but, Becca explained, they took the Word and put their own spin to it, which was fine since it's all the same bible.

"We'd be obliged to drive you back to Law'nce should you choose so," said Toby in an accent familiar from John Ford westerns, a comic character destined to die gulping from a canteen in John Wayne's arms. "We'd be obliged if you'd be a-willin."

"Obliged," said Jackie. She looked over at Alex. "I mean thank you. Maybe we'll take you up on that. We'll see," she said, the last part of the statement a message to Alex.

"Don't worry," said Judith, tipping her head apologetically. "I'll be driving. Promise."

It wasn't a rush to see OOHB that had caused Mark to blast his way through the storm. See, they weren't actually even playing the festival proper. They were playing the following morning, what was called Border Day, the day after a festival when bands could perform unpaid to whatever portion of the crowd remained. Mark explained it like this, "Nah, the OOHB ain't playin' tonight. It weren't recklessness caused us to drive apace. It were a rage against the machine."

A prayer in a giggle, "Rage, rage, against the dying of the light," spoke the little girls. "Rage, rage! Rage, rage!" exclaimed Eden, all up in Lilith's grill.

13.

LINDA WAS STILL on the porch—but no longer working—when Tommy came back outside after an unsuccessful attempt to nap.

"Why are you still down here?" he asked.

"What's your problem? I was upstairs. I made a sandwich and took a shower while you were sleeping. I just came back down to clean up. I'm relaxing. We have a beautiful view, if you haven't noticed."

The porch light made it bright enough that Tommy could see the work she'd done.

"Good job."

"So far, so good—kind of. Come and sit with me," she said, grimacing as she massaged her thin calves. "They're so freaking sore." Her fingers were long like everything else about her, but her nails were bitten down to the skin.

"No thanks. I'm good."

"Don't be obnoxious."

"I was gonna go down to the field but it's already late. I want to get up extra early tomorrow."

"Oh, stop. Go be with your friends. You're being too responsible, you're getting too caught up in this intern business. You don't have to get up 'extra early,' for crying out loud. That's your problem."

"I didn't know I had a problem."

"Bad word choice. I take it back."

"I'm *too* responsible all of a sudden."

"Yes, when it comes to that job—it's not even a real job. Go out tonight."

"I'm still thinking about the man who died, Archie, Sara's husband. The service I went to yesterday."

"That's all you talk about is that place!" she scolded. "It's natural you'd be thinking about him. But you also can't be totally caught up in it. You can't be mulling and fretting over it."

"I'm not 'mulling and fretting.' I feel bad for the woman."

"You've told me all about it."

"In a way, she's my responsibility."

"Oh, come on. In no way is an eighty-year-old woman the responsibility of a seventeen-year-old boy. Just stop. You are there for three weeks and your friend Crazy Cathy only seems to want more and more from you. Thomas, I understand that you care about these people, and that's good. But seriously."

"Seriously what, mom?"

"For goodness sakes. Never mind, you be you. Oh, but by the way, if you are staying home, I bought onion dip if we want to watch TV."

14.

THE MISSION VAN hit festival traffic two miles south of the airfield and from there crawled towards the muddy parking area. Alex and Jackie stuck with the Mission folk, who provided them with a tent and blankets, food to eat, drink to drink, smoke to smoke, and fire if needed. They rolled to a stop a half-mile from the stage and, loaded down with gear, aimed for the music. In their denim skirts, Eden and Lilith carried small tom-toms they banged with whittled sticks as they skipped bare-footed alongside the adults. The progress was slow and muddy, mini-Woodstockian. The music swelled to a happy noise. A band—name unknown and too distant to be made out on the shimmering stage—was strumming to a song pretty obviously titled, the crowd amiably making up lyrics for those they didn't really know:

I was totin' my pack along the Winnemucca road,

When along came a semi with a canvas-covered load.

"If you're goin' to Winnemucca, Mack, with me you can ride."

So I climbed into the cab and then I settled down inside.

He asked if I had seen a road with so much dust and sand.

And I said, "Listen, I have traveled every road in this here land!"

I've been everywhere, man.
I've been everywhere, man.
Crossed the desert's bare, man.
I've breathed the mountain air, man.
Of travel I've had my share, man.
I've been everywhere.

"Yahoo," yelled Toby.
"Testify, Toby!"
"Yahoos" all around.

A ragged line of fans trooped along the northwest ridge. To Alex, it didn't seem quite real. It was too damn pretty. And it was all too much—the Mission, the Avett Brothers, Jackie, the crowd, the stars beginning to poke through the deep blue sky, the dark hills. Wow.

The energy in the tromping crowd swelled and soon the tromping picked up in pace with the music.

I've been to:
Reno, Chicago, Fargo, Minnesota,
Buffalo, Toronto, Winslow, Sarasota,
Wichita, Tulsa, Ottawa, Oklahoma,
Tampa, Panama, Mattawa, La Paloma,
Bangor, Baltimore, Salvador, Amarillo,
Tocapillo, Baranquilla, and Perdilla, I'm a killer.

The stage faced southeast. To its left, the cradle-shaped moon rocked, an interior silhouette of soft blue resting in its cup. The band finished its encore, bowed like a smiling troupe of seasoned vaudevillians then dashed off stage.

At 10:30 the stage lights blinked a spray of colors and the crowd roared in a series of ascending waves. The Avett Brothers Band—the brothers Scott and Seth on banjo, mandolin, and guitar; upright bassist Bob Crawford; and cellist Joe Kwon—waved and grinned, took overly formal bows, and skipped to their spots. Scott walked to the middle microphone and stared into the audience's roar. Finally, "Good evening, and welcome to our little corner of the universe." He grinned towards the bassist: "Good old Fremont, Nebraska, home of the Prairielands Music Festival." The drum beat began and the band members began pogo-ing—jumping up and down, arms close to their sides—and 15,000 souls followed:

> We're walking in the fields,
> We're walking in the forests
> The moon is before us, up above
> We're holding hands in the rain
> Saying words Iike I love you

Alex and Jackie drifted away from the Mission and into the portion of the crowd pushing closer to the stage. They worked their way through, and the multicolored stage lights swelled and dimmed to songs of January weddings and the weight of lies, of the Old Tin Man and of pretty girls from just about everywhere.

Somewhere well after midnight, as the second encore started up, some in the crowd weaved back to their campsites; some settled into stargazing, backs on the grass; some danced more energetically than ever. One by one, until there were dozens, campfires lit around the perimeter. The band, as purged and exhausted as the crowd, silently wandered out for one more song. Sweet and melodic, a lullaby they offered: "Here's a nighty-night for y'all."

> I want my soul to feel brand new
> I want to hold hands and I want to make love
> I want to keep running all day and all night
> Even when my mind tells my body that's enough
> I want to stand up and I want to stand tall
> If ever I have a son, and if ever I have a daughter
> I don't want to tell them I didn't give my all.

Lifted by a thread tied to Venus, the silvery moon gently rocked and ascended; the stars winked and twinkled; Alex and Jackie swayed hip to hip; Monday had turned to Tuesday with no notice.

15.

IT WAS ON every station. The Taliban had given the Marines an ultimatum—either completely withdraw from Bad Pakh or the remaining hostages would be killed. They would be beheaded. Already the American deaths had crept up to sixteen. The message had been delivered in the style of an American western: two of the missing twenty-eight Marines were led into town by two mountain herders. These Marines were dead—they had been hung, the rope still around their necks—but somehow propped upright on the mules that carried them. The Taliban's terms were written and delivered to the Marine commander by the trembling goat herders. Cathy watched on CNN knowing that Henry was at home, staring terrified at his own TV.

As had been her routine for the past several months, whatever Cathy needed for the next morning, she got together the preceding night, before The Late Show came on. Then, by eleven, she darkened the living room and stretched out on the couch, pillow under her head and blanket available. This way, she could avoid walking into the empty bedroom, there would be no decision about when to go to sleep, no need to rise, shut out the lights, walk in the darkness. She might or might not turn off the TV. It was simple. She'd lay on the couch until sleep happened, and hope that when she opened her eyes, the room would be brightened, maybe the sun shining in. It was her ritual-voiding ritual.

In her dream, she was alone and watching CNN from Henry's favorite nook. Wolfe had marginally changed, morphing into a Satanic figure—face red, lips black, eyes white. He announced that a terrible error had been made in the reporting. It was 148 Marines who were missing or dead and "upwards of one-hundred of those 148 are confirmed dead. The names and numbers are being updated by the minute."

Wolf began reading the names of the dead as their photos, photos of them as young men (only two were women), civilians, not in uniform—wedding photos and prom photos, young men holding their babies and 22-year-olds flanked by smiling parents—appeared to Wolf's left: "The 42nd Marine dead, the 43rd Marine dead, the 44th Marine dead . . ." Cathy counted along with Wolf praying she would not see Henry Junior's photo, pleading that she wouldn't. But his name and photo came up.

Number 51 was Henry Junior's high-school yearbook photo: bowtie, diamond earring, his daddy's eyes. Cathy held her face in her hands, but between her fingers she could see Henry coming towards her. He seemed worn and he had lost weight but he smiled with relief, there was joy in his eyes. She would have to tell him though. To give him the news. Wouldn't she have to tell him?

She set her hands on the table, poised to flee, but instead of lifting her, her elbows locked, and her palms anchored her in place. Henry was upon her: "God is good, Cathy. I trust in the Lord. Our prayers are answered. I know Junior is okay, I know it. He is better than okay, he is blessed, Cathy. God is good."

She froze for a moment before speaking: "No, Henry. Junior is not alright. He is not safe, he is not blessed. God is not good. Anyone who believes that, Henry, has just not been watching." But, from behind Henry Tommy appeared waving his arms, rushing towards her, and her words were drawn back.

Frantically, Tommy was shaking his head: "No, no, Cathy. No, don't say anything. It was just a trick, you dreamed it. Don't say anything."

In her dream, she said, "Thank you, Tommy. Thank God it was only a dream." She embraced Henry, who was crying with relief and joy, with gratitude and grace.

Tuesday, July 16
16.

THE MISSION PROVIDED Jackie and Alex with a big four-person tent. They could have slept under the stars but accepted the offer for its privacy: call it Intercourse, Nebraska. They hadn't had sex up to this point but were ready for the challenge. Each on an elbow, they lay facing one another, lips inches apart and tingling.

"I should tell you. Well, I feel like I have to—'owe it to you' is the wrong word—even though it doesn't really matter or at least I think, hope it doesn't but I feel like I should tell you I'm pregnant."

"You're pregnant," Alex repeated. "And you're not kidding?"

"Not kidding, about three months. See I have a little bump?"

Alex's head slid from his palm and he rolled onto his back. Alex, the bio major, knew this: the little something inside Jackie was officially a fetus, no longer an embryo. It was probably as big as his thumb—maybe exactly so, he thought, sneaking a peek at his hand. The creature's toes and fingers were beginning to form and it might already be doing something between kicking and paddling. Its sex would be discernible.

Jackie knelt next to Alex, above him, her butt resting on her heels. She took his hand: "Feel." His fingers gently circled her belly, her T-shirt sliding with his fingers.

Insulated though they were by the tent's walls, they could smell the wood fires and the burning of reefer and cigarettes, hear their neighbors' music, see the flickering light of the surrounding fires.

"It's very weird," Even lying on his back, he was dizzy.

"I guess," said Jackie. "But I still want to make love."

"It's very weird. I mean a little bit of a shock. I don't really know why."

"I know, I do understand." She rubbed the inside of his thigh. "Come on. Let's."

She knelt but straightened her back, butt off her heels, her shirt hanging like a loose curtain to her thighs. "Would it be less weird if I came on top of you?"

"I don't know," he murmured, as she did.

17.

SANDY FOUND SARA working a crossword at a table in the Town Square. The shops had just opened and it was bustling this morning—with wheelchairs and walkers, striders in sandals and tennis shoes—as bustling as it ever got. Sandy was dressed a little more neatly than was his norm—a short-sleeved plaid shirt, navy blue cargo shorts, white ankle socks, canvas slip-on shoes. He had coffee in one hand, Sara's gift in the other in a paper shopping bag. He placed the coffee down, put an arm around her and patted her hand. Before he even said a word, she shrugged: "What are you going to do? Death. Loss. What are you going to do? There is nothing, right?"

Sandy nodded soft agreement. "How are you? Are you okay?"

"I'm okay. Yes. You know, somebody you love dies, it's a shock. I got my own spirituality, though. Then, on the side, I go to Catholic Mass, too," she chuckled.

"Good for you. You seem like a strong person."

"I don't know. I'm strong and weak. I'm both. Are you a strong man?"

"No, no at all." Sara squinted at him in sympathetic disagreement. "I'm trying. I am trying."

"That's good, then. We'll see. How many years did you lose your wife? You still think about her, I bet. I bet every day."

"Carol, yes, ten years. Not just every day, but all the time, *all* the time."

"Like your son."

Sandy's eyes misted. He rubbed the back of his neck.

"I guess so. I guess that's me."

"Yeah, we all married to ourselves."

She patted his hand and he smiled but didn't get her little joke.

"You know, the 'for better or for worse' part."

"Oh, yes," he laughed. "I close my eyes and there's Carol. I'm with her in that way, that particular, peculiar way."

"But you don't believe that you're really with her."

"Believe it like it's reality? Oh, no, Sara my friend. Carol's dead and gone. That's the way it is. That's what's real."

"You experience it and still say it's fake."

"I dream about her still. But, goodness, I still dream about my mom and dad, too."

"And you think 'Oh, there goes my imagination again!' You think that's not real. I don't think that way. See, I think it is real. Everything I experience is real. It's my reality, ha-ha. Usually I keep quiet about that, though. You think I'm crazy?"

"No, you are very clearly not crazy. And I'm not going to argue with you, either. It's a wonderful sentiment."

"Not 'sentiment' the way you say it. I am what's real. With my eyes open, what I experience is real, and with my eyes closed what I experience is real."

"Yes, you are real. And you are wise, too."

"Promise you will try to experience my way. Promise to try it my way."

"I will. I will try to see it that way. I know, I know now that I should change."

"Okay, you have your homework."

Sandy smiled.

"So anyway," he said. "I have something for you, a gift, right here in the bag."

18.

THE TENT, BRIGHT with sunlight, was occasionally darkened by walking shadows which like Saturday morning cartoons passed across the screen. They could hear chatter and bustle around them, and Border Day's opening performers were beginning their sound check. Alex lay on his back, hands on his belly; he didn't think he'd moved all night. Jackie was on her side, her back against him. Alex sensed an alertness in Jackie, that her eyes were open and watching the shadow show. When he shifted, Jackie didn't move. When he sat up, she rolled onto her back and wiped tears from her eyes. He didn't know what to do: to ask, to commiserate, to console, to pull on his pants and leave. She shifted again to face Alex and used her forearm to block the bright sunlight pressing into the tent.

"Yes, I'm here," she said.

"You okay?"

"I'm fine, I'm sorry. I'm fine, though," she smiled. "My heart's garb . . .oops, Freudian slip. My head's garbled."

"Mine, too. We should probably get up, right?"

"Sure."

From seated positions, they pulled on their pants and pushed words into the humid tent.

"They were great. Again."

"Yup, aren't they always?"

"I wonder if this 'Mission' band is any good."

"Yeah, I guess we're stuck here until they're done with their set."

"The Mission."

"Yes, the fucking Mission."

"Sweet but crazy. Crazy-sweet."

They took down the tent and repacked it. Then, rocking left-foot-right-foot, left-foot-right-foot, they hugged and kissed, hugged and kissed, laughing at their self-consciousness. Wearily, carrying their boots and socks, they walked the short distance back to their new friends.

"Hey, hey," called Mark.

"Hey, hey," chirped Eden and Lilith.

Jackie sidled over towards Judith, her almost friend. Raggedy-doll loose and vigorously nodding approval of the universe's benevolence, Becca joined the other two women.

"Just in time for breakfast. Man, your Avett boys were outstanding," said Toby. "I mean, them and the stars! Together. I don't have to tell you."

"When is your band on?" asked Alex.

"The OOHB? They're fourth out of four. They close the show. This is the first group getting ready."

The Mission had breakfast prepared—scrambled eggs and pieces of biscuit and strong coffee in a green and white tin mug for each of them. Nodding and blinking, sniffing the air, muse-searching, transcendental but feral, long-bearded Toby strummed his guitar. On stage, the first band began, playing to a scattered audience of maybe one hundred souls, though even to call the gathering an audience was a stretch. There was simply a smattering of folks in front of the stage, as many sleeping, as many wandering, as were listening, several even playing their own instruments.

Alex stared off beyond the breakfast circle, toward a stretch of trees south of the festival. It made sense to leave, Alex told himself. It really did, to continue west, or at least westerly, to not head back to Lawrence with Jackie, to move on by himself.

19.

"I STARTED THINKING about it before Archie passed," said Sandy, "then afterwards I wasn't sure whether or not I should." He pushed the bag towards her. "You have to respect people's feelings, and I do. But I think it's appropriate and you'll take it in the right way. I mean, at least I hope you take it with understanding and affection as it's intended."

"Oh, of course. You talk too much. Let's see what we have."

"I started working on it last week, using the computer mostly, the internet. I just googled . . .."

"Sandy, shhh. Please. See I'm reading?"

The gift was in a 9x12 wood frame—obviously he'd made a trip to Eclectica Stationary and Gifts. The parchment was grey; the print was in italics, a purplish blue.

"There were so many wonderful sayings—poems and prayers. When I finally chose one, I put it together, the paper and the type of. . . ."

"I am still reading."

"There were so many to choose from."

"Let me read it back to you, out loud."

"It's not exact as written. I changed it up a little bit."

"Shhh. Listen, Sandy."

"The title is mine."

"Oh, my goodness," she said and took a swipe at him, missing his nose by an inch.

To Learn What We Can

Earth teach me stillness
As the grasses are stilled with light.
Earth teach me courage
As the tree that stands alone.
Earth teach me resignation
As the leaves that die in fall.
Earth teach me renewal
As the seed that rises in spring.
Earth teach me freedom
As the eagle that soars in the sky.

"Beautiful, beautiful. I never read this prayer before."

"I changed a few words here and there."

"Yeah, you told me already."

"I just hope it doesn't come across as disrespectful."

"Disrespectful how? It's a wonderful gift. I will put it right on my dresser. Don't blah-blah-blah and ruin it."

"Okay, okay," he said, hands up.

"Let me give you a kiss, Mr. Sandy. You're a very sweet man."

20.

ALEX AND JACKIE wove their way among blankets towards the stage. The first band had already exited to no acknowledgement and the second act took the stage with no announcement. They took a seat in the grass and feigned interest in dulcimer and flute, their silence periodically broken by lame but laughable jokes about Layne, Mex, the storm, and the craziness of it all.

Then, after a short break, the third band of the morning began tuning their instruments.

"Good morning, everyone. We're Mary and John and we're going to play a few tunes for you."

John was dressed in Southern-Gothic black, stovepipe hat and all; Mary wore a below-the-knee dress and scarves of purple and pink and various blues. The first song—listened to by Jackie and Alex with too-obvious attentiveness—was joyous, even a little rowdy in its fiddling, but not contagious. Their second song was tragic and, unfortunately, was contagious.

It was noon, or nearly so, as good a time as ever, Alex thought.

"You know," he said as another slow dirge began. "I'm not sure about heading back to Lawrence. It might make sense just to keep heading west."

"Oh, Alex, come on. Because of me?"

"No, no."

"I'm sorry about my mood. I have no idea what was upsetting me. Hormones maybe. It had nothing to do with you and me. Please try to understand."

"Of course I understand."

"I'll be fine. I'm sorry, I'm sorry. I'm fine."

"Nothing to apologize for."

"Come back to Lawrence, then. You don't even know the town yet. You'll meet a lot of really good people there."

"Yeah, yeah, I know I would."

"You haven't even met any of my friends yet."

"I know. But you'd be okay getting back with The Mission?" said Alex, half statement, half question.

"Okay? Yeah, of course. That's not the point."

On stage, Mary and John announced that they were about to bring out their son and daughter, Punch and Judy. Judy, the older of the two, nearing ten, came out onto the stage with a professional show-biz air, smacking a tambourine against her hip. It was impossible to tell much about Punch, a couple of years younger than Judy, his appearance dominated by the too-heavy guitar slung around his neck. He may have been fatigued or bored or angry or nervous or cool. Whatever, he wasn't sharing in the festive vibe.

John introduced the next song: "We came to write this one when we were playing a roadhouse in Shreveport, Loo-zianna, but both of us were in different bands, amazingly. It was a time when, unbeknownst to one another, we were both heavily immersed in the great Leonard Cohen's catalogue. It freaked us out, didn't it, Mare? Any Leonard Cohen fans out there? Well, yeah, all right, then. Yay, Lenny!"

Jackie and Alex listened in silence. By the time they rose to head back to the Mission, Alex was as good as gone. There was only one practicality to take care of: "Can I give you my friend Billy's address? I know it's kind of a pain in the ass but do you think you can get my duffle bag to him? I think all you have to do is put a tag on it and lug it to UPS. Here's $20. It can't cost more than that, can it?"

"I don't care if it costs more. But you're being foolish. You should come back to Lawrence. This is too depressing."

"It's not. It shouldn't be. You're gonna be a mom with a beautiful baby!"

"Oh, come on," she said, taking the comment as nothing more than a diversionary tactic.

Alex told the Mission folks of his change of plans, of which they heartily approved. "California," they said, nodding at one another. Alex gave a lingering hug to Jackie, as she looked away, then hoisted on his backpack.

"Don't miss Oregon while you're out there, beautiful country," said Becca.

"Amen," said one of the two little girls to the other, who, in imitation of the big folks, began nodding back. "And the road shall lead you on, yup," both girls said, still nodding. "The road shall lead you on."

Two weeks after leaving the cozy confines of Weehawken, Alex saw himself now as a man of the road, weary and experienced, a tested traveler, a young man with a soul older than dirt. He left the airfield and followed a sign towards 30 West. The sun was there, high and just over his left shoulder, but mostly directly above.

21.

FROM FREMONT, ALEX headed due west towards Ames and Schuyler. In a mile, West Military Avenue intersected Route 30; from there the Great Plains imperceptibly rose into the High Plains. Route 30's asphalt was so recently laid that the dividing line hadn't yet been set and the still-shiny black ribbon took on the character of a gently rolling runway through tall grass. The road's shoulders were sandy and pebble-filled, marred by occasional roadkill. Scattered sagebrush and yellowed grasses grew along the shoulders, and the south edge of the road was lined with tall cross-topped poles strung together by loops of utility wire. In the flatlands around Route 30 the range of animal life kept Alex engaged: encampments of pop-up prairie dogs; a distant hump-backed coyote, guilt in his gate; a lone cow wheeling its neck, wondering where everyone went; high-flying raptors over the trees to Alex's north, a mile or so away, which lined the banks of the Elkhorn, one of the Platte River's major tributaries.

After several miles, finally, Alex came to a crossroads, Historic Markers pointing in both directions: Lincoln Highway this way, Oregon Trail that. He continued along Route 30, the Lincoln Highway, passing a dilapidated home and its weed-encroached family burial plot, and beyond that an abandoned farm stand. As the road continued a slow bend south, the trees lining the Platte and Elkhorn rivers bent north, shrunk until they nearly disappeared into the horizon and appeared as a dark seam connecting earth and sky. There were disappointingly few cars on the road, and Alex was quickly wearing out. At a concrete obelisk whose engraved lettering was indecipherable, he set down his backpack and sipped from the canteen. He had another canteen in his backpack, but the only food he had were two homemade granola bars, courtesy of The Mission.

With no phone, Alex didn't know the time. He knew only that it was mid- afternoon and was sure that it had to have been at least two hours since he'd left the world of Jackie, the Mission, and the Prairielands Festival. Where were all the cars? Finally, as fatigue was setting in and the weight of his backpack growing heavy, he saw what looked like a small farmhouse. How far away? Well, Alex had no idea. Could have been less than a mile, could have been two. Whatever the distance, it *looked* like a house—hopefully an inhabited one with someone at home.

It turned out to be a brown-shingled house set at a fork in the road. Route 30 split like a wishbone just before the house—to the right was CR 15, aka Cutoff Road, heading more north than west; to its left, continuing due west, was 30. The sign staked in the front yard read "Hurtley's Ranch—coffee, ice, and quality food. Open All Year." Alex approached from the Route 30 side and knocked on the screen door's frame. From one room removed, "Come on in," a man called, just loud enough to be heard. Alex could see him in the kitchen at the sink washing his hands and throwing the dishrag across the faucet. The man was about as much of a cowboy rancher as Alex could ever have imagined—early fifties, lanky with a small gut, bow legged in jeans and wearing a worn flannel, neatly tucked in at the waist. Alex opened the door but waited at the threshold. The man approached smiling, "Shhh. Come on through," he said. "We got to try to be quiet."

Alex whispered hello and said he was looking for lunch.

Though Hurtley's may have sold coffee, ice, and quality food, this house was a home, not a store. Lying on the living room couch, a pillow under her head, a knitted blanket over her bones, was an elderly woman. As Alex passed, she nodded wordlessly. Beneath the room's spinning fan, a man as old as the woman—all nose and jaw beneath pressed-to-the-scalp dirty grey hair—sat in a wooden chair next to the couch, holding the woman's hand. "It's okay, Charlie," said the fiftyish man to the elderly one. "He's a customer, here for some food."

Once upon a time, there had been children in the house—through an open door, you could glimpse the downstairs bedroom's ballerina wallpaper, and out the kitchen window was a basketball hoop and a swing set with only one of two swings remaining, and hanging by only one chain at that. Right in the living room, other side from the couch, across the worn rug, was an upright piano and a white, child-sized one under the stool. There was a guitar, as well, and a music stand and two drumsticks; there was no drum but the battered edge of the piano suggested it had occasionally served as percussion. Alex passed a steep stairway to the upstairs then entered the next room, the meticulously kept dining room, the family museum.

"Are you coming from that concert in Fremont?"

"Yeah, I am, as a matter of fact." He felt more like guest than customer and was embarrassed that he couldn't present a cleaner and more respectable self to his good-natured host.

"And you're on your own, then? Freewheeling? Where are you heading?"

"California, Los Angeles area."

"Well, good for you. Good for you. Why don't we go out on the back porch? You can put your things down and we can sit. We got shade, we got a little breeze, and we got space—oh, yes, we got plenty of space. Here, you first. You came here on a big day for the Hurtleys. I'm waiting for my daughter Patty to get home. I'm a grandfather as of 12:15 yesterday afternoon."

"Congratulations, sir. A boy or a girl?"

"A little girl. Double sevens—seven pounds, seven ounces. A good weight. Tell me, what can I get you in the way of food and drink? I can make you a sandwich is really about it. I got roast beef and I got

ham, also cheese, white or yellow. It's all fresh. I got whole wheat bread and long rolls. You pay me what you can."

"Oh, sure, I have cash," Alex said and reached for his wallet. "How about roast beef and yellow cheese on a roll?"

"Got it. I think I'm out of mayo—or if I got it, I don't trust it's good. Want mustard? Lettuce?"

Alex eased himself into one of the cushioned wicker chairs. "Sure, and salt and pepper if you got them. How much do I owe you?"

"Three dollars? And I'll throw in a glass of ice water. I may have some lemon to slice up, too. Pickle?"

"That sounds great."

"My name's Fred, by the way. Fred Hurtley."

"Nice to meet you – I'm Alex."

Fred went into the kitchen and Alex watched Route 30's traffic. A few cars passed, more than there'd been a little while earlier. Alex leaned his elbows on his knees, stared out across the yellow grass beneath the cloud-speckled blue sky. He breathed it in, sucked it right into this soul, wondered if this was one of those mini-memories, a spot of time he'd carry to the grave. Echoes, there were, of mortality and a sweet scent there was in the breeze.

Fred brought the food and drink out on a wobbly tray, one that was bent both upwards and down.

"Where you from, Al? Is it Al or Alex?"

"Alex is good. New Jersey."

"Ah, there's a state with a reputation, a stereotype's more like it. I've been out to California and Oregon but never east. Nashville is the furthest east. Unless, I don't know, unless New Orleans is further east."

"I don't know. I think Nashville is more east."

"There's napkins etcetera in that red metal thing, there. Um, I should mention to you about the woman inside. That's my grandma,

she just turned ninety-four. She'll soon be parting us, for sure. She's comfortable, the doctor made sure of that. And she don't know she's dying. That's a blessing in its way."

"Agreed. That's how I'd want to go. What's her name?"

"Gabby. Well, Gabrielle. It fit, too, cause she used to be such a chatterbox. We call her Grandma Gabby or just Granny. She's very much at peace. In a 'reverie' the religious folks around here call it. The old guy, he's my step-grandpa. He'll stay on with us here."

"And your daughter lives here, too?"

"Yes, Patty and her husband. With the baby, after grandma goes, it'll be five like before. One out the door, one in."

"You're a grandpa, Fred." Alex saluted him with his glass.

"A baby girl. Lucky sevens. They didn't know the sex beforehand, I agreed with them on that decision. They had a name for a boy. They we're going to name him Alfred after my son-in-law who is an Alfredo. But they had none for a girl." The sun had moved southwest and now, peaking around the porch, was hitting Fred straight in the face. He shimmied his chair back into the shade. "Now 'Alex.' That's a name could go either way, a boy or a girl."

"Sure. The first girl I ever kissed had the same name as me."

"That's something."

"Yeah, weird."

"I'm thinking you may be a good luck omen. I'm gonna mention that to them. I like that name for a girl, Alexandra, maybe. Makes me see a girl on a tall horse, I don't know why. I have no clue," he laughed. "What's your last name?"

"Moore."

"And that's what it'll be years from now, 'The Legend of Alex Moore.' Some eighty years from today, some new little child will say to

her, 'Grandma Alex, how did you get your name?' And granny'll say, 'Well, honey, there is a legend behind that.'"

Alex grinned, and he scratched his beard in a veteran way. "Well, little one," he said continuing Fred's thread. "It's about a stranger, an easterner, here then gone further west. We call it 'The Legend of Alex Moore.'"

"Exactly, Alex. That's exactly right."

The sun had swung now full onto the porch, and though there still weren't enough cars to please Alex, it was time to go. Could he say a prayer with Grandma Gabby before he left? Sure, he could. Fred led him into the front room. It was 4:00 by the mantel clock.

"Charlie, this young man is Alex, he's traveling. Before he leaves, he wants to know if it'd be okay to say a prayer with granny."

"Sure," he said, softly patting his hands together in a soundless clap.

Alex knelt next to the old woman. "God bless you," she said.

"Thank you."

"Any time," said Granny softly. "Wasn't nothing."

Once back on Route 30, the first vehicle to approach Alex was a blue pick-up. He was about to lift his thumb, but too soon the truck slowed and its blinker flashed. Slowly, it turned into the Hurtley's: must have been Patty, Alfredo, and their baby girl. Sure would be sweet if they wound up naming her after him. Imagine that. What Fred had said. Eighty years from now.

22.

AS THE SUN sailed west, beginning its slide towards the horizon, Alex came upon a small but proud billboard: Welcome to Ames, Population 53. Home of Historic Union Pacific Railroad Station. Alex sat in the

shade of the sign, leaning against one of its posts, slugged some of the water from his newly filled canteen.

A dusty black Jeep Grand Cherokee with Illinois plates slowed as it approached and pulled to the side of the road. Alex hopped up and hustled towards it.

"Heading west?" asked the driver, leaning out the window as Alex skipped towards it. The car was pretty banged up—either the driver was reckless or had found himself in a nasty streak of bad luck. It stunk of what Alex, inexperienced though he was, immediately identified as dirty diapers.

"Yes, sir," responded Alex. "General direction of California, LA."

"Sounds west to me. Hop in then. I can take you most of the way."

The car's interior was a mess—strewn clothes, McDonalds and Taco Bell wrappers, a sun-yellowed Wall Street Journal, a fat college economics text, road maps torn and stained, strips of browned banana peel. In the way-back of the Jeep was a portable baby carrier. In an attempt to protect the baby inside, wheezing as he slept, the carrier was squeezed in between pillows and a blanket. Two bungees were looped through its handle and hooked to the backseat's headrest.

Alex wedged his backpack between his legs. The diaper smell emanating from the back mixed with the car's other smells in varying waves of vileness. The driver was forty-ish, Alex figured. He was lean across the shoulders and down the arms, but heavy in the gut. His cinnamon-colored hair was straight out of a Clairol commercial.

"So can you chip in for gas?"

The guy shifted into drive, turned off the shoulder and into the driving lane.

"Yeah, I can chip in. How much?"

"Depends on how much you got, but don't worry, man, I'm not looking to rob you."

"Well," said Alex—he was half calculating, half pulling a number out of the air. "I can give you twenty."

"Wait, man," said the driver, pulling in his neck, dipping his chin, tilting his head. "Can you do better than that? I'm saying I can take you all the way into Utah."

"Utah's on the way to LA? I thought Utah was north."

"Oh, brother," laughed the driver. "You think maybe you might be in just a little over your head? And you ain't even stoned. Do you even know where you are right now? You're in Nebraska, correct, son?"

"Yeah, correct." Already Alex was having second thoughts about accepting this ride. At the very least, the guy was annoying. "Like I said I thought LA was south of Utah."

"You're lucky I'm the one picked you up cause you're basically lost. Utah is west of Nebraska. California is west of Utah. To get from Nebraska to California, you gotta go through Utah. I tell you what, give me eighty."

Another shift and the car jerked to fifty.

"I can give you fifty dollars," said Alex quickly.

"Oh, man. You drive a hard bargain." Reluctantly, as though just swindled, the driver laid out his palm and into it Alex dropped a fifty dollar bill. "Okay, okay," said the driver. "No need to be like that, though. You're getting a square deal. What's your name?"

"Alex."

"Great name. Always liked that name. My name's Bob. Bob Doe. Feel free to throw a "fucking" in there, 'Fucking Bob Doe' or 'Bob Fucking Doe.' Or just plain 'Fucking Doe.'"

At sixty the car began to shake and Fucking Bob Doe eased back: "No need to rush it. I do not want to get pulled over." They settled in at 50, the speed limit.

On Bob's left forearm was a fading tattoo that looked like a red heart inside a crown of thorns. He wore loafers with no socks, his heels crushing the backs of the shoes. His clothes—a half-buttoned pink Oxford that showed off his sun-reddened chest and pleated khakis worn with a woven belt—were dirty and, from the whiff of them, must have been on Bob for the past week.

"You can put your pack in the back seat, if you want, it'll be more comfortable for you. Just don't toss it into the way back. My boy's back there. That's my whole world there mixed with the junk in the trunk, so to say. You got kids?"

"No."

"Ah, it's glorious."

Bob liked to talk, a lot, to talk about anything and everything, but really all he said served as a showcase for himself. Still, he was no dummy. He knew enough to ask questions, as well. In a situation like this it was to his advantage to learn as much as he could about his passenger. Last name's Moore, you said? From the great state of New Jersey? Weehawken. I heard of that, up around New York City. Traveling solo, then. Good for you. Your friend's a grad student at USC, a Trojan. Great football tradition. He knows you're coming, just don't know when. No phone? No, me neither. You can't disappear if you carry a phone. They can track you by phone. That, my friend, is what the world has come to.

Jayson was the name of Bob's boy in the back, and he was exactly eight months and four days old. If it wasn't for being a dad, Bob would have ended it all. "No, really," he said staring over at Alex who didn't look back. "You think I'm shitting? Huh?"

"No. Why would you lie about that?"

"I been to some dark places, looking to leave those behind."

In a vague nod to those dark places, Bob made clear that while he had no desire to drag "this thing out," he was also avoiding interstates—so things might take a little longer than otherwise. "The interstates are too fucking dangerous," Bob said. "That's where they'll get ya."

When Jayson began to cry less than an hour into their ride together, "Jay-son, Jay-son, come on, dude," called Bob in return. "Please, please, stop crying, little dude. We cannot have this, dude, we are on the road. We cannot, my sweet."

Bob Doe told Alex that he had moved around in his life, at least since he'd left home, Lynchburg, Virginia, at seventeen. Most recently he'd been living in Peoria: "Do you know what it's like to live in Peoria and be an entrepreneur? Not at all what you'd expect, sure not what I had expected." He pointed back at the pile of yellow and pink papers under the economics text. "It didn't defeat me, though—no, no. I got hopes and plans. There's a screenplay back there that's this close to being finished, based loosely on my own experiences. Maybe we'll meet up some day in LA when things are better for both of us."

Bob Doe was divorced, or all but divorced—him and Sheila were still both fighting over this detail and that, Jayson's custody being by far the biggest detail. Right now, he claimed, he had legal custody, had won it only a week earlier, and was taking the baby to see family in Utah, the south-central part of the state, two hours from Vegas and one of the fastest growing communities in the whole country. But what with the kid's crying and shitting and vomiting the whole ordeal was turning out to be a lot tougher than he'd expected. And of course, there was Sheila being the bitch she is by nature. She was the reason he had to get rid of his phone—"to keep her and her minions off my ass." She was also the reason for the Bob Doe "No Interstate" rule.

So, "Fuck her. Let her try and find me. Woman gained thirty pounds in two years of marriage. Nice, right? She's selfish. She's pure

selfishness personified. But I got Jayson, right Jay?" On cue the little
dude let out a shriek and his howling started up again.

Wednesday, July 17
23.

IT WAS DEEP in the night, or early in the morning but no sign of the
sun yet, and Bob had been driving for too long. They'd made it out of
Nebraska and into Wyoming, traveling on Route 30 the whole way,
which, even though it had added hours to the drive (as opposed to
hopping on Route 80) was still too traveled a road for Bob's liking.
Jayson was again screaming his head off, so Bob pulled into a rest stop
just east of Cheyenne. "God damn it," yelled Bob, sniffing the air.

They parked behind the white-lit information kiosk which
would provide just enough brightness for Bob to get the job done—to
change Jason's diaper and get him back to sleep.

"Aw. Aw fuck. Nasty, man. Aw, dude, you freaking stink. God
damn. Aw, look—the mother-fucking rash is getting worse. Now this,
ladies and gentlemen. Just what I need," he pleaded looking upwards,
Moses in the desert pleading for mercy. "Yo!" he called.

Alex was out of the car, stretching his legs, getting some cool,
fresh air, away from the stench.

"In the back seat, by the screenplay, there's some medicated shit
in a tube. Make sure the cap's on tight and then toss it to me." Alex did
as he was told and kept his distance. Bob cleaned the baby's bottom
with the last of dried-out baby wipes and shook some mess from his
fingers, grimacing as he did so. "Oh, God, look at that ass. Just look.
Oh, that must hurt, dude."

Bob untied a bulging white kitchen trash bag. Looking away, he
shoved in the dirty diaper and retied it. "Fuck it," he said, again wiping

his hands, this time on the bag's outside. Holding it at arm's length, letting it wag from his hand, "Nasty as this sucker is, I hate to part with it. It's my last bag," he announced. Grasping it by its red strings, he began whirling the bag around, whoosh-whoosh. "But you gotta do what you gotta do." After a quick look over his shoulder, Bob let sail and the bag flew over a patch of prairie grass and skidded through a floor of pine needles and on past the tree line.

"Alex, my man. You want to spell me? Feel like doing a hundred miles?"

"I don't think so. I'm not used to driving something this big. Plus the dark and roads I don't know and coming up on mountains. No, especially not with a baby in the car."

"Wait, Alex. You're kidding me." Bob stood outside the open car door wiping his fingers on a yellow M&M's bag which he dropped to the ground. "You're seriously telling me you won't drive? We're six hundred miles from my people in Utah and you tell me you don't drive. In that case, I need more money, then."

"We made a deal, Bob."

"Yeah, and you changed the deal. I made a natural assumption that we were splitting the driving. That's the way it is, we both drive. Rules of the road. If I'm chauffeuring, I should get paid more, only makes sense."

"I'm not giving you more money."

"Come on, you must have a credit card."

"No, I don't. I'm purposely not carrying one and I can't afford to give you more if I want to get to LA."

"Okay, boss. Okay, we'll forget it. Let bygones be bygones. Look, do me this favor, at least. Climb into the back seat, Jay's got to be fed. There's still some Chicken McNuggets in the box. Rip them up into very tiny pieces. Remember that you're feeding my baby. He's not really a good chewer yet, but I'm not worried about it. It'll come, babies develop differently. One more thing, there's water in his bottle and next to it somewhere you'll see a bottle of Robitussin, too, just add an ounce or two to his bottle to help him relax into calming sleep. Thanks, buddy."

Alex did as told. When he was done feeding Jayson the chicken nuggets, he fastened the baby as he had been; there, Jayson nodded off even before Alex turned away. After shoving assorted junk onto the floor, Alex got comfortable lying across the back seat, hands behind his head serving as pillow.

From Cheyenne, the plan was they'd continue due west through Wyoming, and at Green River, WY, drop south into Utah. Problem was the No Interstate Rule. Avoiding highways would take them north, west, and south; it would take them onto Wyoming state roads 210, 220, 28, and 372, doubling the time of what would have been a 4-hour Route 80 trip, and it wore Bob out and frazzled his nerves. All things considered, though, Route 80 would have frazzled them more; he was sure Shelia the Bitch had put the law on his trail. He was being smart to play it safe.

An hour after they'd gotten back on the road, Alex learned of Bob's passion for the Beatles: "There was a time—a year and two months—when I had nothing to do with myself. Same routine day after day. . . . Hey, man, look. The moon's traveling right along with us—the moon, myself, Jayson my son, and Alex my friend. Very cool . . . So, anyway. What was I saying? Same routine, day in day out. I went to the library every afternoon from four until supper time and taught myself the entire Beatles songbook. I got real good if modesty allows me to admit. I'm gonna whistle 'Blackbird.' You probably know it. . . . So melodic, ain't it? Such a sweet song: 'Take these broken wings, and learn to fly.' I'll do up another tune, you got any requests. Tell me what you think, your honest opinion. I'm thinking of going on one or the other of the TV talent shows. There'll be no hard feelings if you don't think it's professional whistling. There won't be repercussions."

24.

BY THE TIME Tommy entered Here's 2 You at 10:00 for his rescheduled get-together with Sara (the original date had been on the afternoon Archie died) the first breakfast seating had cleared out of the dining room and the cafe was crowded with those who didn't want to head immediately back to their apartments. Two female baristas—one large and one small, one in uniform, one merely wearing the green and white uniform colors, both tattooed, both in their early twenties— were squawking loudly over the racket of milk fizzing and foaming into tall cups.

Sara hadn't yet arrived but Tommy recognized some of the others. Sandy was alone at a table with his coffee and a newspaper. Ava and Nini, side by side, shared one computer. One of the sisters, Ava, Tommy thought, had a bandage inside the bend of her elbow where blood had been drawn and walked with a slight limp and ankle brace. A cane was propped against the wall nearby. Next to them, efficient and meticulous, Annie was typing. She leaned and squinted, lifted her glasses to proofread her work. Sister Margaret Mary was two computers away, hands serving as blinders around her eyes.

Lurking nearby, Tommy spotted one of the part-time health aides, a heavily made-up woman, "The Fox," Wake called her, Vedunia by name. Still in her thirties, a seductress in nurse's skirt and white stockings, a golden Christ crucified dangling in her cleavage, Vedunia claimed special powers for these computers. She said that's why they were black, not white like the old ones. Vedunia chose her targets only after careful observation.

She would tell these targets—the sad, desperate, willing, illiterate—that if you had proper training in the arts, these computers could talk to God, for a fee. For an additional fee, to the departed. While no one at Bon Secours really knew what to make of her, they all feared her, especially Sister Margaret Mary.

Tommy entered, simultaneously checking for Sara and reading his phone. His mom had sent him a photo as she left the beauty parlor.

"Nice," he replied. "Kinda spiky and punkish."

"Yup, that's the look I wanted."

Tommy scrolled through his emails only to discover that somehow he'd missed the one sent by his brother Monday afternoon from Table Rock. He hurried towards Ava and Nini and Annie.

"Hi ladies. Thought you'd want to know: Alex responded to the questions we sent."

"Oh, wonderful. . .. So sweet and thoughtful."

"Can we find it on one of these computers?" asked Ava, the sister with the limp and cane.

"Yeah," said Tommy. "I just need to log in." He sat in the chair next to Ava and pulled the keyboard forward. Nini and Annie leaned closer.

"Tommy," said Ava, leaning against his shoulder. "Can you read it for us?"

"Oh, stop your flirting," teased Nini. "We all know how to read for ourselves."

"Flirting! What a stupid comment. We're eighty-three, Nini, old enough to be his grandmothers."

"Great-grandmothers."

"Oh, and who could read anyway with your big head in the way? I can't turn my neck, remember?"

"Oh, your stupid neck. The doctor said it was nothing."

Tommy read for them. Alex had done his best to explain his sense of sweet-homesickness and what it was to be alone "out west," and either the ladies managed to intuit his meaning, or they did a good job of creating their own. He described Lawrence and the road to Fremont and the anticipated festival. He described Jackie's looks, a bit of her background, his first meeting her at Cats Who Copy. They chuckled at his half-hearted explanation of just where he was: "Table Rock, Nebraska. That's north of Mexico and south of Canada, east of the Pacific and west of the Mississippi."

Annie, the traveler, always so decorous, suddenly broke down weeping, catching Tommy off guard. Both sisters whispered that Annie's Bill had gone into Memory Care the previous day—"dementia care" was the term the stupid trainee had used while settling him in. "What beauty, what beauty is life," Annie said, before breaking down even further. Even as he avoided meeting her eyes, Tommy patted her on the back, one, two, three soft pats, a little rub mixed in. To ignore her—which until a few days ago would have been his instinct—no longer seemed like an option. "I'm sorry, Annie."

Breaking the silence, Ava announced, "I want to go inside, inside that machine. I want to live there."

"Well, you can't do that," scolded Nini. "It's technology, not magic."

"You watch out for my neck, please."

Smiling, palms together under her chin, sly as a puma after having seen the emotional hubbub, Vedunia wandered towards them.

Nini took note and whispered: "Don't look at her, don't even look at her. She can sense weakness."

25.

WHEN SARA FINALLY arrived at Here's 2 You, she was carrying two large photo albums.

"Come here," she called to Tommy. "Come here, we'll sit here. Okay if we join you, Sandy? I hope we don't bore you."

He put down the newspaper. "Bore me? Now that would be a challenge."

She leaned forward, patted Sandy's head like she was bouncing a beach ball.

"These are pictures of my family I wanted to show this young man. Maybe Sandy wants to see, too. Tommy, I heard you over there talking about your brother. You said he is in Nebraska, near Table Rock maybe. I'm from there, an hour away. Pawnee City."

"Ah, that's your tribe," said Sandy. "You're Pawnee."

"Yeah, Pawnee. And then my father's side is either mostly white or maybe all white. I'm all mixed up on the white side."

"Did you grow up with all Pawnees?" asked Tommy.

"Yes and no. I was a Pawnee in Pawnee City but there wasn't a lot of Pawnees in Pawnee City, not even a hundred and almost all of them in my neighborhood." Sitting, she assumed a position she had copied from the old women back home—her chair removed a bit from the table but her palms flat on it. "I don't know how many are left these days. Maybe we just disappeared, blended into the landscape, into the hills, you know, poof."

She opened one of the albums and from its dozen photos showed Sandy a smaller version of one of the bureau-top photos Tommy had seen in her apartment.

"This one, this is my mother." It was the photo of the more mature of the two women, maybe thirty years old, standing outside a wood cabin, a sheaf of wheat in her arms. "She wasn't from up there. She was from Oklahoma. Oklahoma, that's the real Rez down there. Those old timers, they were real Indians, true Indians. We made fun but deep down we were proud of them, proud and sad for them too, cause when they were dying, they knew that after them, well . . .. We were kids, we really didn't understand a lot of things. My mother went by the name of Brook Whitehorse. I don't know why she was dressed Indian in this picture. That wasn't her everyday. I think she was show-ing off for the camera, haha. But you know all her life up until she died when she was 68, she smelled like Indian, a real Indian. That's a beautiful smell. That's a smell I miss."

"And what was that smell?" asked Sandy.

"That smell, oh, well, that smell. Like the dirt and the trees, like the rain. Like animal hide, like wood fire. If you ever buried your nose in mama's neck, you'd smell it, you'd smell it good. 'Mommy, mommy, we want to smell you, please can we smell you?' Haha."

"She has a wonderful face. It's a strong face, a very proud face."

"Yeah, oh she'd try to scare you. And if she saw that she did, if she got you scared, then she'd call you 'Nancy,' I don't know why, I never did, but she would bust out laughing. 'You little Nancy.'"

"You know when I was a boy and we played cowboys and Indians, I always wanted to be the Indian and not the cowboy."

"Me, too," said Sara. "I wanted to be the Indian, too, except when I wanted to win. Then I want to be the cowboy."

"Your people were treated horribly by the white man."

"Yes. And I'm white, too. Thanks to my daddy. We're all guilty, I guess. The Catholics call it original sin."

"I'm very familiar with original sin. Did you know I was raised Catholic?"

"No, me and Tommy don't know anything about you, do we Tommy? Come on, give us some information. Where is Sandy Cassamarrano from?"

"He's from Asbury Park," Sandy said of himself.

"Oh, the seashore and rock'n roll. The Boss."

"That's right. My pop was a fisherman, in and out of Manasquan Inlet any day the weather would permit. Mom stayed home and took care of us—me, two brothers, and a sister. First the girl, then me, then my two brothers. Sister Pat has passed, brother Thomas has passed. Me and Howie, the youngest one, are who's left."

"Were you a surfer?" asked Sara.

"No, but my brothers, they were. They were five and seven years younger than me. As for me, I kept to kite-flying."

"Oh, me, too!" responded Sara. "Oh, you know, out in Nebraska. What a beautiful picture that was—the yellow prairie, the blue sky, a silly girl in a silly skirt and silly brown shoes, and her kite so high it made her neck hurt to look at it. That was something, those days. And you know what, me and Archie went kite flying not too long ago, maybe like three or four years ago. He didn't know what he was doing, haha."

"Yes, to fly a kite well, you've got to know what you're doing," said Sandy. "I was quite good, expert I thought. Son, do you ever go kite-flying?"

"Nope," said Tommy. "Once in third grade they had us make our own kites, but I don't remember ever finishing the project. Maybe we did."

Sara disapproved.

"What? Never? Not ever?" she scolded. "You say you and your friends go to play right by the river, a baseball field by the river—that's right?"

"Yeah, that's where we go, we hang out there."

"And you never thought maybe to fly a kite? Oh, that's a sin and a shame. You even sure you know what a kite is?"

"Yes, Sara, I'm sure." Tommy smiled.

"Well, that's good at least. Sandy, me and you are going to have to teach these kids a thing or two about kites."

26.

ALEX AWOKE AT the Value Gas Station, an oasis and wasteland in one, just south of Green River. Still lying across the back seat, half asleep, he lifted himself on an elbow to get a better view. To the northwest, hills like crinkled, gray paper cut a hazy margin between earth and sky. The windows were rolled down and the air cool. To the caw of a crow, the smell of gasoline, the rumble of truck engines, Alex sat up and ran his hands through his hair. Jayson was sound asleep, wheezing like an old man on a drunk.

Alex swiveled his head to find Bob at the pump, filling the car and whistling to the Stones "Honky Tonk Woman," the song playing inside the attendant's empty cabin. "Yo, son, remember the fifty dollars you gave me? Watch it disappear in a single gulp," called Bob, tipping his head towards the ticking pump. "Fifty-five, there you go, and the world just keeps on spinning. Fuckity-eight, fuckity-nine." The final click came at $66.20. "Uh-oh. Shit, man. Alex, look at this horseshit. It won't accept my card, dude. 'See attendant.' Yeah, right, like the fucker can speak English."

One way or another, cash or credit, Bob was going to be looking for money. Alex rubbed his eyes, pretending to be more out of it than he was. "So, pay inside," he replied. "It's not a big deal. Just pay cash."

"Yes, it is a big deal. I'm holding onto my cash. Cash works regardless of circumstance and leaves no tracks."

"Christ," muttered Alex, frustrated with this fool.

"I'm not using up all my cash and the card don't work. It's simple," Bob said, showing his hands. "I knew it was gonna get denied sooner or later. You're late on one payment and look what happens. Come on out here and stick your card in the machine."

"This is bullshit and you know it."

"Don't blame me, dude."

"I told you I don't have a credit card."

"You got cash."

"I'm not using up my cash, either."

"Then use that debit card you got in your wallet," he said pointing. "Come on, do this and we're on our way to southern Utah, and points beyond. No need to quibble over pennies."

Alex didn't slam the door behind him. As annoyed as he was with Bob, he was unsettled, too, even frightened.

"Tell me, dude. Do you even know where you are? Do you know what state you're in?"

The sun, a pale yellow, had fully cleared the hills and was now in the process of burning off the haze. "We're in Wyoming and those are the Rocky Mountains. Here," Alex said, handing Bob the card.

"Close, but uh-uh. We're south, in New Mexico. Remember, we're heading for southern Utah. What's your pin?"

"Never mind, give me the card back. I'll do it. Give me the cash I already gave you back. And you're making sixteen more dollars on this deal as it is. Give me my fifty."

"Absolutely." Bob pulled the fifty from his pocket. "Here ya go," he said, slapping the money into Alex's palm. "Hey, you forgot the receipt. Here ya go, buddy."

"Keep the damned receipt!"

Bob bent over with laughter, hands on his knees. He stretched out and happily smacked Alex on the shoulder.

"Let's just go," Alex muttered. "And no more money."

"You're right about that, good buddy. We're good. You know what, I got to change the little one. Do me a small favor, pretty please? Get me a cherry Coke. A big one like the sign says, Guzzler 99 cents. Go ahead, go ahead. Don't give me a look. There's change in the ashtray, take all of it if you want. Oh, and while you're in there tell Ali Fucking Khan that Afghanistan's a long way off and we're all paid up so the terrorist bitch can stop watching us already."

27.

BOB HAD OF course lied when he claimed they were in New Mexico. Maybe to confuse Alex, maybe just for kicks, maybe a genetic default to lie. But Alex had been right about Wyoming.

Twelve miles south of Green River on WY 530, after passing a bullet-pocked sign welcoming them to Flaming Gorge Recreation Area, blue and orange lights flashed behind Bob's black Jeep and a Wyoming State Police car sent out its initial woot-woot. Fuck—no way to outrun them Bob knew. He tapped the brake and pulled onto the shoulder. Bob raised his right arm and touched the ceiling with his fingers. His left arm waved for the approaching trooper. The officer was short and bulky, wearing black slacks, a grey-blue shirt—achievement and rank patches up near the shoulder—and a tall Canadian Mounties-type hat that made him seem even shorter. A second trooper, the driver, waited in the car.

Bob gave a thumbs up, then a peace sign, then offered the trooper his hand, "Good day, sir."

Though now past noon, the air was still crisp. There were a few wispy clouds—white strokes with too little paint on the brush—floating above this stretch of dusty, barren mountains.

"What stupid thing did I do now?" Bob asked.

"Well, you were driving pretty erratically, sir."

"Erratically? These roads are rough, and you can see I'm not from this neighborhood. I thought maybe I was pushing the speed limit."

"No, speed limit's fifty and you were under. Problem is you got only two lanes on this road. You're supposed to be in one at a time. There is no third lane. This is the shoulder where we are now, the shoulder isn't a lane. The way you were driving, that's trouble waiting to happen."

"'Trouble waiting to happen.' That's an excellent way to put it."

"Yeah. Can I see your license, please, and registration?"

"Sure thing, I already got 'em for you."

"Robert, have you gotten much sleep?" asked the trooper as he read the license and registration. "You look tired."

"It's a cumulative thing, officer. I slept three hours maybe last night and that's the most sleep I've gotten of the past three nights. It is wearying. I guess maybe that wasn't enough. You see my friend Alex here, he don't drive."

"You got quite a long name there, Robert B. I'm thinking you better take a rest for another while. I mean right now." He handed documents back to Bob.

"You got it, man. I'm glad you pulled me over before I hurt myself or someone else. Is there a rest stop shortly ahead?"

"Yeah, five miles. We'll trail you . . . Woh, I just caught a whiff. What do I smell, is that diapers?"

"Could very well be. I hardly notice it anymore. I got my little guy in the back."

"Oh? Where in the back?"

"In the way back. You mind if I show you?" Bob stepped out, hands in the air, smiling. "He's Jayson. Come on, look and see. I got him hooked in pretty good. Very good, in fact. Protected with blankets, pillows, boxes, whatnot," he said as he lifted the hatch. "I also, you can see, I also got the cradle tied around the back seat there, the head rest."

"No, no, no." The officer shook his head. "You been driving all these miles, and now through the mountains, with the baby like this? These are some treacherous roads."

"Yes, I have. My dad was a trucker and I knew how to load a trailer truck when other kids were throwing teddy bears into their little red wagons."

"Jayson, you said was his name? And you've been driving from Illinois—your plates. . ... Gimme a second." The trooper stepped away and listened to a message on his portable police radio. "Get back in the car and let me see that registration once more."

"Of course." Bob sat sideways behind the wheel with the door open, one foot dangling in the air, one on the ground. He handed the cop his registration.

"There seems to be a mix-up with the plate. Did you buy the car used, or how did you get it?"

"Damn, when will I learn? I knew that was stupid. You can't trust people. I should have known that little Italian prick was no good."

"Yo, kid." The officer tapped the top of the car, calling to Alex. "Sit up straight. You got anything to add?"

"No, sir."

"What's your name?"

"Alex."

"You got a last name?"

"Alex Moore."

"I picked him up hitchhiking," said Bob. "Got him in Nebraska. He's a nice kid."

"And you're doing what?"

"Heading to California to meet a friend."

"And you been in the car for how long?"

"Yesterday evening."

"Mmm, yesterday evening. Bob, I'm going to have to run this license. Give me just a minute. I'll come back for your insurance if you don't mind taking it out for me."

"Understood."

"Would you turn the car off, please?"

"Of, of course. Didn't realize I'd kept her running."

"Jayson's last name?"

"Same as mine. Jayson Bargonovich."

"License plate check notwithstanding, you're getting a violation for the way you got that baby flopping around in the cargo area. That's really stupid and really dangerous."

"And probably illegal, if I can tell by the tone of your voice. But I mean trust me, he's very well secured back there. I wouldn't mess around with something like that."

"Give me the keys, please."

Shocked by the request—or "as though" shocked by the request—Bob looked at the keys he held in his hand. "You afraid I'm gonna try to pull a getaway?" He asked before slapping the keys into the trooper's hand. "Hey, ain't this America anymore? Land of the free, and all."

"It's something we do every stop."

"No, problem, as long as it's in the name of life, liberty, and yadda-yadda, haha."

Alex turned to watch the short, bow-legged officer amble back to his car. When he turned back, Bob was staring into the mirror. Blindly,

Bob reached his hand into the console between the seats. Grabbed something there. When Alex looked again at the State Troopers, he saw the other officer—Native American or Mexican-American, same size as the other cop, but in a white short-sleeved shirt—get out of his vehicle and straighten his gun belt. He approached the passenger side of the Jeep as the first cop waited at the back on the driver's side.

The ignition fired and in that instant the Jeep jerked ahead, knocking Alex's head first forward then back as the Cherokee reversed and rammed the troopers' car before speeding off. All the gear and all the boxes and the rest of the mess in back alongside Jayson were whipped around just as Alex had been. As the Jeep raced down the highway, Alex turned and saw the cops standing beside their steaming car, guns drawn but held at their sides.

"Fucking ball busters!" screamed Bob waving a finger out the window. "Fuck you! Fuck you! Haha-hahahahaha."

28.

IT WAS THE dark of night and distrust levels were high when they stopped at a dilapidated General Store—cigarette and Lottery advertisements covering the front windows, outdoor trash cans overflowing with plastic liquor bottles, a rusting gas pump out front. Bob bought two bottles of water from a vending machine. Alex, sitting in the car, began calculating—time and miles and dollars. But his calculating lasted just a minute because regardless of what the calculating would show, he vowed that come sunrise, as soon as they came upon anything resembling a main road, Alex would be done with Bob. Sixty-five dollar investment or not, this was dangerous. Bob was crazy as a loon and desperate. It was settled. And that was a relief.

Bob went to the back of the car with the two water bottles. In a lady's cosmetics bag tucked beneath a large suitcase were six small plastic medication bottles—Bob's stash. Out of Alex's view, Bob crushed a quarter Valium and half a Percocet and shook some of the powder into the opaque baby bottle, which Jayson took while remaining mostly asleep. He then poured six crushed Valium into one of the water bottles for Alex. Bob, with his first slug of water, gulped down three Ritalin.

Twenty minutes later, Alex and Jayson were both out cold.

"There is no song in the entire Beatles catalogue more beautiful than this," Bob announced as whispery as a public-radio dj while they wound through the woods. "It's called 'Norwegian Wood,' and I'll whistle it for you now, softly, like a lullaby."

Alex had been a cash source and an amusement at first. Then, shortly, he had become a nuisance, but now, ever since the run-in with the law, he wasn't trustworthy. If he got away from Bob, he'd go straight to the cops. Alex—sweet, innocent Alex—even though drugged and snoring, was as sullen and twitchy as when he was awake. Damn Ritalin, Bob thought, always gets me spooked.

As the road grew narrower, the speed limit in Flaming Gorge fell to thirty, and Bob did his best to keep to that number, but too often he'd find himself nearing fifty and at some unexpected bend he'd have to jam on the brakes. The road followed the Yampa Valley between Diamond and Cold Spring Mountains; there were still lots of steep inclines and frequent hairpin turns to come. Worse, since night had fallen, a hundred miles into Utah Bob began to see phantoms— shadowy pedestrians and Big Foots hulking across the road, glowing animal eyes and forks in the road that were no forks at all. Then the road worsened. No longer paved, it was dirt and gravel and domed at the center. After one tight turn, Bob mistook a hiker's trail for the road and busted his right headlight on an already busted pine tree—three feet of stump holding up six feet of splinter. The Jeep was able to back out of the shallow ditch, after which Bob shut off the car and settled back into the seat. His precious cargo still slept. Time for him to get some shut eye, too. He was sure as shit that, if he could fall asleep at all, he'd wake up sooner than the drugged Alex and Jayson, and he was even more sure that things would look brighter in the morning just like they always did.

"Here comes the sun, here comes the sun, And I say, It's all right."

Thursday, July 18
29.

THE EARLY MORNING sun twinkling yellow-gold through the green of the forest woke Bob. Alex and Jayson were still knocked out six hours after being dosed. Bob figured they were at least three hundred miles from their stated destination, the home of Bob's "people," Richfield, Utah. He backed the Jeep onto the gravel road in the middle—or, for all Bob knew, the north, south, east, or west edge—of Ashley National Forest. They had been on Route 191, last Bob recalled; whether or not they were on it now he didn't know. Nor did he know how long the road would continue—a dead end would have been about the worst case—or what surprises the road ahead held in store. He knew it was dawn and that the sun rose in the east; and he knew that the sun was behind them which meant they were more of less traveling west. That wasn't the worst thing, but, to his thinking, it wasn't the best either, Richfield by his reckoning was due south.

Fortune shone on Bob Doe—the gravel fire road he'd somehow found himself on finally merged back with Route 191 and, as they continued through sharp curves and steep grades, the speed limit rose from 30 MPH to 45. There were no crossroads or intersections on 191, though, and an hour later they simply continued along the same winding course.

Alex awoke, groggy and more fearful of Bob than he'd been to this point. Even in his near-panicked state, though, Alex knew that jumping out of a moving car traveling along the winding road in a state forest—mountain rocks on one side, thousand-foot drop on the other—wouldn't be the move to make. He had to bide his time—stay quiet, cause no problems for Bob who, for his part, had one essential piece of business to take care of ASAP, and that was to get rid of the Jeep before all of Wyoming's State Police, and whoever the fuck else might be on his tail, got hold of him.

30.

SIX KIDS FROM Christ United Day Camp, eleven- and twelve-year-olds, descended on Bon Secours, there to help the residents with the Helen Wysocki Memorial Display Case. Helen Wysocki had been an early leader, one of the founders, in fact, of the Residents' Council, and in the role of Council President she'd fought for that display case for the better part of a decade. In those final years, when, as she said many a time, her friends were dropping like flies, that mission was the only thing that kept her going.

The showcase was in an otherwise unused stretch of wall between the reception desk and the Town Square, situated such that it could be easily seen and just as easily passed by. Supervision of the upkeep was technically the job of Sister Margaret Mary. Sister, though, found the quarterly change of the showcase too stressful, and that morning had sent an email asking Cathy to be in charge. But shortly after that, Cathy called Henry. She wouldn't be in, maybe she'd make it later in the afternoon.

"She been with me a lot these days recently," Henry told Tommy. "We're helping one another out, well mostly she helping me out. But I'm doing my share for her, too. You know about my son Junior?"

"Yeah, somewhat."

"MIA, Missing In Action, in Afghanistan." It had been little more than twenty-four hours—twenty-four gnawing, sleepless hours—that Henry knew his son was not among those safe. "He's gonna be okay. Faith in Jesus, son. Me and Cathy, we pray together. But Cathy's just worn out. Things getting to her, maybe. But I do think she'll get herself together. I expect she'll be in in a few hours."

"Yeah, I heard about Junior. I bet it's stressful, even though I'm sure everything will turn out okay in the end."

"Yes."

"I'll pray for you . . . Nonetheless," said Tommy.

"Thank you, young man. You're a very good assistant to Cathy. She told me so, and I can also see it for myself."

"Really?"

"Yes, Cathy says she wishes she could keep you on. And, hey, remember to say that prayer."

"Oh, for sure."

And so, after Sister Margaret Mary, after Cathy Degnan, it fell to the intern Tommy Moore. Well, now he could add Volunteer Coordinator to his growing list of job responsibilities. Two adults, one male, one female, both black and wearing jeans and basketball jerseys, had ushered in the kids from Christ United. The receptionist pointed them in Tommy's direction. The female—the one in the Lakers jersey—handed Tommy a pink form and a pen and tapped on the line for his signature. Then she and the big guy in the Bulls jersey disappeared, headed to the church van parked in the lot at Waterfront Park.

The kids, supposedly there to help residents by helping the Bon Secours staff, did little, and what they did added to rather than reduced Tommy's work. According to the list Henry had handed him, Tommy' first task was to clear out the old display—the Spring Ceramic Arts Showcase. It took the kids thirty minutes to do what Tommy could have finished in ten, but already they had earned a reward—drinks all around from Here's 2 You Cafe. Tommy assigned the task of getting the drinks to one of the girls, who immediately determined that what Tommy really meant was for her to invite a friend, one of the two boys, to go with her as there were too many old white people lurking about for her liking. On cue, the one remaining boy disappeared into the men's room after placing his drink order. Three girls remained. Two of them worked. Well, one girl worked for real, the other assumed a working posture but did none. Occasionally she'd wrap a ceramic clown in white paper but mostly she kept out a sharp eye and mean look for anyone who might approach her. The third girl sat at a table by herself, head lying across folded arms—stubborn and miserable, dead or dying.

Ultimately, the tasks of vacuuming and wiping down the display case fell to Tommy, not the Christ United team. The kids who'd vanished had yet to return. As though annoyed with her own arms, the sleeping girl turned her head from left to right and right to left, huffing as she went. The two working girls showed no interest in participating in the cleanup, instead spending their time admiring pieces of pottery even as they faked dropping them, occasionally bursting into fits of musical giggles.

By 10:00 a.m., residents—more than the ten who'd originally signed up—were drifting into the Town Square, the majority carrying shoe boxes or canvas bags, their faces lit with the excitement of the secrets in their hands. The summer showcase's theme: Toys of Yesteryear.

Sara arrived at the showcase event carrying a crocheted blue and rose-pink bag with a braided leather handle. She sat at the table nearest the display case and began unpacking, removing from her bag a half-dozen small objects, newspaper-wrapped and candy-bar sized.

A few moments later, as Tommy and his not-so-hard-working crew were about done with the clean-up, Sandy and Wake entered from the far side of the grand fireplace. They halted and surveyed. Wake wore his brand new 40th Anniversary Steppenwolf T-shirt—a wolf howling atop a mountain amidst a blizzard of silver specks. Sandy patted Wake on the back and gave him a little nudge in the direction of Schmidt's Deli, then moved forward and waved to Sara as Wake ambled away. Soon, under one of the Sabrett's Hot Dog umbrellas outside Schmidt's, Wake took a seat and nursed an espresso, read CREEM, observed the soft parade.

Carrying a snap-and-buckle satchel that was nearly as old as he was— its brown leather cracked as a baseball glove left half a century in the garage—Sandy joined Sara.

"Oh, so you brought something after all," greeted Sara as she made room for the satchel on her table. "I'm surprised and very glad. I'm proud of you."

"Yes, yesterday afternoon. That's when I decided. I'm surprised, too. May I?"

"Yeah, yeah. I made room."

"I told you I was a kite flyer. Alas, none of the kites themselves made it through the years. But I thought, well, some of the things might be interesting. I have you to thank, it was your influence. I don't know, though. I don't know if they're anything that belongs in a showcase."

"Well, come on, now, let's see it. Open up your treasure chest."

Sandy began unbuckling his satchel.

"Oh, so you made kites, too. You didn't just fly them?" Sara asked. She made a motion like she was holding onto a tugging kite string, her shoulders wriggling.

"Yes, me and my best friend, Phil Marx. He's in bad shape now, his mind, but, well . . . We were a good team, Phil and I. We built them and we flew them."

Sara reached for the book Sandy removed from his bag. "This may be the first book I ever bought in my life," he said. "1935." The book was titled "A Kite Story," and it followed one boy through 2,000 years of kite flying. Some of the pages had folded corners which, if straightened, would have snapped off like flaking plaster. Sandy pulled out a second book, this one a faded blue notebook with unlined pages. It was something Sandy had created himself, a real book, or as real a book as a nine-year-old with neat penmanship could muster, complete with a "Table of Contents" and a one-paragraph "About the Author" end-page that sandwiched its four chapters: "Why You Should Fly a Kite," "Getting Started," "Types of Kites," "Eight Things All Kite Flyers Should Know." And there was one more book in Sandy's bag of tricks, this one nearly as large as the satchel itself. It was a black-covered sketchbook filled with Sandy's own artwork. Most of these were simple crayon drawings of different types of kites, but two were more ambitious, these in charcoal touched over in color. In one drawing, there was depicted a two-inch-tall boy in a bottom corner connected by a string that passed over yellow-green grass into a powdery blue sky, where at the opposite corner a long-tailed red kite flew. The other major work of the young Sandy Cassamarrano was a two-page spread showing three boys and three girls across the bottom of the page, the kids' backs to the viewer, their intertwined lines lifting to six colorful diamond kites that bordered the tops of the two pages.

"Oh, ya know," said Sandy digging deeper into the bag as Sara carefully flipped through the books. "I was sure I still had *things* . . . Certain *things*. Strings and scissors and such. And now," he shrugged, "I guess not."

"This one, with all those kites. You did it with regular crayons?"

"The colors are all pastels which are like softer crayons. First I'd do a little pencil outline, then charcoal—I called it underlaying, then the pastel colors on top."

"We only had the little Crayola boxes in Pawnee City—sixteen colors and not the really cool ones. To get the big boxes you had to go all the way into Lincoln. That was expensive! But, Sandy, my goodness, you are a talented guy."

"That was a long time ago."

"Oh, come on. This is something, a treasure trove. You did every-thing with kites—you drew them, you wrote about them, you made them, and you flew them."

"That's right, me and Phil. Phil was the best—I can picture him racing the wind. We had the beach right there. We had everything we needed. . . . The beach, the breeze . . . "

". . . Young legs," added Sara.

"Yes, yes," said Sandy, looking down at his pink, slightly swollen ankles. Still searching for his *things,* he unsnapped the inside pocket of the old book bag. "There they are, that's where they've been hiding." Onto the table he laid the scissors, sewing thread, a strip of white bedsheet gone yellow, three-inch pieces of leftover spine and spar, the vertical and horizontal framing. He stuck his fingers into the scissor holes and click-click, click-click. "Yup." Click-click.

"Do you still remember how to make them?" asked Tommy.

"The kites you mean? Oh, yes, Tommy. Like it was yesterday. What went up and stayed up seventy years ago will go up and stay up today. It's the laws of physics. They're the same today, at least I think they are. Now, Sara, show us your things. What did you bring?"

"Wait, I'm still studying yours."

"No, mine don't need studying. Show us. What'd you bring? Let's see," he demanded with an enthusiasm which, for all its genuineness, he was frightened by and had to force up and out. "Let's see, now, let's see!"

"Okay, let me show you. I brought a lot. Wait till you see, Tommy. And even you, old timer, even you are going to be impressed."

"What do you mean even me?"

"You know. You know what I mean. I'm gonna show you right now. You ever heard of clothespin dolls?"

"Yes, I think. But show me."

"Okay, if you're so interested you better pay attention. This is my perfect little collection of clothespin dolls. I don't know if this is a Nebraska thing or an Indian thing, I don't know. But, oh, how us kids loved our clothespin dolls." Sara unwrapped the dolls and laid them side by side.

"Oh, they're lovely. I'd like to hold one."

Sandy stretched out a hand.

"Go ahead, you pick."

There were seven dolls, all made from the one-piece, long-legged clothespins that worked without a spring, by the wood's own tension. The hair was made of yarn, their clothes of calico fabric or soft hide, their faces were painted onto the wood.

"They all got names, you know. Hey, you listening, Tommy? Okay, just checking. This one that Sandy is holding, that's Fancy Lady. See, you see the one he picked, ha-ha. The one you are touching is Chief Stuck-Up, the real big shot. This one is Plain Lady—see how different from Fancy. This guy, he's just The Doctor, he didn't come out too good. He was supposed to be Abraham Lincoln, but I was embarrassed to my girlfriends. This, of course you know, is Raggedy Ann. And last but not least"—she picked up and held this doll to her chest—"he is Lover Boy. Now, shhh, his real name is Red Moon but I never told anybody that before. He's all mine. Sandy, have you ever seen clothespin dolls before?"

"Oh, years and years ago, in trinket shops. After the war or maybe it was the 50s. They used to sell them on the Asbury Park boardwalk. They were mass produced, nothing like these—these are works of art, Sara, art and history."

She looked him in the eye and smiled: "Oh, are they? Yours, too."

31.

BOB FOUND HIS opportunity to rid himself of the Jeep at one of the Ashley National Forest's camping grounds. Ahead, he noticed a muddied Ford Escape SUV turn onto a rocky, uphill road toward Dear Run Campsite. It looked like two adults and two kids inside. With the campsite area—a grassy high plain, a hundred yards from the nearest trees—in view, Bob quickly turned the Jeep onto a "No Access" road, as the campers' SUV continued its climb toward the open field.

Eyes opened, trying to figure out why the sudden turn and stop, Alex roused and shifted to his right, his window side. He felt what he thought was Bob's finger poking into his ribs, but it wasn't a finger. It was the barrel of a .38 Colt Automatic.

"This is just a precaution, Alex. No need for alarm. Man's gotta do what a man's gotta do, and guess what? I gotta *do,* right now."

Twenty yards in, the No Access road was blocked by a hung chain: "No Admittance: Park Personnel Only." Bob turned off the car and stepped outside. "You stay put, Alex. I can't have you running around. I can't have it." Gun in hand, Bob walked to the back of the Jeep, and from the floor behind Jayson's carrier pulled out a short-handled sledge hammer. As he walked past Alex, he shook the gun at him in a half-joking manner. He reached the steel pole to which the chain was linked and gave it two quick strikes with the hammer. "Fucker, aaaand, mother-fucker." Pleased with his success, he came back to the car smiling broadly. He drove over the chain and into the woods.

32.

CLIPPITY-CLOP, CLIPPITY-CLOP CAME the swift feet of a Christ United girl in black patent-leather shoes and yellow socks.

"What are they, what are they?" The closer she got the more dainty she became. "They are so adorable! Tanisha, Tanisha. Come here, come here. Come *on.*" She stomped her foot. "Come over here, T! What are they, Missus?"

"These are clothespin dolls. That's what I call them. I made these, me."

"You?"

"Yes. I, me. Sit down. What is your name?"

"You can call me Gabby."

"Okay. This is Tommy and that is Sandy. My name is Sara."

Tanisha arrived and looked curiously from behind the first girl, her chin on that girl's shoulder.

"Get offa me!"

"Brittany! Brittany!" called Tanisha to the sleeping girl. "Wake up, lazy. You're supposed to be working. Come here. Come over here and hurry up."

Gabby, the first girl, took the table's fourth seat.

"These are clothespin dolls and this lady here made them," Tiffany explained to Brittany, who seemed as nerdy and under-nourished as she did sleepy.

"They're *so* cute," replied Brittany.

"Do you know who invented the clothespin?" asked Sandy.

"Um, you mean somebody invented the clothespin?" Tanisha asked skeptically. She had a great-grandfather Sandy's age, and his marbles weren't all there.

"Of course. Don't embarrass us," said Gabby, who, seated at the table, now seemed to think of herself as one with the original group, and of her girlfriends as Johnny-come-latelies. "How else do you think they got here if somebody didn't invent them?" She asked sternly, shaking her head, looking at Sara for acknowledgement.

"But it counts as an invention? It's not like a light bulb or a computer or something," asked Tanisha of Sara.

"Anything not found in nature is man-made, and that makes it an invention. But we don't know who invented them. Excuse my simple little friend," Gabby said teasingly to the geezerly white folks.

"Well, actually yes we do. The Shakers invented them," said Sandy. "The Shakers invented many things and the clothespin was one."

Tanisha looked at Brittany who looked at Gabby. "I don't think you mean the Shakers, sir. I think you mean the Quakers."

"No, I mean the Shakers."

"What's the difference?" asked Gabby.

"Well, the names themselves should tell you," said Sandy. "The Shakers shake and the Quakers quake."

For a second, they stared stone faced—was the old man telling the truth or was he plain and simple crazy? Or was he making a joke? Then they erupted in laughter followed by some shaking and quaking of their own, all four of them: Gabby, Tanisha, Brittany, and Sara Berry.

33.

THE JEEP ROLLED deeper into the woods, Bob steering with his right hand, and leaning his left elbow out the window. The gun was held loosely in that hand and was turned back into the car, pointed in the general direction of Alex. When satisfied that he was deep enough into the woods, Bob stopped the car and gave Alex an order: "Grab that bandanna," he said, nodding towards the back. "Roll it and tie it over your eyes."

"What are you going to do? Come on, man. Just drop me off and leave me here."

"Oh, I'm not going to do much at all, 'man.' Just be good and go along with the program. You'd wind up dead if I left you here, and I don't want that, bud. Come on, just grab the bandanna. Roll it, tie it," Bob said, wagging the gun more purposefully. "Don't be scared. Do what I say. Good, that's it. Tie it, tight. Triple knot it." Alex could hear the metallic jingle and was alarmed but not surprised when Bob ordered, "Hands together on your lap, wrists together."

Two quick snaps and Alex was cuffed. "Let me check that blindfold." He pulled the ends tight. "Relax, okay, just take a deep breath. Every game's got it rules. Just o-b-e-y. Listen, we're both much safer now. . .. Lean forward and towards me a little bit. Come on, come on. That's good." Two more snaps and a second pair of cuffs locked the first set to the steering wheel.

"Just let me go. I'll head to the road and hitch another ride."

"Can't right now. This is remote country, son. It's complicated. You're not hearing me, man. Give old Bob a little time to figure things out, to plan and strategize. I need to think everything through," said Bob as he popped two more No Doze.

"I'm going to be gone for a short period, my friend. When I'm back we'll be in a much better situation. I'll be more clear-headed and then we can discuss what to do with you. Oh, when I say 'we,' I mean me and the other me. Think good thoughts. Here, hey, let me crack the window for you." Bob exited the car. "How long has Jay been sleeping back there, forever? Look at that boy, not a care in the fucking world. I would never let harm come to him."

The vacationing family was parked nearly half a mile through the woods in the middle of the grassy rise surrounded on one side by a gently bubbling brook, on the other side by an arc of woods that edged up towards jagged mountains. The husband and wife—nerds in khaki shorts and safari jackets—were unbolting the overhead storage. The kids helped, sort of, for a few minutes. Then, with their parents occupied, off they ran into the woods, not far from where Bob, hiding impatiently, waited. A moment after they disappeared into the trees, the boy, the younger of the two, yelled to his parents: "Dad, there's a bear out here! No, really, there is, a bear or something."

The mom located her son's voice. "There is no bear, Colin," she called. "Just come back here, would you please."

"Yes, there is," yelled the big sister. "Even I see it. It's brown or black."

The parents huffed and rolled their eyes. "We'll be right there, then," The mom called back. "Dan, you better bring the rifle."

Dan unzipped the gun case and lifted the rifle from the Escape and he and his wife hurried off towards their kids.

As soon as the parents entered the woods, Bob ran towards their car. The kids led their parents deeper in. It would have been nice if the nerds hadn't already dumped all the provisions from the SUV, but that was no priority. Getting the vehicle and getting the hell out of there was the only one. And in that regard, the parents had set Bob up splendidly.

There was just one bungee left to be unloosed from the car, the keys were in the ignition, and "Rocky Raccoon" played from the radio.

It was forty minutes from the time Bob left Alex and Jayson in the Jeep until the time they pulled away in the stolen SUV. When they did, one set of cuffs was on Alex's wrists, and one was on his ankles. Jayson had shit his diaper, but his whimpers and the stink would have to wait. They had to get out of there.

Another thirty minutes and the whimpers turned to howls, and Bob, with no choice but to change the baby, pulled over. He threw the dirty diaper into the woods and dabbed at the kid's ass with sheet after sheet from a box of baby wipes, Jayson screaming bloody murder throughout the ordeal, his behind sunrise red and beginning to blister. Each time Bob tried to dry Jayson's butt, the baby's anguished screaming would get worse, and so instead, he lifted the baby over his head and swung him back and forth like a hung towel on a breezy day. He cleaned the plastic seat of the baby carrier with the last paper towels he had. Given the alarming state of Jayson's butt, Bob didn't want to put the little dude back into one of those humidity-building plastic diapers so he took off his grimy T-shirt and used that as a loose, make-shift substitute.

Their elevation dropped from 6,000 to 5,000 to 4,000 feet, and by mid-afternoon the temperature had touched ninety. The cops knew—and Bob knew they knew—that he had slammed the Wyoming State Police car after the traffic stop, and it wouldn't take the law very long to realize that it was he who'd stolen the nerds' SUV. Alex, for his part, was still blindfolded as well as handcuffed, and had only a general sense of where Bob was heading—southern Utah—and that was questionable as nothing out of the man's mouth could be trusted. In fact, Bob had changed his plan—Richfield, Utah, was still his destination, but only for a quick visit. If he stayed there, he figured he would have to kill

Alex since he knew the general whereabouts of Bob's people. And Bob didn't want to commit murder. The best bet, it seemed to Bob, was to strand Alex in a spot where, by wit and luck or lack thereof, he would or wouldn't find a way to save himself. Rid of the kid, he'd stop to see his people in Richfield—for money, for a shower, for rest, for a night of booze and reefer and singing, just like the old days—but stay there for only a matter of hours, not days, then continue south, to Mexico if need be. Or north, to Montana, if need be, or to Washington or Oregon or Canada.

"Alex, we hardly know one another. You want to talk music, bud? I'm open to your taste. That band you were at the festival to see, what, the Amen Brothers, they got any Beatle-like songs? Anything like say 'Hey Jude,' anything like 'Ticket to Ride,' anything like 'Come Together?' Come on, dude, talk. It's gonna work out. I got this all figured up here, my man. I was lost, but now I'm found. Hey, relax, cool it with the leg tapping, you're jingling the cuffs and shit. You're making me nervous and you don't want to do that. Don't be all doom and gloom, for Chrissakes. Hey, we're in this together, A-dog. I got concern for you too, not just me and the dude. A few more hours and we'll be out of this whole mess. And now, ladies and gentlemen, back to the music."

34.

BY LATE-AFTERNOON THE kids were gone and the showcases filled with two doll-houses, a Tinker Toy Ferris Wheel, a grandma and grandpa Teddy Bear, three model WWII fighter planes, seven clothespin dolls, all things kite, and more. The Christ United kids may have done little in the way of actual work but their interaction with the residents, once things got going, had been great. Much better than Tommy had expected. He was picking things up, getting the hang of things. Definitely. Of course, it was possible that he had nothing to do with the success. But maybe. Could have been. He gave himself credit.

Wake approached Tommy as he was finishing the clean-up. "Hey, kid. You did good," he said, stretching out his arm to fist bump. "The people enjoyed it, both young people and old people. I was keeping an eye on it from afar just in case you needed a hand. Remember, you done good. Wake Parish told you so."

"Speaking of seeing things, have you seen Cathy? Did she ever come in today?"

"I been keeping an eye out but haven't seen her. If she's here, she's probably with Henry. You know his kid's deal? The two of them, him and Cathy, they been praying like banshees. I'll reconnoiter, though."

Tommy picked up the last scraps of tissue paper and headed for the nearest wheeled garbage barrel.

"Yesterday I caught the two of them praying in the chapel," continued Wake.

"'Caught' them? I say good for them."

"Come on, bro. Don't tell me you believe that religious mumbo-jumbo."

"I don't believe it as in 'believe in it.' But it serves a function."

"That would make you a hypocrite. Just one man's opinion."

"You have to see it from their point of view, Wake." Tommy grabbed two garbage barrels; Wake grabbed onto the third. "Cathy and Henry, they're each helping out the other."

"You must have noticed I didn't bring anything down for the whatever, the Toy Day."

Tommy, Wake, and the three barrels squeezed onto the elevator.

"I wasn't too into toys as a kid," continued Wake. "Wasn't my thing."

The elevator hit bottom at LL2, and they pushed the barrels towards the Recycle and Disposal Center, a stuffy low-ceilinged room made even lower-ceilinged by the insulated pipes that ran through it, a room large enough to serve as the collection place for all the floors' individual disposal rooms.

Confident that his mere presence was a form of assistance, Wake sat in a molded-plastic chair, chains dangling, boots firmly planted, hands on his knees.

"I guess you can tell I'm not really much of a social being."

"I've noticed. But you're social in your own way."

Tommy dug into the barrels they'd brought down, searching for anything plastic that had found its way to the bottom and would have to go into its own bin.

"I'm social in my own way?"

"Sure."

"Yeah. I like Sandy especially, him and the Indian gal, and you're okay. The South American dynamic duo, they're kind of hot in their own right."

"What about those kids today? Did you like them?"

"Not much of a work ethic. But, yeah, on the whole I liked them."

"There you go, see what I mean?" Tommy interjected.

"They provided amusement. They were goofy but sweet. Even Cathy is basically okay. She just happens to be a mental mess, has been since I laid eyes on her. She was always a little high strung, but now, I don't know, that string looks about to bust. Did you know her husband killed himself?"

"No."

"Yup, about a year ago. She had the trembles bad."

"I didn't know. No, I didn't know. If there were anything I could do . . . ."

"Yeah, believe it or not, I feel bad for her. I guess Mr. Wake Parish isn't so stone cold after all."

Tommy pushed down on the lids of the big barrels to lock them.

Wake explained that music was his thing and that the only physical objects he could have brought down for the display were his collection of chains. "People call them heavy-metal chains, but that's a misnomer." Wake started collecting chains in '64–for personal adornment and self-expression— back before the term heavy metal was even created, back when there weren't even any head shops this side of the Hudson and to find a decent chain you'd have to go to a biker shop.

Tommy and Wake and the three empty barrels arrived back at the main floor.

Chains were just an accessory, though, Wake continued. Music was his real thing—his heart and soul and spirit. Now that he'd learned how to do it on the computer, he even composed some music of his own, and was willing to burn a cd for Tommy, a mix of originals and some by the core classic groups: Pink Floyd, King Crimson, Jethro Tull, Soft Machine, Zep.

All the while—as they pushed the barrels through the Town Square and into the hall behind Henry's office—Tommy kept an eye out for Cathy.

"I'm gonna make that cd for you," promised Wake.

"Thanks, but you know tomorrow's my last day."

"What the hell?"

"Yeah, this is just a high-school internship thing for me."

"You're going to leave?"

"Yeah, this is a three-week thing. Time's up."

"That's sad, after us bonding like this and all."

"I think I'll be back, though. I don't know how much," Tommy said, hearing his mom's disapproval of such an idea—clearly she didn't want him to keep returning there. "But I think that I will. I'm going to check the chapel, see if Cathy and Henry are there."

"Okay, but give me your number and keep your phone to the ready. While you head that way, I'll check the stores, the cafe, and other adjacent areas. And remember, you done excellent work today, handling those young ones. Respect," he said.

35.

HIDDEN BEHIND THE counter at Cats Who Copy, following google leads to try to track down her bio dad, Jackie sat at a computer that was functioning so poorly it didn't even make it to the merely semi-dysfunctional table of computers a customer might find herself in front of.

She cleared her throat before answering the store phone and slipping into a robotic voice: "Good afternoon, and thank you for calling Cats Who Copy, just outside the campus of The University of Kansas, in delightful Lawrence, Kansas. We're all busy or out of the office right now, but if you leave your name and phone number and a short message, we'll get back to you as soon as we can. Your message is important to us. BEEP."

"Shit. . .. Hi, my name is Linda Moore. I'm calling from New Jersey, and I'm trying to reach someone who works there by the name of Jackie. I believe she's friends with my son Alex . . ."

Quickly, Jackie switched to her normal voice.

"Hey, hi. Yeah, this is Jackie. I just came running in, you'll have to excuse me, I'm all out of breath. Yeah, I know Alex."

"I'm so glad I reached you."

"Everything's okay, isn't it?"

"I hope so, I believe so," said Linda. "I have no reason not to think so except I haven't heard from him in a few days. You know the way moms are."

"Sure. Let's see, I was with him Tuesday, up until noon or so. We were in Nebraska to see a show. The place was Fremont which is like a couple of hundred miles north of Lawrence."

"Yeah, his brother said something about a festival. You're not with him now?"

"No, no, unfortunately. He didn't come back with me."

"He stayed in Fremont?"

"No. He was going west, he was hitchhiking."

"Oh, my God."

"No, don't worry, it's safe out here in the Midwest. Eventually he was going to meet his friend in LA. But I don't know for a hundred percent certain when."

"Well, Nebraska to California is a very long way. You have no idea where he is?"

"No, not exactly. He just walked off, him and his backpack. Well, my backpack, actually. He asked me to ship the rest of his stuff to him in Cali," reported Jackie. "I know that he was gonna hitch along Route 30. "

"So, okay. As of Tuesday morning, or Tuesday afternoon he was hitch-hiking west from Fremont along Route 30."

"Exactly. It wasn't as crazy as it seems. Really it wasn't crazy at all, and Alex is such a great guy."

"Can you give me Billy's address in LA?"

"Sure."

36.

IT WAS EVENING when they entered Vernal, Utah. There, behind an abandoned car dealership—just a long shell of white cinderblock, its windows blown out—Bob cleaned and fed his son. The kid's ass was even worse than it had been earlier in the day—little bubbly things the size of mosquito bites all over it—and now his neck was breaking out in red blotches and two shiny canker sores, one on each side, were blooming on his lips. It seemed he had given up crying; instead he stared blankly at his dad who spoke back to him: "Hiya, hiya, Jay. We gonna get you some good care, dude—some nice soft sheets and blankets, some baby powder, some ointment. We'll be very gentle with you, my boy. Hey, hey, are you okay? Is anybody home in there? Oh, you a good boy," he said as the baby's eyes slowly rolled towards him. Bob then kissed his own fingertips and patted the boy's head with them, the only reaction from the boy being a weak cry. "Got to toughen you up, my little dude."

Jayson resisted his baby food, gurgling out anything Bob spooned into his mouth. Bob offered Cheez-Its, but the salt and cheese dust must have burned because the baby suddenly screamed and tears poured from his eyes as soon as the first square touched his lips. The sudden cries startled Bob. He licked his fingertips and dabbed Jayson's lips with them.

Bob used a napkin from Taco Bell to wipe the baby bottle's nipple clear of little bits of grass and rug-dust, then sat, feet dangling, on the edge of the trunk holding Jayson. He wrapped his baby's dappled pink and white tiny fingers around the bottle, partially tucking it under Jayson's folded arm. He swapped a plastic diaper for the T-shirt he had used earlier as a replacement and, the dumpster locked, tossed the urine-heavy shirt against the dealership's cement back wall.

The sunset created a soft glow at the western horizon, and the moon was a thick crescent. It was one of those nice moments, one of those beautiful moments between a boy and his dad: "Who loves daddy? Does Jay love daddy?" It was something rare and beautiful in this damn world filled with falsity and greed. He cooed to his son:

> Little darling it's been a long, cold, lonely winter
>
> Little darling it seems like years since it's been clear
>
> Here comes the sun, here comes the sun
>
> And I say it's all right.

Friday, July 19
37.

THE NEBRASKA STATE Police were trying to locate a missing person named Alex Moore—stringy light-brown hair, 22 years old, a gangly 5'11". The kid was hitchhiking west from Fremont and his mom was worried half to death. Bored and eager for their shift to end, two troopers sat in their car, a quarter mile east of Fred Hurtley's place. It was a non-emergent situation and protocol called for them to wait until eight a.m. before disturbing citizens. The 54-year-old male trooper had a fever and wanted nothing but to get home and into bed. Ten months and he'll be retired. The female trooper was 37. Her daughter was away at camp for the first time and had texted her mom at midnight, at one a.m., and at five a.m., begging that she come and get her. To make matters worse, the sick cop had fallen asleep, no longer merely spreading his germs but snoring them as well. By 7:45 the female trooper had taken all she could and drove up to Hurtley's.

They knocked on the door and peered through the screen to find a full living room.

Grandma hadn't died yet. She was tipped into a corner of the couch and covered in a crocheted blanket, but she was sitting up and fairly alert, holding a tea cup in two hands. The new mom, Fred's daughter, was sitting in an overstuffed chair feeding her infant daughter. The new dad—a big guy, a barefooted, out-of-shape athlete wearing a Green Bay Packers jersey over jean shorts—was in the kitchen fixing eggs. Fred answered the door and the trooper explained why they were there. The female cop accepted the coffee she was offered. The male cop—tissue to his nose—declined then abruptly excused himself back to the car. Granny looked on smiling at the woman Halloween-costumed in full trooper gear.

Moments later, when she returned to the car, the trooper called her lieutenant to let him know that they'd picked up Alex Moore's trail, that as of late afternoon Tuesday, all was good with him. Like the girl in Lawrence had told his mother, he was hitchhiking west and all was perfectly fine.

"Yeah, it's all well and good that he was all well and good on Tuesday, but we're a step ahead of you," said the Lieutenant. "We just heard from the FBI."

The FBI had made the connection between Alex and the debit card that had been used at the Value Gas Station outside Green River, Wyoming, and that led to the connection between Alex and the incident with the state police vehicle. This put him in the company of Bob Doe/Bob Barrymore/Bob Harding/Bob Bargonovich. And this put things in a very different light. Bargonovich was wanted in Illinois for child abduction and kidnapping. He had a record of drug offenses and a variety of misdemeanors as well as an outstanding warrant for armed robbery. The FBI had information from his ex-wife that Bob had family or friends in Utah, around Richfield, south-central part of the state.

"What about the kid's mother?" asked the female trooper as her partner slept. "Has she been updated?"

"FBI's gonna take care of that. You guys can call it a day."

"Amen," said the female cop and quickly phoned her home-sick daughter.

38.

ALEX WAS ONCE again blindfolded, as he'd been on and off at Bob's whim for the past sixteen hours. Bob patted Alex on the shoulder, squeezed his neck in a comforting way. He promised Alex he'd be free by nightfall, free and unharmed. Just obey. All he had to do was what he was told. Bob's plan was a simple one, he promised—just be cool for a few more hours.

A single traffic light marked the town center of Fort Duchesne, Utah. Just past the intersection was a strip mall consisting of a laundromat and five stores, the largest of which was a Family Dollar Store. It wasn't clear whether "Jesus Is Lord" was a proclamation of faith or part of the store's public relations or both. Bob parked at the far end of the lot, forty yards past Chuckles GoGo Lounge, which even at this afternoon hour had six cars or pickups in the dirt lot. Bob hid the SUV behind a trio of long dumpsters out of sight and out of shouting range. He pulled down Alex's blindfold, then took the pistol from his waistband and pointed it at Alex as he handed him the key to the handcuffs. Bob oversaw the process as Alex, still handcuffed, struggled to unlock the cuffs around his ankles.

"And don't try to be cute. The horn hasn't worked for a year," He then recuffed Alex to the steering wheel, pulled the blindfold back up, and locked the SUV before heading into the Dollar Store.

Bob couldn't believe how well stocked the store was for this-out of-the-way nowhere location. And it was clean, too—you could smell the Spring Waterfall Lysol and insecticide. Indians seemed to run it, Indians from India, skinny twenty-something men in rubber sandals, khaki shorts, football jerseys with shoulder stripes and numbers but no team name, and belts too large. Bob got a kick out of it. Indians from India here of all places on an Indian reservation. He couldn't help but crack a joke, but all he got for his attempt at levity was a snicker and an unappreciative, "This fucking guy," from one worker to the other.

Bob filled the shopping cart—it was a small cart, bigger than one of those supermarket kiddy carts but not by much: diapers, medicated cream, butt wipes (those cracks around Jay's butthole could get infected and that was stressing Bob out: the wipes even had Aloe and Vitamin E in then—nice!), a half-dozen towels (bundled together, great price), a hooded baby's robe. Next came plastic baby bottles—yellow and powder blue—then cans of generic-brand Similac, Imodium liquid, Miralax powder, a can of sliced peaches, a can of mandarin oranges, an unknown brand of gluten-free crackers—all healthy stuff for Jayson. For himself and Alex, he bought trail mix and water, four Lunchables, a couple of Payday bars because he knew peanuts were a great source of protein and calcium, and a large bag of chips. After paying, he grabbed a folded Rand McNally map of the Western states from a stand near the register and shoved it in his bag. Once he returned to the car, Bob removed Alex's blindfold and gaily handed him a candy.

Route 153 East took them to Starvation Lake National Recreation Area. There a sign with six destinations and distances greeted them at the entrance. Five miles into the rec area, they arrived at the turn-off for Pink Willow Road and that road took them up two more miles to the hill's crown, overlooking the ravine.

"Where are you going, Bob? What are you gonna do?"

"I'm not gonna do anything except set you free."

"Here?"

"Beggars can't be choosers. A few more yards and you'll be a free man."

Bob took the car as far off road as he considered safe, then, leaving the motor running, led Alex, still handcuffed at the wrists and ankles, hopping his way through the brush and towards the ravine.

"Okay, we'll stop here, Alex. Listen. Here's a bottle of water—full, clean, and large, and this is a pack of Endurance Trail Mix—I'll leave you both packs, to my own risk," he said. Bob laid the food and drink on the ground. "Watch me now, this is the important part. You looking?" He took the single key that would unlock both sets of cuffs and hurled it further into the ravine where it landed in a patch of tall, dry grass next to a short, windswept tree, its growth heavily weighted to the left or east. "Now it's time to say goodbye. I told you I'd leave you free and unharmed. That's not so far to the key, then a few miles and you'll be back on the road. I just need to make sure I have a good head start. That's why I'm strategizing in this manner."

Alex pleaded with Bob. He'd never find that damn key.

"Hey, that's on you. You're an equal partner in this game of life. You got plenty of daylight left. You saw where it landed, be careful heading down to it. 'Til we meet again, Alex. Jay and I will miss you. We had some times, didn't we?"

39.

TOMMY KNEW SOMETHING was wrong. He'd said his goodbye to Wake—and accepted his parting gift, Wake's personally curated cd. He'd said his sentimental goodbyes to Sara and Sandy, Nini and Ava and Annie. But, though he knew she was at work, he hadn't seen hide nor hair of Cathy. What the hell was that about? This was his last day and, while he didn't expect her to throw him a full-blown Bon-Secours party, he had expected heartfelt thanks, a hug or two, maybe even a few tears. He and Cathy had become a team, and these three weeks had taught Tommy more than a decade of Collins' lectures would have. Tommy for sure didn't love her, but, yes, he liked her, respected her, sympathized with her, understood her, wished her only the best, hoped to see her again.

* * *

At the end of the day, Tommy had already given up his search for Cathy and left Bon Secours when finally she and Henry returned from Riverfront Park where they'd been walking, walking, walking, nearly to Edgewater and back. They headed straight for the Prayer Garden of the Blessed Mother. There they knelt on the white pulldown kneelers and prayed, overseen by the Blessed Virgin statue and accompanied by the recorded piano music.

"Ah," Cathy sighed. "Do you smell the ocean, Henry?"

"Yes, the salt. Sometimes the tide comes up the river like that."

Large silvery clouds floated in from the west, over the Palisades. Between clouds, the sun shone over the Blessed Mother's shoulder. When Henry moved to a seated position, Cathy remained kneeling, cheeks flushed and shiny, beads of sweat on her temples, red streaks, as though she'd been scratched, across her forehead.

Henry was exhausted. It had been too many days for him with no word of his son's fate: negotiations, threats, deadlines, third parties, but no news, no news of when or how or if he'd see his son again.

"Cathy, we can go inside now. We can continue our prayers later. I want to watch the news, and it's too hot out here, anyway."

When finally Cathy lifted her head, she faced the sun directly, eyes open. Seconds passed without her blinking. Slowly, she brought her hands to her face, and suddenly, she jerked her head back as though a sharp pain had flashed through it.

"Cathy, what happened? Are you okay, dear?"

She stared at the sun then slowly turned her head towards Henry, her eyes tearing but unmoving, tracking nothing.

"Cathy, Cathy?" called Henry, his hand on her arm.

"Henry, God has come into my heart and I know Junior is okay. I know it, I know it for certain. He is well and he has been spared. Don't suffer, Henry."

"Come inside, Cathy. We been outside too long. There's too much of an ache in your heart and that has you all confused. And the heat, too, honey. The heat has you all confused. We better get inside and cool off."

She reached for Henry's hand, and when he took hold of it, she squeezed with all her strength.

"Come on, come with me. We'll sit in the cafe and get something."

"Hold onto me, Henry. I can't open my eyes."

"Cathy, your eyes are open, honey."

"No, I can't see Henry," she said, her face a single joyous smile.

40.

KNOWING WHAT SHE now knew—that Alex had been abducted by some maniac and that he was heading for somewhere in Utah—there was no way Linda could do nothing. She couldn't sit on the couch and wait. She couldn't sprawl across the porch and paint. Tommy was on his way home when she called him. They were flying to Salt Lake City that night, pronto. Tommy understood. Of course he knew she could do Alex no more good from Utah than she could from New Jersey, but he also understood that she needed to go, they needed to go.

The blood work hadn't looked very good. Once having seen it, Dr. Hammond ordered an immediate biopsy. Results weren't in yet, but simply and certainly, Linda would have to cancel her Monday follow-up appointment with the doctor. Getting the biopsy results would have to wait.

The FBI offered to put them up at a Holiday Inn between the airport and Provo. Their Continental flight was scheduled for a 10:10 p.m. take off, but she wanted to be out of the house no later than six. Tommy needed to hurry home and pack.

41.

BETWEEN PARK WILLOW Road and Starvation Lake the road dropped a thousand feet. Campsite A was too near the ranger station. B, C, and E were labeled "Developed." Bob chose campsite "D"—a primitive site whose only amenities were a weed-overgrown parking area and a wooden bulletin board--and which abutted the bow tie-shaped lake at its narrowest point.

Bob drove the Escape down a trail into the woods, where he changed into clean boxers and a pair of plaid shorts he'd stolen back in

Missouri. He gently picked up Jayson, grabbed a few things from the shopping bag and then emerged from the woods, sucking in the cool cedar-scented air. The bulletin board cast a long shadow onto what passed as Starvation Lake's beach—a twenty-yard margin of rock and gritty sand between the parking lot and the lapping water. Bob knelt and raked the sand with his fingers. He laid one of the brand-new towels over the groomed sand and folded another, making a pillow for his boy. Onto the towel he tossed the container of butt paste—that's what the shit was actually called, Bordeaux's Butt Paste—and the wipes and Johnson's baby oil.

Bob ambled to the water and stumbled in up to his shorts. Cold— wicked cold—way too cold to bathe Jayson. So Bob laid him on the towel and wiped him down with a damp cloth. He knelt next to his son and gently dried him off, oiled him, wrapped him snuggly, and cuddled the boy close, whispering words of love which Jayson couldn't understand but which, Bob was sure, his son would carry inside him forever and ever. Relieved, at peace and in love, feeling safe, he smiled and he breathed, and, oh, did he breathe.

42.

THE PULASKI SKYWAY was smooth sailing and the taxi delivered Tommy and Linda to Newark Airport Terminal C in a little over half an hour. The crowds there were thick, though, and the lines wound through the terminal in fits and stops. Still, they arrived at the boarding lounge with plenty of time to spare, just as a stream of passengers departing the just-landed flight were exiting the loading bridge. Moments later the attendants from that flight pulled their wheeled bags into the crowd, leaving Gate 86 a virtually empty station.

There were a few sleeping souls among the boarding area's scattered newspapers and coffee cups, but Tommy and his mom took themselves to be the first passengers there for Flight 909, Salt Lake City. Chatting on their phones, two cleaning women—one sloppy in her uniform, the other as dolled up as you could be in brown work shirt and slacks—entered the area with their dustpans and brooms. From a half dozen hovering TV screens, John King was closing the seven-to-eight o'clock hour with a report from Bad Pakh.

43.

AS HE LAID Jayson onto the blanket, Bob nudged his son awake, just enough to get some formula in him. The lotions and the cleaning up, the smell of the freshwater lake and the soothing early evening breeze had surely helped the baby Jayson, and a moment after he'd done with the formula he was back asleep, clean, wrapped in his new powder-blue and white robe, a goofy smile on his skinny un-baby-like face. Alongside him, Bob opened supper for himself, a ham and cheese Lunchable and a blue Powerade. He sat with his legs crossed, a map of the western United States in his lap.

"Here we are," he said softly. "Starvation Lake Park in Utah. We'll only stay here 'til dawn. We're not going to go to Richfield, though—too dangerous. We'll make do for now with the $200 I still got stashed. From this here Starvation Lake, we can head anywhere we want—north, south, east, or west. I don't know where we'll go. I thought Mexico, I thought California, but I'm also thinking of throwing them a curveball and turning back up to the north, any one of those northern states. The ball's in our hands. How hard you think they'll look for us, Jay? I don't think so hard, and then the case will go cold as long as my boy Alex makes it to safety and gives a good report on me. I hope he does, as a friend. They won't really care what your mother says. They won't give a rat's ass about her, they'll see she's a bee-atch.. And anyway, if she loves you even a little bit, she'll know you're better off with me. Nobody was hurt on this adventure of love. No malice intended, no harm done. Your old dad had this all the way."

Bob finished the crackers and went back to examining the map.

"Wyoming was pretty, wasn't it? But I don't know, they might be on the lookout for me there," he said to himself.

Night hadn't fallen, but the ring of mountains surrounding the lake put the entire area in deep shadow. Bob laid on his back and stared up at the sky. The first star appeared and then a second and a third and a fourth.

"Lookie, lookie, come sit with daddy. Come here, big boy," As Bob lifted Jason, the boy's head fell to the side, and to Bob's surprise Jayson didn't startle when his head jerked to a stop. He laughed at how dead-to-the-world his son was. "You got it made out here, don't you? Maybe you gonna be a little cowboy, huh? Home, home on the range."

Bob carried the Lunchable box and the near-empty can of sliced peaches over to the trash barrel aside the bulletin board. On it was a trail map, identification of the types of dangerous critters in the area, the number to call in case of emergency, and an open envelope, "Amanda S" written on the outside, empty inside.

When he got back to the blanket, Bob lifted Jason again. He noticed a light and he turned around. "Shit," he said. "No. Come on. Oh, oh, fuck. We just got here," he said, more to himself than to the cops. "We just got here, a man and his son. Oh, God, please. After all I been through. Come on, please? Oh, God, please. Officer, there must be some mistake. God, damn."

44.

ALL OF THE TV's in the now-crowded boarding area showed the same image: a U.S. military transport and medical trucks kicking up dust as they bounded through the Afghan hills.

"Tragedy and relief once again conjoined in Afghanistan," announced Anderson Cooper. The video from Afghanistan receded with a whoosh and Anderson flashed front and center. "Good evening. We begin with news about the US. Marines who have been held captive by the Taliban around the western provincial town of Bad Pakh. On the line with us now is Anour Karachi, our senior correspondent on the ground, reporting from the NATO outpost set up ten miles outside Bad Pakh."

The screen went to split image—Anderson on the left, Anour on the right.

Anour was in his thirties, balding. He hadn't shaved in several days and the sweat made his dark complexion shine. He looked weary and war-torn, the opposite of an adrenalin-pumped combat reporter, his professional voice belying the despondency in his eyes.

"Good evening, Anderson. In just the past few hours, the U.S. Marines have reduced the number of men listed as missing from sixteen down to eleven. Five missing Marines were either freed or found in an action taken by NATO forces who stormed a mosque located in the center of Bad Pakh. One Marine did not survive the action, four were freed. The four surviving Marines all suffered wounds in the fire-fight that Marine brass described as being 'not life threatening.' Anderson, I can now give you the names of those four Marines," said Anour, lifting a sheet of white paper that he held in both hands.

"Please," said Anderson.

"All of these. . ."

"I'm sure America is praying . . . .Sorry. Go ahead, Anour."

"Yes, all of these Marines, those I'm about to name, are alive and safe," Anour looked at the paper and moistened his lips. "Corporal Randy Fisher of Leavenworth, Kansas; PFC Juan Jose Gomez of Prescott, Arizona; Corporal Henry House Junior of Kearny, New Jersey; and Sergeant Michael Tempesto of Athens, Georgia."

"Thank God," whispered Tommy.

"What, honey?"

Tommy explained—he knew the father of one of the Marines found safe. "He's an impressive man. I bet he's been on the phone with Cathy since he got the news."

"Oh…." Linda paused. "I'm happy for him, them. I really am. God bless the man. But I can't really process what with my own MIA son. You're not disappointed in me, are you."

"Of course not, Mom," he said, putting an arm around her shoulder, kissing her cheek. "I get it. I really do. He's our Alex," he said, kissing her once more.

"The name of the one Marine killed has not yet been released pending notification of his family."

45.

TWO COPS ON foot, guns holstered, amiably but cautiously approached Bob, and four police cars rolled in—three state police and one park ranger, two in the lot, one on the beach, one by the woods next to the Escape—and turned on their beams. There were eight cops in all. Through the headlight's glare, Bob could see that the four in the lot had rifles trained on him.

"Bob, put your son down, please. Just lay him on the blanket."

Bob nodded and did as told. This sucked. This sucked as much as anything in the world had ever sucked.

"Mind if we search you?" The cops approached slowly. They were brawny guys, tattooed over their biceps. Could have been older brother and younger—both sun-burned, thick at the waist, looked like they could easily wrestle most anyone down.

The older of the two cops waved for the snipers to come in closer.

"Sure." Bob lifted his hands and spread his legs. The cop approached and patted him down.

"Where's the gun?"

"In the car, the SUV, in the glove compartment."

An ambulance pulled into the lot.

"Anyone else with you?"

"Nope, just me and my son."

"Come over here to the car with us, please." The older cop did the talking. "No, no. It's okay, leave the baby there."

"Are you guys dads?"

"We'll have one of the EMTs look after him. He'll be fine. Come on over to the car."

"Can I put my shoes on? I feel naked without them."

"You don't need your shoes."

Bob stepped out of the sand, over a log, onto the parking area's broken asphalt.

"Turn around now, Bob. Hands behind your back. We've got to cuff you," said the cop, his younger sidekick seeming to grow more angry with each passing second.

"This is a shame," Bob whispered. "Really and truly a shame."

"Where is Alex Moore?"

Bob's attention was on the EMTs who lifted Jayson and brought him into the vehicle. "Yo, Bob. Alex Moore. Where is he?"

"Okay, let me begin at the beginning . . . ."

"No, let's begin at the end. Where is Alex Moore right now and has he been physically harmed?'

"He's not physically harmed. I've never harmed anyone. It's not in my makeup. He's a nice kid, someone right on the cusp of life. Me? I had my heyday, not that I don't still . . . I'm looking for a life of peace."

The younger cop stepped forward and smacked Bob across the head. "Look, asshole, we could give a shit about your life story. Where is Alex Moore?"

"There was no need to hit me!"

"Don't whimper, you little shit. I'm sorry if we ruffled your feelings. I'm sure you'll have plenty of opportunity for therapy in case you're traumatized. So, where?"

"He's up at I think it's called Pink Willow Ravine," said Bob. He was finding it difficult to hold his voice together. It wasn't only that he was going to jail, and, at this moment, it wasn't only that they were taking Jayson away from him. It was that the cops despised him so much. Why? Why was that? He could have been them, for Chrissakes, and they could have been him. Why'd they see him as scum, as worthless? Why was that? "I could take you there. I didn't harm him. I'll show you where I left him."

"You left him over at the ravine? Jesus Christ. Anything else you want to tell us?"

Bob explained about the handcuffs, that they were around wrists and ankles. That he'd left the keys to the cuffs there but had kind of made them difficult for Alex to get to.

"And how'd you do that? What do you mean 'difficult to get to'?"

"I threw them off. Away a little bit. You see I realized . . ."

"Shut the fuck up! God, you are pathetic. It's getting dark soon. It's fucking dark out and there are predators up there," said the younger officer, faking a smack with his right hand, hitting Bob with his left.

"We're gonna need the helicopter to find the kid Alex," said the older cop.

"Look, about Jayson. That's my flesh and blood. He's my only son, my boy."

"You know what," said the younger cop. "I would bet you, Bob Doe. I would bet you that today is the luckiest day of that kid's life."

"Go call for the copter before it gets dark," said the older cop. Then, to Bob: "You better pray that kid is okay."

46.

TOMMY EAVESDROPPED AS his mom called Dr. Hammond, but she got the doctor's answering service rather than the doctor. She cancelled Monday's appointment at which she'd been scheduled to get the biopsy results.

"What was that about?" Tommy asked when she closed out the call.

"I told you I had a follow-up."

"No you didn't."

"Yes, I did. Lab work. It's nothing to be concerned about."

"You just said biopsy, not blood work. I heard you."

"Whatever. It's all the same. Tests, tests, tests."

Linda hadn't even gotten the phone back in her bag when it rang in her hand, startling her.

"Oh, God. Fuck, fuck. . . . Hello." Shhh, she signaled to Tommy.

"Is this Mrs. Moore?"

"Yes."

"Hi, Mrs. Moore. This is the UBI, Utah Bureau of Investigation."
At the other end of the line was a woman with a husky voice and a
cowgirl accent. "We have good news. Your son has been found. He's
safe and in good condition."

"He's safe," she said for her own benefit. "He's okay," she
told Tommy.

Tommy stood up, sat down, stood again and walked to the wall
of windows overlooking the airfield. Hands in his pockets, the roll of
jet engines vibrating through his feet, he observed the twinkling blue
and red tarmac lights and the distant white stream of auto traffic.

"He was picked up along a road in Utah by the FBI, not far from
a state park we had targeted. Yeah, Alex went through some pretty
harrowing experiences at the hands of a real low-life," said the UBI
woman. "But he's good. He's fine. I mean, he's got some bumps and
bruises but he'll be okay. You have nothing to worry about."

"I have nothing to worry about. Thank you, God."

*"Good evening, ladies and gentlemen, and welcome to Continental
Airlines. In a few moments we'll begin boarding Continental Airlines
Flight 909, Newark to Atlanta then on to Salt Lake City with transfers to
Seattle and Los Angeles. At this time, we'd like to call forward any flyers
with Special Accommodation Boarding Passes."*

The walking wounded who'd been hidden in the rows of cushioned seats rose and struggled forward.

"Are you still planning on coming out to Utah?"

"Oh, yes—me and my younger son. We're at the airport right
now, about to board. We'll be there in five hours."

"Yup, that's what we've got. Continental Flight 909 to Salt Lake.
We'll be there to pick you up and drive you over to Provo. We're taking
Alex to Heber Valley Hospital, that's twenty minutes south of Provo.
From what I hear, you should be able to visit him tomorrow. I can

imagine how nervous you must have been so I just wanted to make sure you knew you could relax. Everything's looking good, but we still need to keep an eye on him. Like I say, he's pretty beat up. But he'll be fine. Youth's in his favor."

"Oh, thank God, thank you God."

Saturday, July 20
47.

ALEX'S ROOM WAS a sixth-floor single in the Trauma unit looking over Provo and its outer burbs, then on to the northern hills. He'd remain in the hospital for one additional day for observation.

Following an x-ray and scans done that morning—that first morning-after, the morning Linda and Tommy paid their first visits—and a cognitive test done by one nurse, Alex was scheduled for an additional soft-tissue scan of his abdomen in an hour. His IV was still in, due to dehydration. Next to Alex on the bed were two clickers, one for the TV, one for the nurse. On the roller table alongside the bed were an orange-brown container of ice-water, a paper cup half filled, two small packets of saltines, the hospital magazine, and some papers attached to a red acrylic clipboard which the nurse-in-charge had left for Linda and Tommy to review. There were four sheets on the clipboard: first an overview of the hospital's visitor policies, the second a summary of the treatment Alex had received upon admission to the ER, the third a definition of terms. The fourth was the one which held their attention; it was a listing of Injuries and Areas of Concern:

Concussion, Level 2+, likely brief loss of consciousness. Headaches.

Sudden sharp pain in abdomen, approx. 8 cm below right rib cage, bruising present.

Blurred vision out of right eye

Four stitches along right eyebrow.

Eight stitches to right forearm.

Three stitches to right hand knuckle #2

Moderate dehydration.

Superficial abrasions to forehead and right cheekbone

Periodic loss of mental focus.

Alex had seen the general area into which Bob had thrown the key; he'd been able to follow it until just before it broke the line of grass. That patch consisted of tall, light brown, nearly white grass, pebbles, and smooth boulders, all on a steep downhill slope, the slope making it more difficult and dicey to hop and shuffle his way to the area of the key, all at an altitude of 5,000 feet.

The key was to Alex's left, somewhere near a dying, bonsai-looking tree. Unable to use his hands for balance or grasping, it was a treacherous twenty yards down. Already he was sweating through his shirt and was exhausted but relieved when he reached the tree and rested his back against it. For half an hour, sometimes standing, sometimes on his knees scratching through the grass, Alex had been circling the tree to no avail, each loop he made around it more rushed, less cautious, Alex nearer to panic with each revolution.

He needed to rest, to relax, to settle himself. To regain some remnant of composure. He worked his way uphill to a flat rock twenty feet above the tree. When he reached it, he spun round on his heels to look back towards the tree. He saw a glint—it was the key he'd been looking for so desperately. Joyously, he headed back downhill, forgetting that his ankles were shackled. He tumbled head over heels. When his feet hit the ground again, he tried to upright himself, but there was no way he could. His momentum overwhelmed him, hurling Alex face first into the rough bark of the tree, then tumbling another twenty feet down the hill.

Bloodied, bruised and dazed he clambered back to the tree, quickly found the key, seated himself on the ground and proceeded to unlock the cuffs. Alex then climbed to the spot where Bob left the supplies, downed some water, and began his limp back towards the road.

48.

LINDA LEFT THE room for the cafeteria. Tommy was in the chair next to Alex's bed.

"I talked to Billy last night," said Alex.

"Everything good with him?"

"Yup. The temporary job USC gave him is good, he's excited about starting classes, he likes the people. His apartment's nothing special, but fine. 'Thank God for the air conditioning,' he says."

"Sounds like he's settled in pretty well."

"Yeah, I'm going out there to see him."

"Look at you! You're battered to bits, and you're gonna what?"

Alex laughed. "Gonna give myself a couple of weeks back home, then fly out, stay with Billy at first."

"Jesus." Tommy moved closer. "And what are you going to do for money?"

"I should still have a few hundred dollars after the flight, and Billy can get me a temporary job with him. They save money by hiring temps."

"Uff," went Tommy shaking his head disappointedly. "How long is this gonna be for?"

"Don't know, but I want to see the whole state, and it's a big state."

"My god, look at what just happened to you."

"No, no, no. I'll be more careful. No hitchhiking this time. And anyway, at least a month of it will be in the safe confines of Billy's place."

"Listen. Listen, Alex. I'm worried about mom. I don't think she's doing so good."

"Wait. What do you mean? The cancer's back?"

"I think so. I'm not sure."

"Well, then why are you scaring me?"

"Just listen," said Tommy. Alex had the look on his face of a big brother being told by the little one to "just listen." Tommy went on. "Mom was supposed to get biopsy results tomorrow but we came out here."

"A biopsy? Fuck. She got the results, or is going to be getting the results?"

"I said—tomorrow."

"You're telling me no actual facts, just conjecture."

"They don't do biopsies for nothing."

"Tommy, in the medical field they're extremely, extremely overly cautious."

"You're a cancer expert, now?"

"Compared to who, compared to you?"

"No, compared to Dr. Hammond, obviously."

"Listen," said Alex, "I'll stay home as long as I have to, but I'm not letting you decide that for me."

Tommy stood. "I can't believe how juvenile you are," he said as he was leaving the room.

"I told you, I'll stay as long as I have to. I'd never leave Mom if she needs me. I'm not an asshole."

UNION CITY HIGH SCHOOL

CENTER FOR ACADEMIC AND STUDENT SUCCESS

LIFE SKILLS: Summer Internship Evaluation

STUDENT: Thomas Moore

I WILL BEGIN by stating that I have a great personal affection for Thomas—yes, a special affection that rises above and beyond what I have for *every* student under my tutelage. I have invested blood, sweat, and tears in this young man's academic and personal advancement. It is therefore with a measure of disappointment that I write this final evaluation of "Tommy's" 120-hour internship at Bon Secours Continuous Care Facility on the Hudson.

There is no question but that Thomas was reliable and well-liked at his work-site. He received a sparkling, though voluminously incomplete, evaluation from his work-site supervisor Cathy Degnan, Director of Whole Persons, who scored him as excellent on all five rating scales: ability to learn; reliability; willingness to assume tasks; focus and attention to detail; and cordiality and respect. No doubt, the young man carried himself well.

However, there were several weaknesses in Thomas's internship contract that, alas, were starkly evident to me, and which I, as someone both pedagogically and personally committed to attention to detail and thoroughness, could not overlook; weaknesses which I had to calculate into my grading calculus. To wit:

There are four parts required by the Life Skills Internship Contract, three of which must be completed by the intern her/himself:

1) Daily Log, 2) Weekly Report, 3) Capstone Report, and, (4) two-part Final Evaluation, to be completed by the work-site supervisor.

1. No daily logs were submitted, though numerous times per week I would contact Thomas—via phone, via text, via email—to please come to my office to pick up these forms which would chronicle his hour-by-hour tasks assigned and completed. I was relentless;

2. Two of the three Weekly Reports were completed, but these were loaded with what I call "lalala writing," random details and meandering philosophizing, and the third of the Weekly Reports remains missing;

3. Due to the weakness of (1) and (2), Thomas's Capstone Report carried even more weight than this component typically does. To commence, this important report was submitted three days late, a failing which Thomas laid at the feet of a difficulty his brother was having in Utah and which forced him, so he wrote, and his mother, to travel to that western outpost. Life Skills, at least as this instructor teaches it, aims for overcoming obstacles, not succumbing to them. Even when I did finally receive Thomas's Capstone Report, it was an unimpressive mess of the rushed, the meandering, the indecisive, and the confused, that is, written as though there were other, "more important" things on the lad's mind;

4. As referenced priorly, Ms. Degnan scored Thomas very highly on all of the contract's ranking scales. However, Ms. Degnan did not submit the all-important narrative portion of the Final Evaluation (more on this below), and with this failure she did Thomas no favor.

Thus my dilemma: Did Thomas Moore meet the NJ State Mandated requirements of a Life Skills Course Internship? Unavoidably, the answer is no. In the integrity of my heart, I find it impossible to give Mr. Moore a grade higher than a "D," a grade which will require a repeat of either the course or a second internship. All is not bleak for the young man, though, for I myself do have a creative proposal!

Apparently, towards the end of Thomas's internship, Ms. Degnan had what can only be described as a nervous breakdown. (I do not know all the details.) Soon, though, she will be, or at least hopes to be, returning to work. She has requested (even before having knowledge of Thomas's need to repeat his Life Skills work) that he be permitted to return as her part-time assistant, or, as she put it, "to be her eyes." Apparently, since her breakdown, she has been blind—in other words, without sight. She believes that with Thomas's help, she will be able to return to work very soon—coinciding with the beginning of our fall term—and that together they would be better than she ever was alone, or so she predicts. Yes, I endorse this plan.

To wit: I recommend that this fall term, Thomas be given the choice of repeating the standard Life Skills course offered by Union City High School, or that he redo his Internship at Bon Secours Continuous Care Facility.

It is with some measure of regret, but with my integrity intact, that I hereby record Thomas Moore's Summer Internship experience as Deficient, final grade as a "D."

Graciously,
Mr. Avery. B. Collins
Coordinator of Life Skill
Weehawken High School

EPILOGUE

October 2

THE BREEZE WAS exactly right, steady and stiff, perfect for kite-flying, explained Sandy. Together with Sara, he led the way. Sandy carried the kite—a diamond kite, three feet tall, two feet wide. Royal blue, it would set a sharp contrast to the silvery gray-blue sky and the morning's slow-moving, wispy clouds. In one hand, Sara carried the kite's tail, in the other the string and reel. Next were Ava and Nini, flanking Wake who held their hands. Ava was in an electric wheelchair, and there were needle bruises—red and blue and mustard-colored—on the back of her free hand. She clutched a lacy handkerchief in that hand in case she had to wipe her mouth. Behind those three were a dozen kids from the South Bergen Recreation Program and a pair of diligent teenaged counselors. These kids were 6- to 9-year-olds, younger than the summer group from Christ United. Pulling up the rear were Tommy, Cathy, and Alex. It was a new scene for Alex, but a familiar one, as well, given that Tommy had described it so often and in such detail.

At first, Tommy's new plan sat well with big-brother Alex. These eight Bon Secours weeks of part-time work would be a good experience for Tommy. He seemed at home here, this was a required course for graduation, and by doing the internship he wouldn't have to sit in class with Collins, that useless ass. It was all good except for the Tommy/Cathy relationship, which left Alex uneasy. He couldn't put his finger on it exactly, but he had talked to his mom and knew that their concerns, though difficult to organize into words, were mutual, fearing that this was just too much for the kid. Too much, too soon. Here was this seventeen-year-old, and a particularly naïve one, at least still so to them, working with the elderly. As admirable as that was, it was, or *certainly should have been*, a mere school requirement, a do-over of a dumbass non-academic course he shouldn't have been required to take to begin with. Bon Secours should have been barely a blip in his life, a story to tell for a few years, but then, and not in the too distant future, a tale buried in the underground of his life story, many new chapters piled atop it. But it wasn't a blip, Alex and Linda Moore both realized. It was more than that. Yeah, but how much more, especially given their sense that Blind Cathy was driving this train and Tommy a passenger? No, it was troubling where this *blip* could lead.

This was not a vocation. Tommy was not ready for one. This both mother and her eldest son knew: the more often Tommy walked into Bon Secours, the more difficult it would be for him to walk out.

* * *

Sandy halted the march, and Sara turned to everyone and indicated the short table that would be their workstation. Sandy, sporting a blue Asbury Park baseball cap and a white cable-knit sweater on this cool October day, completed the final touches. Having already finished the hardest parts of the job—tying the horizontal and vertical sticks of wood together, using string to construct a diamond frame, stretching and gluing the royal-blue paper sail to the cord frame—now he checked for tautness and give, balance and bend. Sara's job was to pin the tail.

* * *

"Let's sit. Is there a bench nearby?" asked Cathy, wearing dark sunglasses, still holding Tommy's hand.

Together they sat.

"I'm so glad you came back," said Cathy. "There's so much we can do."

"There is. It's kind of daunting."

"We'll get it done," she reassured.

"By whatever means necessary," answered Tommy.

Seated at their own bench, watching Sandy and Sara prepare for lift-off, were Wake, Ava, and Nini.

"Excuse me, ladies. I'll return shortly," said Wake. "You're okay? Everything's okay?" He wore a black and silver REO Speedwagon windbreaker, baggy black shorts that came down past the knees, high black Converse.

"Yes, go ahead," said Ava. "But we expect you right back."

"Not a problem, ladies. Let me see if I'm needed at the flight area," said Wake. He called to Sandy and Sara, "You guys need a hand? I'm here!"

Sandy called back: "We can use your height, big fella. Come here and take the kite. Grab it like this, Wake." Sandy raised the kite above his head, slightly tipped, tail towards the ground.

The teenaged counselors—nearly the same age as Tommy—had ordered the children to sit on a patch of grass and to do nothing but watch. Any time a kid tried to move from the group, one or the other of the counselors would take a jab step towards him or her to get the kid back into the circle. Keeping the kids amused, somehow, was Wake. Every kid in the group giggled at Wake's efforts. There was nothing in particular that he'd done, nothing funny or crazy, but they all recognized that in Wake there was something worth giggling about—a combination of good-heartedness, bitterness, naivete, bluster, and an appeal for acceptance and appreciation, but only on his own stubborn terms. A hulking cowardly lion, dressed in black, at your service.

Alex leaned his elbows onto the railing of Riverview Park, looking across the Hudson onto Manhattan's upper west side. His mom's biopsy had proven to be cancerous and presumed to be aggressive.

Surgery was performed on August 25th, again she needed a temporary ileostomy afterwards, and the surgeon was only 75% certain that in removing her tumor he had gotten all the cancer. While she was in the hospital for six days, both boys visited daily but at different times to double the contact. Then early in September, Linda had begun her twice weekly chemotherapy. With Tommy back in school and having to redo his Bon Secours internship, it was Alex who had taken up the responsibilities of household chores and of serving as Linda's chauffer and primary caregiver. Linda's chemo treatments were early morning, Monday and Thursday, each infusion lasting for three hours. She had difficulty with the treatments—sleeping through long afternoons and unable to eat the days after chemo; and the day following that, fevered, vomiting, still fatigued, eyes red but not overflowing with tears, fearful of her own despondency, bitter towards her fate. For four days a week, Alex stayed close to his mom. He might leave the house for a few hours at a time either for errands or to drive round and round—never with a destination in mind. The rest of the time he was in the house, watching TV, reading, playing video games, playing cards with his mom, cleaning, cooking, napping, mapping out plans, though the ink was draining from the pen.

From the time of his return to New Jersey in July until early September, he'd call Billy out in California just about every day, getting updates and making plans, and that seemed to give him a lift. But that number had dropped to once a week on average, and there was no lift apparent or experienced.

The breeze was blowing southeast from New Jersey's northern palisades across the river towards lower Manhattan. If this whole plan worked, the breeze would carry the kite down river, towards the harbor.

"This is perfect," said Sandy to Sara.

"Yes, the breeze is perfect . . . if the kite goes up. The kite still has to go up, you know?"

"Oh, don't you doubt me. It will go up! The third post, Wake— you're going to take the kite to the third post next to the statue of the boy," explained Sandy, holding onto the reel, the same type he'd used as a kid—a thin clothesline reel with a dowel through its center.

Wake did as instructed. Kite above his head, awkwardly, he walked backwards towards the spot Sandy'd assigned. With one hand, Nini covered up her own laughter; with the other, she covered Ava's.

"Ready, chief," called Wake.

"Can you hold it higher? Sandy, should he hold it higher?" asked Sara.

"If he can."

"This is as high as my arms go up, folks. I'm trying to help here."

"Okay, okay, Mr. Sunshine, you're doing good," teased Sara.

Wake shook his head. "That's always been my cross," he muttered, "Sensitive and misunderstood."

"Wake, listen. Press your side to the rail, lean into it and start walking backwards quickly, slide along the rail. Quicker. As quickly as you can. Keep going. Okay, now let go. Wake, let go of the kite!"

The kite jumped from his hands, and after a few struggling seconds of flipping and flapping, it settled, even keeled, lifting, smoothly sailing skywards above the water.

"It's up," screamed the camp kids, jumping to their feet. "It's up, it's up!"

"It's up," yelled Wake, on his tip toes, clapping hands. "Now what do I do?"

"Get out of the way," called Nini.

"I'm finished?" asked Wake, excited by his success but disappointed that his acclaim and usefulness had been so brief. Twisting, still trying to keep an eye on the kite, he returned to Nini and Ava's bench.

"Don't worry," whispered Nini, "Sandy will give you another turn."

"Oh, yeah, Sandy's the man. And he's my best friend. I trust him. A father-figure may be what I need."

"Higher, higher," demanded Sara. "Get it into the clouds."

* * *

An hour later, the fun was done. Wake and Sara as well as a few bold kids and their counselors had all had a turn before the kite was reeled into Sandy's waiting arms. Heading back to the facility, Tommy, Cathy, and Alex were at the back of the pack. Tommy led Cathy by the hand, Alex trailed.

"Come on, Alex," called Tommy.

"I'll be there in a minute. It's beautiful out here. I'm chillin."

All the kids from the program crossed River Road except for one girl who'd fallen behind, a knock-kneed kid in a blue head wrap. As she hustled past Alex to catch up to the group, she turned to him and with a thumbs-up shouted, "Thank you, mister! That was the best show I ever saw!"

Alex returned the thumbs up, then leaned again on the park railing, looking towards the city. A moment later he bent down, stepped between the horizontal pipes of the railing, and jumped onto the black gravel separating park from river. He grabbed one, and two, and then a third handful of the flat stones and, one after the other, skipped them onto the Hudson while behind him, arm in arm, Cathy and Tommy disappeared beyond the sliding doors of Bon Secours.